Praise for Billy Mott's

The Back Nine

"Poised and cinematic. . . . Mott captures the dialogue of the caddy bench." —*The Times* (London)

"Mott's debut novel has a unique rhythm and beauty that is akin to gazing upon Fred Couples swing a five iron during his glory days. . . . Great stuff." —*Entertainment World*

"This remarkably assured debut stands out from the pack because it takes the game seriously as a subject of literary fiction and then delivers a story that can carry its thematic weight and a character whose humanity is as palpable as his golf swing is smooth. . . . *The Back Nine* is golf's *Hustler*." —*Booklist* (starred review)

"Written with expertise yet very easy to read. . . . You find yourself imagining the film version as you go along." —*The Arizona Republic*

"A well-written and endearing novel that mixes elements of *Rocky*, *Hoosiers* and *Field of Dreams*." —*Bookreporter*

BILLY MOTT

The Back Nine

Billy Mott was born in Pittsburgh. He currently lives in
Santa Monica, California.

The Back Nine

BILLY MOTT

VINTAGE CONTEMPORARIES

Vintage Books

A Division of Random House, Inc.

New York

FIRST VINTAGE CONTEMPORARIES EDITION, MARCH 2008

The Library of Congress has cataloged the Knopf edition as follows:
Mott, Billy.
The back nine / by Billy Mott.—1st ed.
p. cm.
1. Golfers—Fiction. 2. Caddies—Fiction. 3. Golf Stories. I. Title.
PS3613.O84B33 2007
813'.6—dc22
2006017009

Vintage ISBN: 978-0-307-27786-2

Book design by Robert C. Olsson

www.vintagebooks.com

Printed in the United States of America
10 9 8 7 6 5 4 3 2 1

For
J. Siobhan Mackey

This book is dedicated to anyone
who has ever dragged a bag.

ACKNOWLEDGMENTS

Thanks to Dawna Kemper, Dr. Jack, Kathy Raborn, Steve Lovett, David Gernert, Gary Fisketjon, and Liz Van Hoose.

The Back Nine

Prologue

Larry Siegal had been asked to do a favor. Play a little match, eighteen holes is all, humor his opponent, an actor, a genuine movie star and a decent player; beat him but make it close and as long as the chump was nice, spare him any humiliation. Larry hated such arrangements, but it was a good turn he was obligated to fulfill. And make no mistake about it—he was obligated.

The game was match play, each hole counting only for itself. Win the first hole and you're up one; lose, you're down one; tie and it's like you never played it. Move on. If a player gets down more holes than there are holes left, the match is over. Simple, just the way Larry liked it. Outside the game he had a hard time keeping things straight. There was too much booze, too many drugs, too many women, and Larry couldn't resist any of it. So, on the golf course he kept things simple.

The night before, his challenger lay awake anticipating playing a round of golf with "the legend." He knew of the reputation, had been told a million times how, for years, Larry had beaten literally everyone—hustlers, top amateurs, pros, and millionaires with plenty of money but not enough game. He had no chance to win, no right to even be on the same course with Larry Siegal. But he was one of the lucky ones. Born with model good looks, he'd arrived in Hollywood from Missouri and fell into the good life, was filthy rich but a six handicapper masquerading as a one.

But when they met on the first tee, the movie star was deeply disappointed. He even thought for a moment that this was the wrong guy. This guy was a mess. He was ugly and he was fat. His hair stuck out every which way from beneath a floppy plaid beach hat and he hadn't bothered to shave. He was chain-smoking Pall Malls and he looked half drunk. And his caddy wasn't any better.

Through the front nine Larry did as he was told—he lay low, took it easy, missed shots he could make with his eyes closed to keep the match close. The movie star was two up at the turn, and though he'd been warned not to get hustled, serious doubt about the "legend's" ability had crept into his head. For Christ's sake, he'd out-driven Siegal on every hole by ten yards. The guy was supposed to be an unbelievable putter, but not today. So as he waited on the tenth tee, the movie star came to the conclusion that the legend wasn't all he was cracked up to be. He was over the hill.

When Larry missed a short putt on eleven, the movie star went three up. Hope blossomed in his breast as he strutted to the next tee, his imagination running wild, picturing himself at his home course with his friends gathered around him at the bar as he described how he'd whupped Larry Siegal.

He split the twelfth fairway with his best tee shot of the day. Just a few more holes, he thought, and I'll own this fat fuck.

But even as Larry stepped up to his ball, he changed. Like John Wayne galloping over the hill, arriving in the nick of time, the real Larry magically appeared. His whole demeanor shifted. His body, fat and loose a second ago, suddenly appeared solid, ominous. His drive flew his opponent's by ten yards, then bounced and rolled another twenty.

The movie star, instead of sitting back and enjoying the show, felt he'd been played for a schmuck and got pissed. Victory evaporating and his cool blown, he dumped his second shot into a greenside bunker. Larry hit his approach to five feet, strolled to the green whistling, marked his ball and flipped it to his caddy.

After two shots from the sand, the movie star grudgingly conceded the hole. Livid, he flung his wedge at his bag and stormed onto the green. "I'll bet you a thousand you don't make that putt," he said, flashing his straight, too-white teeth.

Larry forced his lips into a smile but his eyes went dark, wild, almost hypnotic and the movie star found it hard to hold his gaze. "You know, you're better-looking in person than in the movies," he said, "but you bet like a little bitch."

Grunting, he bent over, re-marked his ball and moved it halfway to the hole. "There," he said pointing. "Two and a half feet, straight up the hill. Simple, huh?" He reached into his back pocket, pulled out a roll of cash in a rubber band and dropped it on the green. "Jack," he snapped, and his caddy reached into his bag and dropped another wad on the green. "That's twenty thousand. Ten on yours, ten on mine."

The movie star tried his best not to swallow, but he did, and Larry's smile now spread completely across his face. "You know, you're just a country-club six handicapper," he said. "Another idiot who thought he could've been a pro if he'd just practiced a little more, could putt a little better and hadn't been a movie star. You insult the fuckin' game. Now, do we have a bet?"

His face on fire and his hands ice-cold, the movie star could muster only a tiny shake of his head. Larry held his hand to his ear, cupping it. "What? I can't hear you."

"No bet," he murmured, and licked his damp upper lip. "Jack," Larry said, and his caddy scooped up the money.

He drilled his putt in the hole and backpedaled toward the next tee. "And now I'm going to have to beat you bad," he said. "I didn't want to embarrass you, but damn it, you pissed me off."

Imagining Jackie Gleason, he did a graceful little two-step, his belly jiggling. He laughed wickedly, then smoked his tee shot down the middle thirty yards farther than he had all day. He flipped the driver to his caddy, lit a cigarette and turning to the movie star said, "You're up, good-lookin'."

An odd scent was in the air and Charlie MacLeod wondered where it might be coming from. From off the ocean it rode the wind and swept over him, faintly medicinal but pleasing, and he inhaled deeply to fill his lungs. Towering trees with long strips of peeling bark lined a narrow two-lane street and hugged the edges of a dirt path worn into the overgrown grass. Long, straggling limbs drooped low, so that Charlie had to brush them out of his way. He'd been traveling for days now, constantly on the move—a bus, two trains, then another bus. He'd walked for hours this morning, his belongings in an old canvas bag slung over his shoulder. He trudged up one last steep hill, came to the end of the path and stopped to catch his breath.

A dirt road split off into the forest of trees, and at the intersection stood a waist-high marker made of rough, uncut stone. Exhausted, he removed his old wool cap to cool his head, leaned against the stone and dropped his bag at his feet. He rubbed the week's worth of stubble on his face, a beard grayed by the passing of time and the pain of his memories. Dread that had been working on him since the moment he awoke finally swept over him and seized his body. His heart pounded into his throat as he tried to stop the utterance of a name, but failed as miserably as ever.

"Helen," he whispered, and realized he'd traveled thousands of miles for nothing. "Christ," he said, as tears filled his eyes and spilled down his face. His legs weakened and he slid down to his haunches, the rough stone scraping his back. His head throbbed, blotches of light bordered his vision, and his hands and feet tingled as though a thousand needles had penetrated his skin. He covered his face with his hands and waited for his anxiety to pass.

Past episodes had taken hours—the worst ones, days—to subside. He spent hours shaking, wandering through his house late into the night until, finally exhausted, he fell into bed and passed out. When he finally awoke it was impossible to get up. The only time he felt good was at work. He labored in a foundry shoveling sand and grinding metal, and though he was slight, he was strong. Charlie could work for hours. But when the whistle blew and the men dispersed he would sink again. Even as he put the key into the door of his new house, the panic would return.

The wind rocked him and he came to; how long he'd been out he didn't know. His neck and face were dry. He pulled a clean towel from his bag and rubbed his hair, then draped it over his shoulder. He stood tentatively and circled the marker. A bronze plaque, dark and weather-worn with simple, bold lettering, stated what was stretched out beyond him over acres of green land. His spirits lightened. Amused but not quite believing, Charlie read the plaque again, then turned around to find himself before a wall of giant trees and dense foliage.

Maybe the place is closed, he thought, or maybe they just don't want anybody to know about it.

A horn startled him as an old Chevy carrying four grown men slowed behind him. From the front passenger side, a bony-faced man eyed Charlie, then took a drag on his cigarette, and the sun-bleached blue car, engine tapping, brakes squealing, turned and spun up the dirt road.

Inside the tree line, smooth blacktop stretched out before him. The foliage on either side formed a tunnel blocking out the sun and wind, and though it was colder here, the quiet was welcome. So he kept walking. Shortly the road widened into a parking lot, where the sun cast bright light over a small Tudor building at the far end. It looked warmer there, and Charlie picked up his pace. Parked alongside a small prefabricated aluminum building were tractors and riding mowers. Dark-haired, dark-skinned men with white-collared shirts, floppy hats and rubber boots sat at a picnic table drinking coffee on their mid-morning break.

"You here to loop?" someone asked, and the question turned Charlie around. A short, chubby, gray-haired, red-faced man dressed in worn khakis, a blue polo shirt and an argyle sweater was jiggling a considerable key ring, trying to find the one that opened the trunk of his Chevy. "Forgot something," he said, and pushed his wire-rimmed glasses closer to his face. "Aha!" he said, holding up the key. He stuck out his hand. "Al Hrabovsky. I'm the caddy master around here."

"Loop?" A smile sprung to Charlie's face.

"Yeah, loop. What? You're not a caddy?" Al pulled a pair of old tennis shoes from the trunk and held them up. "One of the guys needs them." He spoke quickly, nervously. "Look, if you're here for the grounds crew you'll have to talk to José over there. But they're mostly Mexicans. And the pay, well, it's shit."

"No, I just hadn't heard the word for such a long time. Loop."

"I saw you out there with the towel on your shoulder."

"Yeah, right, the towel," Charlie said, trying to catch up to the conversation, lost in memories of yellow flags dotting deep green Pennsylvania hillsides. His left hand slowly rubbed his right elbow.

"You all right?" Al asked, and Charlie looked up. "You hurt your arm?"

Charlie let his arm fall. "You saw me out front," he said.

"We passed right by you. I thought you were a caddy."

"I am, I mean, I did when I was a kid."

"Oh," Al said, and slammed the trunk shut. "I'm sorry, but you got to know what you're doing. I only have twenty or so caddies.

They're all older and for the most part, when they're sober, they know what they're doing. I'm always looking for another good one, though."

Charlie looked down at himself. He'd been wearing the same clothes for three days. His hair was too long. He couldn't remember if he'd ever looked so bad. "I've been on the road," he said softly.

"You look fine," Al said, pointing at Charlie's clothes. "I don't care how you look and neither do the members. You should see some of these guys. We're not hung up on all that stuff. But you got to know what you're doing."

"I know what I'm doing," Charlie said with sudden certainty. "If I know anything, I know this." He pointed at the clubhouse and grounds around him.

"You got to know your yardages, clubs—"

"Reading greens, keep 'em clean. Flat yardage, playing yardage. Wind, hills, speak when spoken to."

"Yeah," Al said.

"Anybody can pick up a bag. That ain't caddying."

Al shook his head. "No, it isn't."

Charlie sighed heavily. "To tell you the truth, I wasn't really looking for work," he said, loving what he saw and feeling calmer than he had in recent memory. "But I'd like to."

The two started walking. "How'd you hear about this place?" Al asked.

"I didn't," Charlie answered. "I stopped and leaned on the marker out there. I was tired. Your car came by."

Al laughed. "All right, now I know you're a caddy. I think that's how we all got here. By accident." They headed toward the clubhouse. "You play?" Charlie shrugged and Al raised a hand. "Don't worry. We got a caddy shack full of secrets. You're safe here."

As they walked toward the clubhouse, Al explained, "You can wear anything except shorts."

"Who lets their caddies wear shorts?" Charlie asked.

"Well, there's been a trend lately but this membership isn't much into trends. They like things the way they are. You'll find that out."

A few steps past the clubhouse Charlie passed into sunshine and took in the huge expanse of green land opening up before him. It was not like the green of home but more washed-out, the terrain flattening and fading endlessly into the horizon. The hazy sun muted the edges of the landscape. Gentle hills rolled away from him, more of the same kind of trees interspersed with giant stately pines separated the fairways. Clouds hovered high above, and below them a wall of fog looked as solid as the ground beneath his feet.

"That's the ocean, that way?" he asked, taking a deep breath.

"Yep. That's number one," Al said, pointing to a small, well-clipped tee box.

"Beautiful," Charlie said.

The course followed the lay of the land, as if the builders had laid it gently, not wanting to disturb a thing. "No flowers," Charlie said.

"Just golf."

"No tennis courts," Charlie said.

"Just golf."

"Kids?"

"Hell, no."

"How many members?"

"Not many."

A small building sat off to the right. It had two doors. Al pointed at the near door. "Pro shop." Then he pointed to the far door. "Caddy shack. That's where you go. Don't get the two confused."

Before a tall hedge, a few of the men sprawled on a wooden bench like they were waiting for a bus.

"Have a seat," Al said.

Charlie felt stuck. There was something odd, indefinite and

preposterous about Al's request. He wanted to ask, "For how long?" or "What for?" But just as he was about to speak, he recalled his first caddy master, old and craggy, a crumpled, sweat-ringed ball cap on his head, a cigarette burning between his lips, mouthing the first words Charlie ever heard on a golf course: "Boy, you're a caddy, a mule. Speak when spoken to."

Assaulted by questions all day long—from members, from staff—the last thing a caddy master wants to hear is another question he can't answer. It's what he hates most of all about his job, the caddies asking when they'll work, if they'll work, the members asking how long it will be before they can tee off. When? How long? Over and over again. And the truth is, if it ain't right away the caddy master doesn't know. He may act like he does, and he might—and often does—lie, but the fact is he doesn't know. At this golf course, it's a wait-and-see deal. There are no tee-times here. It's first-come, first-play. If Mr. So-and-So shows up with the rest of his foursome in front of the caddy master, then they'll play first and everyone else is going to have to wait. The caddy master might have some idea but, until the players are standing in front of him, he doesn't really know shit. People call and say they're coming, then don't. Or they show up out of nowhere wanting to know when they could get off.

There are busy times and slow times, and no one can predict the amount of play. A caddy has to wait and see, learn how to pass time, without going any crazier than he already is. That's the trade-off for being able to leave anytime and for as long as you want. And as far as the caddy master's concerned, you don't ever have to come back. Don't let the door hit you in the ass. And nobody can up and leave faster than a caddy does.

The men drifted easily between the bench and inside the shack. They read newspapers, ate fast food and sipped coffee, their mood at this mid-morning hour quiet and tranquil. No fewer than three chessboards were set on the bench between them. As Charlie approached, they moved quietly apart to make room for him. Welcoming the much-needed rest, he sat down and leaned back, blending in, anonymous, safe. His worry slowly began to peel away, like the strips of bark from the giant trees, and for the first time in a long while he imagined that someday he might just leave it behind for good.

2

The sun peeked out, then hid behind the incoming fog as caddies and players marched by in a sparse parade from the ninth green to the tenth tee and off the back nine.

A twosome came trudging down eighteen with their caddy—older men, stooped, gray and wind-burned, their age having betrayed them.

Leaning forward into the prevailing wind, they were bundled in wool pants and sweaters to shield themselves from the elements, but it was far too late; their faces and hands were a road map of wrinkles, the wind and the sun having taken their toll.

Striding steadily before them with a large leather bag on each shoulder was a tall, broad man in khakis, an old gray sweatshirt and a red baseball cap. Well ahead of his players, he dropped the bags greenside and waited patiently as the two old men struggled up to their balls. The first took two shots to get out of a sand trap, cursed, then three-putted; the other merely three-putted, shrugging his shoulders as if he'd expected to all along. They laid their putters against their bags and huffed and puffed up the short, steep hill to the clubhouse as their caddy raked the trap smooth, replaced the flagstick, shouldered his bags and in a few quick strides caught up to and passed his players.

That's how it's done, Charlie thought.

The caddy stood his bags by the pro shop and the men paid

him. "Thank you, Henry," one said, and patted him on the back. "Same time, tomorrow. Good day."

Henry nodded, took a spot next to Charlie and pulled a tattered paperback from his back pocket and red-framed half-glasses from his shirt pocket.

"You all done, professor?" Al asked from the pro-shop door.

"Yes," Henry said quietly.

Al tapped the face of his watch and glanced at Charlie. "Three hours. That's movin' 'em," he said.

Unaware of the compliment, Henry thumbed a page or two, found his spot and held it with a finger. Sensing Charlie, he greeted him with a bashful nod, sighed contentedly, and began to read.

An hour passed, then another. Noon approached and cars began to roll in, each caddy knowing every car and the member who drove it. A trunk popped open and a thin, baby-faced kid in his twenties with shaggy brown hair and freckles jumped up and ran to it. His sudden movement sent a ripple of head-shaking and snickers down the bench, but that had no effect on him. He retrieved the bag, set it between the first and tenth tees, quickly returned to his spot on the bench and, like a beagle eyeing a rabbit, waited for the next car.

"Stop pressin', Billy," someone said from behind a newspaper. "It's fuckin' embarrassing."

"Fuck you, Figgs," he replied.

"Starin' at the parking lot don't make 'em come down the road."

"Some of us don't have steadies like you."

Jimmy Figgs folded the paper exposing his narrow, mean face. "You been here since you were a kid. You don't have steadies, you're a duck."

"Leave that boy alone," someone mumbled.

"Eat shit, Spider," Figgs replied, and resumed his reading.

Sitting at the far end of the bench, Spider rolled the toothpick in his mouth from side to side as he measured his response. Black as night, he was dressed in white from head to toe: floppy white sun hat, white pants, white shoes and socks too. A white Ban-Lon shirt stuck snugly to his skinny torso, rubber bands at the wrists holding the long sleeves in place. Jewelry hung from his neck and wrists, and thick-framed sunglasses concealed his eyes. He'd been slumped on the bench all morning, his head tucked in his shoulders like a turtle. "Sure," he said, "motherfucker." These words seemed to sap all his energy and he returned to his nap, waiting.

If there was a basic difference among these men, it was between those who "pressed" and those who didn't. The more a guy pressed, the less he seemed to work. It showed a lack of confidence that, once he did get a job, would make it difficult for him to relax and do well. There are only so many players in a club, and news about a caddy, good and bad, travels quickly. The best ones are in control of their wits, able to stay with the shot and think ahead at the same time. They're admired, revered, and paid for their cool, for the knowledge and ease with which they carry out their tasks. They keep every club clean, are there when needed, and most important, know when to leave their player alone. And a good caddy always knows where the ball is; no matter how far off line, deep in the rough or the woods, he'll find it and within seconds know the play, always aware of his position on the course and what shot to hit. He'll know if his player should try to run the ball up to the green or just punch out, take his medicine and try to save bogey, maybe hole a putt and make par. "No, no," he'll quietly insist. "You can't make birdie. Forget it. Play for par." He gives just the right amount of information so his player can swing freely, play to his strengths and avoid his weaknesses. A nervous caddy makes mistakes, says the wrong thing and gets blamed for a bad shot or, worse, the whole round. And in a way, he is responsible. Indecision and lack of clarity are at the root of every bad shot. Players can get too quick. In his take-away or with his putter, in his mind and in his hands, a player wants to get there before he is there. Impatience, that's the demon. It seeps into his mind, disconnects what the eye sees and what the body knows, throws everything off and what was certain a second ago spirals into chaos. This player's lost, so the man holding his bag has got to step up and say the right thing, concisely, without a waver in his voice. He must know both the problem and how to relieve it, even by lying if he has to, anything to give his player the temporary fix and get his game back on track.

There are always some in the yard who never worry. They take care of business either honestly or dishonestly. They're either good caddies or they slip the caddy master a twenty day in and day out. There are no rules here, no union, no rights, and nothing fair or unfair. Their welfare hinges on the caddy master: his moods, his whims, his sense of fairness or bias; his judgment of each man. He might not like Mexicans or blacks; he may favor them. He might have a thing for white boys or Asians; he may despise them all. He might talk kindly, gentlemanly, with a smooth Southern accent, and be a thief. That doesn't matter, because until the caddy gets that bag on his shoulder, this man is his boss.

To simply get work means waiting day after day, hour upon hour in order to slip those bags on your shoulders, not just one but preferably two, twice a day on the weekends but at least once, looking for the right car to roll in, hoping your man shows up and you get the nod that means Yeah, you got a job today. Jimmy Figgs already had a loop and always would. Billy, as if born into his predicament, would always struggle, waiting and wanting, eyeing each car that pulled up with a forlorn hopelessness.

Al bounded out of the pro shop and stood in the grassy area amidst all the bags studying a clipboard.

"Hey, guys!" someone shouted into the shack. Sounds of shuffling feet, chairs scraping, and locker doors slamming echoed out the door. A dozen or so more guys came out of the shack, squinting and stretching, and all were present and waiting even before a flood of players began walking toward them from the clubhouse in groups of two and three and four. Some of them turned away as they spoke to Al. Others stared unabashedly and pointed. It was as strange a sight as Charlie had ever seen, and not something he remembered.

"Figgs," Al called first, and Jimmy folded his paper and tossed it at Billy. "Read, learn something you duck," he said. He maintained his snooty manner even as he met his players and shouldered two bags.

"Where am I goin', Al?" he barked.

"Get 'em to one," Al answered. "Tuck your shirt in."

Men rose as their names were called, grabbed one bag or two and off they went. The whole thing was reminiscent of some long-ago era when workers had no rights and nothing to say about how they worked, like dockworkers or coal miners long before labor organized. Charlie had grown up in the cradle of the union movement, where work and morality tied together. Labor versus management divided friends and family along the same lines, and to cross them brought ferocious consequences. But here the line had never been established. This was a society all its own. One man, appointed, stood before all the others doling out their fate for that day and for as long as they came around. There was no equity here. No "time in," no seniority, no recourse. It was day-to-day, each man pitted against the rest.

Names were called and the number of remaining players quickly dwindled. A few caddies tried playing it cool to protect their dignity, calmly chewing their lunches, while others completely forgot who they were and what they were doing, trying desperately to catch the eye of anyone who could get them out of the caddy shack or off that bench.

"William," Al called out, then "Sam Deacon."

A massive man, towering and broad with dark, smooth skin, William Moorer rose from the bench and in a few strides was standing before Al, removing his ball cap, revealing what was left of his snow-white hair. A small man, tanned, thin and ruggedly handsome, came slowly to his side and they stood there as if they'd always been together.

"Sam, you take Daniels," Al said. "And William, you take Snyder and Maggs." Al thought for a moment and shook his head. "Or do it however you want to."

William pulled a small green bag off the ground and slid it onto his friend's shoulder.

"Th-th-th-thank you," Sam said. His speech impairment was jagged and hard, more stammer than stutter. No one reacted to it, but when William Moorer lifted a large brown leather bag and mumbled something, the whole bench cracked up.

"What'd he say?" Charlie asked.

" 'Fuckin' trunk,' " someone answered.

"What?" Charlie asked.

"The bag's heavy," Henry whispered.

William handed a scorecard to his man, and he and Sam sauntered to the tenth tee.

"They make that look easy," Charlie said.

"They should," Henry said without looking up. "They've been doing it for forty years."

"That's a long time," Charlie said.

"Nobody knows how old William is."

"Fuckin' ancient. Before the sphinx," Spider said from his malaise. "Was an old man when they laid the block for the Golden Gate."

"Well, no, he wasn't old," Henry said.

Spider raised his head. "He worked on that bridge."

Henry nodded. "Yes," he said, "he did."

Indeed, Charlie could picture a younger William Moorer as a comic-book hero, slamming blocks of stone into place.

"Shaw's family built the motherfucker," Spider said.

"He's a member," Henry informed Charlie.

"He may own the company," Spider said, "but William's sweat is all over them fuckin' stones."

"It is," Henry answered softly.

"Thank you," Spider said, and with his purpose fulfilled, began to nod off again.

Out in the tenth fairway, Sam Deacon came to his player's ball and stood the bag beside it. The man pulled an iron from the bag and, after Sam backed away, took a smooth, easy swing.

Nice swing, Charlie thought. Good golfer. The ball went flying straight and true, landing on the front of the green. Sam held out the putter, exchanged it for the iron, then sauntered forward and scooped up the divot with it. He then laid the divot back in place, gently tamped it down with his foot, hoisted his bag and headed to the green. Charlie watched his every move until he was out of sight, a contented smile parting his lips.

3

The bench was empty. Hours had passed and men were either on the course or had given up for the day and left, some working twice while others didn't work at all. Al had gone into the clubhouse for one of the caddy master's perks, a free lunch. A lonely cold settled into Charlie's bones as he paced back and forth. The contentment he'd found in the anonymity of this place had proved fleeting, and he contemplated following the others through the blacktop parking lot. But to where? He was as far from home as he'd ever been. What more could be gained but sheer distance? Nothing around him was familiar, but the same old feelings that had driven him west began to resurface. The wind gusted, a shiver rattled him and he ran a few steps in place. "Christ! I thought California would be warm!"

"You might warm up if you got walking," a man said, dropping his bag to the ground. "I'll be right back! I gotta hit the head. I'm Danny! Nice to meet ya!" he called over his shoulder as he jogged into the clubhouse.

Daniel Lang was bowlegged, an inch or two shorter than Charlie, but much heavier, with big hands that drooped too low. His shoulders and chest were considerable. He wasn't a young man, and Charlie thought he must've lifted weights daily to have kept his bulk. His handsome face was lined with a square chin that jutted out, not naturally, but rather from habit. His blue eyes were piercing and cold, his blond hair a bit too long and shaggy. He was the only person Charlie had seen that day who wasn't wearing a hat. It fit him, though, for it could be felt in an instant that Daniel Lang was, above all else, defiant. His pace was quick and strong, packed with purpose and intention, not a move wasted. Even as he stood before Charlie his presence was imposing and potent.

"Afternoon," he said as he wiped his hands in the wet grass and then on the towel draped over his bag. "Who's caddying for me?" he asked without looking up.

"Charlie." The two shook hands.

"Danny. I don't know why but most people call me Daniel. Do what you want." Charlie shouldered Daniel Lang's bag. It was light. He'd taken only what he needed and that seemed to fit him too.

Why do people have so much crap in a golf bag? Why so many pockets, places to bury and lose possessions? Why are the newer bags so awkward and unyielding? Who designed those things, and what was their reasoning? By rule only fourteen clubs are permitted, and any fourteen will do. Carry what you will. The choices are endless. Three or four, even five woods if that better suits your game. High handicappers can leave the two- and three-iron at home; they're dead weight. Hybrid clubs are easier to hit, though to the purist that's not golf. But legal is legal. An extra wedge would benefit any player, or better yet just one you can trust from sixty yards and in. We're not that good and the game's being taken too seriously. Be honest. Buy less, practice more. A lot more. How many balls do you need? Three, four at the most. Tees are weightless. A marker is the coin in your pocket. Sunscreen. All else is ego in an egoless game. Waste in a game of economy. Free your caddy! Release him from that weight and he'll serve you better. And there is a high correlation between low handicappers and light bags.

"Hold on," Lang said. "You got two. And if no one's coming up nine we'll sneak off ten."

A tall, lithe and handsome man, dressed smartly in gray wool trousers and a black turtleneck, trotted out of the clubhouse, green canvas golf bag in tow, like a quarterback being introduced in a football game.

"Grant Evans," he said, standing his bag at Charlie's feet and pulling out his driver. "What are we doing?"

"Let's just play a Nassau. Fives," Daniel said. He sunk a tee into the ground, placed a ball on it and backed up behind it. "Front, back, eighteen."

Three bets, Charlie thought, relieved to hear a game he was familiar with.

A shining metal driver in his hands, Lang moved quickly, cat-like, to his ball. He took no practice swing.

"Two a side," Evans said.

"You're a four now?" Daniel asked, even as he waggled the clubhead over the ball. "You were a scratch two months ago."

"I get a stroke on ten and seventeen on the back," Evans said gleefully. "And two and eight on the front." He turned to Charlie. "Wife had a kid three months ago. Killing my fucking handicap." The familiar banter, old as the game itself, lit and buoyed Charlie's spirit. "Daniel, you'll be glad to know I lost a lot of money getting there."

"Not to me," Lang answered. "Taking all my money."

"That is impossible," Evans said.

Lang's stance was too upright, his grip strong. His left hand was placed well over top of the shaft; his right hand lay easily below. He wore no glove. He had an old-fashioned waggle and a short backswing, but his thick body was more flexible than it looked and his shoulders turned easily. At the top of his backswing he hesitated for a moment, then brought the club down quickly, powerfully, his whole body flying at the ball. There was nothing smooth about it except that everything—his hands, the clubhead, the right side of his body, his hip and shoulders—came together at impact. With a dull clang the ball rocketed down the fairway, arcing from right to left, drawing toward the middle, bounced once, then sat softly in the fairway.

Charlie was shocked at how far the ball had flown. The distance was disproportionate to the effort, and the hollow clang unnerved him. "Nice drive," he murmured. Lang tossed him the club and Charlie caught it and, engaged by its lightness, held it with both hands. Though he didn't take a stance, Charlie's bearing altered, mutated. His jaw tightened, the skin between his eyes furrowed deeply, and he studied the club as though it were sorcery.

"Good-looking grip," Lang said. "Do you play?"

"Can you feel the ball off the face?" Charlie asked.

Though he felt ignored, Lang let it go. In Charlie he detected something formidable. It's what he did and how he made millions: he read men, their strengths and their weaknesses. "Well, no. Not like the old wooden clubs. But it goes farther. A lot farther and straighter." He smiled devilishly. "You can get away with a lot more." Charlie slid the club back into the bag but kept a hand on it.

Evans came to address. He was the taller of the two and a good deal younger and his swing was schooled and studied, smooth, contained. With another clang his drive split the fairway and he posed his finish a bit too long. "Easy game," he said, and the two laughed like little boys.

As they marched off the tee, Lang turned to Charlie. "So you haven't played in a while?"

"A long time," he answered pleasantly. But the dark scowl remained. Lang let him be.

As he approached Evans' ball Charlie started looking for yardage markers. He found a sprinkler head, but there was no number giving him the distance to the green.

"What do I have?" Evans asked.

Charlie felt his face flush. "I can't find a marker," he said.

"There aren't any," Evans said, and folded his arms. "Didn't they tell you?"

"Charlie's new," Lang told him.

"Oh," Evans said, trying to maintain his patience. "Well, I'll tell you what. Inside that pocket is a yardage book. Have a look at it." Evans pulled a club. "About one sixty you think, Daniel?"

"Sixty-five," Lang said.

Evans addressed his ball, Charlie unzipped a pocket, then another and Evans backed off.

"Charlie," Daniel said, holding a finger to his lips and giving him a good-old-boy wink.

Evans made another smooth swing; the ball flew high and landed softly some ten feet above the pin.

"One sixty," he said, as he leaned the club against his bag. "Not a yard more."

"This it?" Charlie asked, offering the book.

"Keep it," Evans snapped. "Putter? Never mind, I got it."

"He didn't know," Daniel said.

"I'm not pissed at him. But I am going to tell Al about it. I mean, what the fuck are we doing here?" He turned to Charlie. "It's not your fault. How the hell would you know? We're the only place in the country without yardage markers. You know, the whole Scottish thing," he said with a bad accent. "Let's just make the best of it and get on."

Charlie hoisted the bags on his shoulders. Daniel followed and with a good, hard nine-iron, hit the green too. This time Charlie, ready and waiting, held out the putter, an antiquated club with a hickory shaft and flat-metal finish.

"And don't laugh at Daniel's putter," Evans said. "It's older than me and he's deadly with that thing."

"You can't putt, you can't play," Daniel said. "Right, Charlie?"

Daniel's inclusion brought relief. "May as well stay home," Charlie said.

"I'll tell you what," Daniel said. "Go to the next tee, you'll see it. Leave our drivers there and walk down the right side about two hundred yards. It'll give you a little time to look at the book while we putt. All the yardages are off the traps or a tree and measure to the middle of the green. If you play you'll get it, and once you got it you'll never forget it."

Charlie reached down for his divot but Daniel took it from him.

"When you're carrying two bags the player takes care of that," Evans said. "How are you going to get to the next ball before your other player? How are you going to have the yardage? Can't be done. Slows everything down, and around here we're sticklers about pace. When you have two bags, the player gets the divot. You can do it when you're carrying one."

The fog flew by and the men huddled their shoulders against the wind. The conversation was nonchalant, their pace purposeful but easy, and Charlie fell into the rhythm as Daniel instructed him.

"Keep the clubs clean. A pro never puts one back without cleaning it. And put it back in the same place. I don't want to be digging around looking for a club."

"Never hand me a club," Evans chimed in. "I don't care if you're right, just lean the bag. Give a yardage when asked. Flat yardage, then how far it's going to play. Big difference." Charlie nodded his head in agreement. "Get to the ball before your player. Sometimes that isn't possible and if the balls are too far apart a player should take a club or two. He's a fucking idiot if he doesn't, and you should tell him."

"Not that he's an idiot," Lang said, "That he should take a club or two."

"Some of the members, that might be hard not to do," Evans added. Listening closely, Charlie nodded as one by one, each of the old rules, the code of conduct that he'd followed years ago, was renewed. Lang's interest quickly waned. He listened, but with one eye on his caddy.

"Know where all the balls are at all times. Cheat when you

can, move when you shouldn't, but don't get caught. Get a step or two ahead. As soon as the ball is hit you should be moving. Watch and move. If you're out ahead and a player is ready to hit, make sure you're still or can't be seen. Duck behind a tree or something. Get small. That way you won't be disturbing play. It may also prevent you from getting hit. Tell him your favorite, Daniel," Evans said.

"No running, God damn it," Lang said. "You want to run, go play basketball."

Evans took over again. "If you need to, walk quickly. The caddy should set the pace, Charlie, not keep up. Always a step ahead. We can't go anywhere without you, and you have to know everything before we do. I don't want to think about it between shots. That's why I have a caddy. If you lag, we all lag. Set the pace." Then, as if reciting a creed, he said, "Golf is a game to be played at a pace."

As his players approached the green he sped up, followed his orders and tramped through high rough to the bend in the fairway of the next hole. There he set the clubs down and pulled the book from his back pocket. But each time his eyes left the page to search for markers he glanced at the two sets of clubs. Lang's set was new, high-tech, the latest design, the shafts made of light graphite and the heads of composite steel. But it was Grant Evans' set, as old as Charlie, refinished and polished to a shine, immaculately clean, that had his attention. He stole a look back and the tee was still clear, so he unsheathed a two-iron. Wiggling his fingers, he adjusted them, and in a matter of seconds they settled as if on their own.

"God," he whispered as he instinctively took a stance, set his feet and took a swing. When the clubhead swept through the grass, his right elbow brushed against his side freely, painlessly, and that startled him. From the tee a metallic clang resounded and he fought through his confusion and the bright blue sky to spot the ball. It landed and skipped in the fairway and a second ball quickly followed, soaring over his head and landing in the fairway twenty yards past the first.

"That's Lang's," Charlie whispered as he gathered his bags and hustled up the fairway.

4

The sixteenth hole was a par three beautifully nestled between steep hillsides, with a narrow two-tiered green sloping severely back to front. But Charlie hardly noticed. Daniel had dumped his tee shot in the sand and played out within a couple of feet of the cup. Evans had hit it tight but was puzzled by a short, but difficult, downhill putt. "What's this do, Charlie?" Evans said. Charlie laid the bags down greenside, his mind still reeling back over the years, trying his best to conceal his confusion. But he could not fool Daniel Lang. "Now you ask him," Lang joked, trying to lighten the mood and give Charlie a moment to collect himself, or even bail him out. "When you're two holes down with three to go. Nice."

"Fuck you. Let's see what he knows," Evans said smartly. "Charlie?"

Charlie felt lost, bewildered, but even in this state he stepped forward and with the butt of a club pointed to a precise spot halfway to the hole. "Here," he whispered and backed away. It took most caddies years to learn the subtle breaks on these greens and Charlie had barely looked. But his conviction was so strong that Evans decided to take a second look.

"I see," he said, and shot Charlie a wary look as he addressed his putt. But Charlie's concentration had shifted again; he was lost in thought, oblivious to his surroundings.

The putt was well struck, and the ball rolled nicely over the spot and with its last revolution fell into the hole.

"Putt. God-damn good putt. Nice birdie," Daniel said, but his mind was on Charlie.

"Nice read," Evans said.

But it was as if Charlie had expected the putt would drop, even knew it. Distracted and apparently unconcerned, to the point of insult, he nodded his thanks, his thoughts set adrift once more as he returned to his duties.

"Your putt's good, Daniel. Pick it up," Evans said. "I'm down one."

Since he'd lost the hole, Lang picked up his ball. "We'll take our drivers and walk back to the tee," he said, pointing in the opposite direction from where he and Evans were heading. "You can fore-caddy on this one, Charlie. It'll save you a couple hundred yards."

Charlie quickly moved through a grove of trees into a clearing, then down a short hill. Above him the fog rode the wind in sheets, but here all was quiet and still. He stood his bags, took shelter behind a thick eucalyptus and pulled out the two-iron again. He held it carefully, nervously.

"Tempo, Charlie," he whispered, waggling the club side to side. Voices from his past, when he was a boy, surfaced in his mind like scattered pieces of a shipwreck washing ashore, bobbing and floating, half-drowned, haunting and tempting. "Balance, son, this game is all about balance. In your feet. In your head. You got no balance, you got nothin'." Again Charlie drew the club back and took a free, easy swing. Puzzled and troubled, he angrily slammed the club back in the bag. "How can that be?" he hissed.

Behind him the underbrush rustled, then there was a snap. Startled, Charlie spun around but saw nothing. Lang and Evans had just arrived at the tee, so he took another look.

Camouflaged in the trees was a thick, powerfully built man with wild black hair down to his shoulders and layers of dirty, ragged clothes hanging loosely on his broad frame. He glared out at Charlie, whose blood ran cold. A ball was struck but Charlie dared not move. The stranger immediately picked up the flight of it and Charlie followed his eyes, then picked it up too as it descended into the fairway, hit and rolled in the deep rough. Another shot and again the man spotted it against the blue sky, his mouth open as he looked up, his eyes squinted, battling the sun spiking through the branches, until it came falling down close to the first. He then backed away, still staring at Charlie, his filthy clothes blending instantly into the brush, until he was gone. The cold wind swept across the narrow valley, and with one eye on the woods Charlie made his way to the fairway.

The hole was a long, sweeping par four that curved to the right and slightly uphill. The green looked tiny and the pin was tucked in the back right corner. Three small, deep pot bunkers guarded the left front corner.

"What am I, about two hundred?" Evans asked as he pulled a club from his bag.

Charlie nodded.

"I have what I need," Evans told him.

Lang stood with his back to them, scanning the woods as if daring whatever was in them to come out. He paid no attention to Evans' shot, which fell short and right of the green.

"Did you hear something?" Charlie asked.

"What's that?" Lang said, still gazing into the woods.

"I saw somebody in there. Some guy."

"You did?" Daniel said. Facing Charlie, he seemed incensed. "Homeless. They're everywhere," he muttered, then jerked a club from his bag. His anger evaporated in an instant as he sized up his shot, took his first full practice swing of the day and picked out a target. The distraction was gone.

The ball was struck and the sound echoed through the hollow like a muffled firecracker. It flew out of the rough low and hard, arcing left to right, through the moist air and the wind, whistling down the fairway and up the short, steep hill. When it landed it bounced just right of the bunkers, caromed off the edge of a mound and rolled gently onto the green.

"Christ, Daniel," Evans said. "I want another stroke." Lang flipped the club to Charlie and forced a smile.

After they putted out—Lang made par, Evans bogey—and headed to the next tee, Charlie backpedaled, weaving through the trees to a spot where he could see the tee shots. "Don't lose the fuckin' ball," he whispered, trying to keep his mind on the job at hand. "Number one. Don't lose the fuckin' ball."

Finally he stopped and waited. Back on the tee, the seemingly staid Grant Evans was emphatically making a point. He pointed at the clubhouse then back into the trees. Daniel leaned on his driver and listened, nodding his head. Evans became more animated, then shrugged and addressed his ball.

After they hit their shots, Evans veered toward Charlie and his ball while Daniel headed down the opposite side of the fairway. His huge drive gave him plenty of time to walk and think as he looked back across the fairway and into the dark woods.

5

That's it. We're done," Lang said as he plucked his ball from the cup on eighteen. Charlie was looking forward to seeing the front nine and to finding an opportunity to sneak another swing, but that would have to wait. Lang was in no mood, having abruptly changed his mind about playing on. "I take my clubs with me, Charlie," he said. "Always."

Off the course, the commonality was broken. Players and caddies who conferred for hundreds of hours over a year, laughed and shared a million stories, were suddenly strangers. That's how it is.

"All right, then." Grant Evans held out a hand to Charlie, whose pay was pinched between his thumb and forefinger. Then he shouted, "Good man here, Al. A keeper."

Inside his little hut, Al stood too quickly and knocked his chair over. "Huh?" he said as he stumbled through the doorway adjusting his glasses. "Oh. Yeah, Charlie, yeah."

Evans gave a two-fingered salute and went into the clubhouse.

"How'd you do?" Al asked. Charlie spread the money in his hands like a deck of cards. "Got the freight," Al said. "Not bad for a rookie."

"That's what they always pay?"

"Yep. Not everyone pays for eighteen unless they play at least twelve, that's the standard, but those two do. If you do a good job."

"Good deal," Charlie said.

"Can get addictive," Al warned.

Al went back to his office, resumed adding things up, counting stacks of money at the small desk, scribbling notes. Charlie was alone once again. Everyone had gone down the road with a pocket full of cash, with wet, dirty towels draped over their shoulders, heads down against the wind. William Moorer and Sam Deacon caught the train back to town, then went their separate ways. Jimmy Figgs drove off in an old broken-down BMW, Billy riding shotgun. By now they sat in a bar drinking and telling stories about their day. Figgs' man had missed a three-footer for birdie and all the money on eighteen. Billy bragged about guiding his man away from trouble as only he could, and how his man hadn't forgotten that when it came time to pay. They always boasted about their paydays. Somehow Jimmy Figgs always came out on top, and Billy wondered if he didn't just carry more money with him.

In another part of town Henry met friends in his neighborhood bar for a beer, then strolled home to his apartment in the Castro district, enjoying every step freed from those bags on his back. It was a clean, quiet place with a small garden in the back and Henry loved to sit alone and read late into the night, bundled up in an old gray sweater with Dickens, Steinbeck, Melville, Faulkner, and Maugham at his fingertips. His eyes danced across the pages as the characters sprang to life inside his head, and he underlined passages he wanted never to forget. Before going to bed he carefully laid out everything he needed for the next day: a clean towel, fresh socks and a clean pair of khakis.

The parking lot was still half full with cars. It was a Friday night, and many members stayed for dinner and drinks. Later they'd retire to a dark room with card tables and a fireplace, drinking more and playing well into the night.

The sun began to set. Lights from inside the caddy shack spilled through the doorway onto the green grass. Charlie slid his hand into his pocket and felt the money there. It felt good to work again, to get paid for his labor. It was all Charlie ever wanted and something he could always do. Find a job. Make money and survive comfortably. He was taught that if you work hard, good things will come. But it hadn't happened. More was expected of him, and when he failed to find reason to take action he'd lost everything. And here he was, in a new place where the best he could feel was guarded.

The caddy shack smelled of old wet shoes and was littered with discarded food wrappings, cans, bottles, and cigarette butts. On an old sofa in the corner, a tall, skinny caddy lay sleeping with his head resting on one arm and his feet hanging over the other. An old Yankees baseball cap, sun-bleached and tattered, covered his face from the nose up. His pant legs were spotless and his shoes sat clean and dry at the foot of the couch. His feet were bare. Charlie remembered him on the passenger side of Al's car but couldn't recall him standing with the other men when the jobs were being assigned.

He stirred, sniffed and wiggled his toes. "You new?" a voice came from beneath the hat.

"I got here today," Charlie said.

"Back East?"

"Yeah. Well, sorta. Pittsburgh."

"That's East. East of here," he said in a hard-edged Jersey accent. He coughed again, a deep, phlegmy smoker's cough, then swallowed hard. "Motherfuckers around here think anything beyond Oakland's back East." He pulled his hat down to his chest, exposing a weathered, smug face. "They don't get around much," he said and laughed at his own joke.

"Why's that?"

"None of 'em ever leaves," he said. "They all think they found heaven."

"It's nice. The weather."

"Yeah? You should've been here in January. Rained for three fuckin' weeks."

"You're kiddin'?" Charlie said. "In California?"

"Hell, yes." He rubbed his face, trying to wake up. "Mother-fuckers starvin' around here."

"The caddies?"

"Yeah, the caddies," he said. "No work. No money." He sat up slowly and stiffly. "Fuckin' tired," he growled. "You got a smoke?"

"No," Charlie said. "The money's pretty good here, though."

"Best in the West." He offered his hand and Charlie took it. "Jack. Nice to meet you, Pittsburgh. I don't think we have anybody from Pittsburgh."

"Good," Charlie muttered. A stranger mentioning his home made him sad.

His haunted look was one Jack recognized. Many of the men here had no past and were called by a single name that most times was fictitious. "You're in the right place," he said, and this brought Charlie a degree of relief.

Jack took an ashtray filled with butts off the coffee table and started poking through them, picked one out and fired up. "Don't worry, nobody knows you're here. Not unless you tell 'em," he said and took a deep drag. "Hell, even then they wouldn't be able to find you," he said. "Nobody knows where this place is. Whoa!" he barked, blowing out a cloud of smoke. "That's fuckin' nasty! You saw the marker outside?"

"Yeah, the stone thing."

"Me too. It's like a fuckin' magnet."

Jack took another drag, burning the tobacco down to the filter, and then crushed it out. "This place is habit-forming."

"So I've heard," Charlie said.

"Oh yeah?"

"Al said the same thing."

"He don't know shit. Worked here for a year and they made him caddy master. Kiss-ass motherfucker."

"Must've been a good caddy."

"No, he sucked. But that ain't the fuckin' point. Henry or Spider, though they'd never hire a spook, shoulda been caddy master. Henry's been here twenty fuckin' years. Smart, too. Hell, I been here longer."

"You want the job?"

"Fuck no," Jack said as he resumed his search for a smoke, inspecting each butt, estimating whether or not he could get a drag from it. "Have to be here every fuckin' day—twelve, sixteen hours a day with all those members pullin' at you. 'I want, I want, me, me, fuckin' me,' all day long. Fuck that. I mean, face it, that's why we're caddies. We can't be or don't wanna have to be anywhere." He looked at Charlie and smiled. "Oh shit, Pittsburgh, what are you gonna do, huh? You're damned if you do, damned if you don't. Stay, go, what the fuck."

His act was catching and lightened Charlie's disposition.

"What are you gonna do?" he said again as he picked up another butt then tossed it back. "Christ, I'm havin' a nicotine fuckin' fit. If I was on Powell Street I wouldn't have this fuckin' problem. You been to the city yet?"

"I came in early this morning. It was dark. I didn't see much until I got around here."

"Well, Powell Street's the steepest motherfuckin' street in the world. The cable car, you know, Rice-a-Roni and all that shit. Well, when you're in the city and you're broke and you need a smoke all you gotta do is go about twenty steps up Powell Street and stand there." Jack reached underneath the couch and pulled out an old black leather gym bag, cracked and worn, and began digging through it. "At the foot of Powell are a lot of office buildings. Financial types, big-money, high-pressure motherfuckers come out of there, pissed off, freakin' the fuck out and fire up feelin' like

I do right now. They walk about ten steps up Powell, start pantin'
like a motherfucker, look at that smoke between their fingers and
throw it down. Easy pickin's. A couple times a day you'll see 'em
toss the whole pack right on the ground." Jack laughed again,
coughed, then pulled out a pack of cigarettes from the bag,
tamped it, opened it like a sleight-of-hand magician, rapped it
again on the heel of his hand and with his teeth pulled out a fresh
smoke, then returned the pack and threw the bag to the floor.
"Aaah!" he barked as he blew out the first drag. "There you go!"

"Why didn't you smoke those to begin with?" Charlie asked.

"They ain't mine," Jack said. "He won't mind."

"Whose is it?"

"I don't know. A friend of mine."

Charlie walked to the door of the shack.

"You ain't gonna say nothin', are you, Pittsburgh?"

"Who would I tell?" Charlie leaned on the doorway. "I don't
know anybody."

Jack sat back, relaxed. "Well, there's a certain comfort in that."

The sun had dropped behind the trees; streaks of orange and
red smeared a great width of deep turquoise sky. The wind settled
and the temperature seemed to rise and drop by the minute. "It's
getting late," Charlie said.

"You stayin' at the hostel?" Jack asked.

"I don't know. You mean a youth hostel?"

"There's a good one in Fort Mason. It's cheap."

"How do I get there?"

"Take the train to town. Walk up the road there and you'll find
it. You get a bus from town to wherever you want."

"Can I walk it?" Charlie asked.

"From town, yeah, but it's a good walk," Jack answered.

"That's all right. I got some shit to work out."

"Don't we all," Jack said, resting comfortably on the couch.

"Some more than others," Charlie said.

"And shit don't always turn out for the best."

"No, it does not."

"This is a pretty good place to work it out, Pittsburgh. You just gotta know when to leave."

"Yeah? How am I gonna know that?"

"You'll know. You might not go, but you'll know."

"And you're here because . . . ?"

"I'm still workin' it out," Jack said. "I'm easily distracted."

"How'd you get here?" Charlie asked.

"Bus."

"I mean . . ." Feeling he'd somehow broken a secret code of conduct, Charlie raised his hands, surrendering. "Sorry."

Jack waved him off. "I know what the fuck you mean," he said easily. "I was livin' on Long Island buildin' houses, poundin' nails, makin' some money, caddied on weekends since I was old enough to pick up the bag. I had a kid. Me and my wife were into some heavy shit. She gets pregnant and says, 'I gotta quit. I gotta quit the drinkin' and the drugs.' I said, 'I ain't.' That afternoon I bought a bag of dope, caught a bus and got out here before I run out of real estate."

"Right in front of that monument?" Charlie asked.

"A little south of here. I got sidetracked for a while, but eventually, yeah."

"You ever go back?"

"Never," Jack said.

"Ever wish you did?"

"Every fuckin' day."

"So, why don't you?" Charlie asked.

"Why don't you?"

"It ain't that simple."

"Never is. Used to be, when we were kids."

"Simple enough a couple of years ago," Charlie said.

"You musta been a kid."

"I'm forty."

"I'm sixty."

A minute passed slowly between them, like a funeral procession for someone neither of them knew.

Jack sat on the couch, suddenly looking his age as Charlie gazed into the night.

"Great golf course," he said.

"None better."

"So, do the caddies get to play on Mondays?"

"That's our day," Jack said.

"You play?"

"Slap it around," Jack said. "I'm a caddy. You?"

"I'm a caddy."

Charlie picked up his canvas bag and started up the road. He came to the end, crossed over a busy four-lane street, heard a train screeching to a halt off in the distance and walked toward it.

6

Charlie emerged from the underground train to find towering buildings and narrow, crowded streets, a stream of different languages spoken as people hustled by. Gone were the aromas of pine trees and cut grass; here the odors of rotting garbage and urine wafted on the cold stiff wind. Terribly ragged men and women, high or drunk, lay on the sidewalks or leaned against buildings holding out paper or metal cups, some with their hats turned upside down on the ground before them. Charlie side-stepped through the crowd and found himself at the foot of a cement staircase. At the very top, lined by streetlights and framed between buildings, a wisp of clouds passed before a star-filled night sky. Out of the darkness and fog an open-sided trolley clanged by, starting up the hill, jammed with people sitting and reading or hanging on. Charlie walked. Halfway up his lungs and legs began to burn and his back tightened. Glancing up occasionally but never stopping, he reached the top. From its crest, the street appeared to plummet down into the bay, a freefall into deep and frigid waters. Fort Mason was over here somewhere; he'd seen it on a map posted in the subway station.

Go to the water and turn north, he told himself. He found a quiet street and started his descent, passing three- and four-story houses that clung to the hillside. He and Helen had spent count-less hours perched over the river, gazing peacefully at the lights lining the many bridges, the boats pushing coal barges, even as they counted how lucky they were. It was a simple place; two stories with an attic bedroom, built on thick limestone a century ago, a foundation that secured it forever to the steep terrain that overlooked the city. Charlie wondered if he would ever look out over a landscape without thinking of his life there.

But then the bay of San Francisco unfolded before him with a full moon reflected in the water, vast and ominous in the night, its immensity obliterating any thoughts of home. Out on the horizon, the silhouette of a huge oil tanker trolled out to sea like a slow-moving dinosaur, trailing a gigantic ship, on whose deck trailers were stacked like so many toys. You could fit twenty barges on that thing, Charlie guessed. Maybe fifty.

As the terrain flattened, the streets once again became busy with tourists and locals enjoying a night out, hopping from one bar to another listening to live music that leaked out into the streets. Charlie thought of spending the night at the hostel and sharing a room with some stranger.

"Not tonight," he said, and headed across the street to a small hotel. Behind the counter a girl sat wrapped in a baggy black sweater, engrossed in a paperback. Charlie waited, and even though he was weary he got a kick out of how engrossed she was. Finally, he wasn't sure she'd noticed him come in. "Good book?" he asked. She held up a forefinger, answering his question of her awareness, read one more line and closed the book. "Wow," she said through tear-filled eyes. She swiped a strand of light red hair from her face, hopped off the stool and leaned against the counter, smiling as she pushed a piece of paper in front of him.

"I'll just need a credit card and driver's license," she said. "Oh! Sorry. You do want a room, don't you?"

"Yes," Charlie said. "What if I stay a week?"

"I can take off ten dollars a night."

"I'll do that," he said as he took up a pen. He was tired, fading by the second.

She noticed his calloused hands as he removed his hat and ran them through his dark hair. "Tired?" she asked.

Charlie looked up and, through his fatigue, forced a smile.

"The rooms are nice," she assured him. "My mom owns the place. It isn't that big, but it's a lot of work. We really take care of it." She turned the registry around. "You've come a long way."

"Feels like it."

"Well, now you can rest."

"I don't think I've ever been so tired," he said, his voice trailing, his mind drifting off. "I could work doubles six days," he said, confused, practically asleep on his feet. "My dad used to look so worn out when he came home."

"I'll get you a key," she said.

Inside his room, Charlie dropped his bag to the floor and sat gingerly on the bed. He meant to take a nice long bath and get something to eat. His legs were stiff and as he lay down on the bed he craned his neck to work out a kink.

"Those bags," he whispered as he pulled a pillow under his head. He put his hand to the side of his neck and felt his pulse, a habit he'd picked up since his heart raced wildly at times. But for now it was strong and steady. As he relaxed he felt it slowing. He sighed and for the millionth time recounted the time past, carefully brought to mind the faces he missed, and wondered if the ache would ever go away. Still, it was better than panic and sharp pain, the cutting glass in his throat; it was better than the tears. It was part of him now. His fingers worked as he counted. One, two, he thought, two and a half years, and drifted off to sleep.

7

The patch of ground in front of Al's hut was filled with golf bags, the bench full of caddies. Older men sat or stood to the far end, closer to the first tee. For a moment Charlie entertained the idea that maybe there was an order, with the oldest, most experienced caddies sitting down there. But Sam Deacon and William Moorer were together, Sam sitting and William standing at the near end. No, Charlie thought, there is no order here.

Others filed in from the parking lot and milled around. It was Saturday morning and it seemed everyone was playing. The clubhouse door opened and the players began rolling out. The pace quickened and the whole yard took on a busy feel.

"Henry," Al said, "you're with Jenkins and Greer." And Henry picked up two bags.

"Mitch," Al called, and a large white man in his forties with a puffy red face lumbered slowly to his bags, smeared sunscreen on his nose, then snapped the lid shut on the tube and popped it into his rear pocket. He wiped his hands on the wet grass, dried them on a towel draped over his shoulder, then picked up both bags and threw them over his right shoulder. The first foursome of the day was off.

One by one they were picked off the bench. Some knew who they had and Al said nothing or whispered as they walked by. More and more members poured out of the clubhouse, some still half

asleep, drinking coffee, others rummaging in their bags for whatever they needed—sunscreen, Band-Aids, a new glove, a fresh
sleeve of new balls or old ones that still looked okay. Players
headed to the driving range to warm up. The first ball was struck
and then another, and soon it sounded like a string of dull fire-
crackers going off.

Smoke was everywhere—cigars, pipes and cigarettes. An older
man with gray hair and thick glasses hobbled to his bag and
William Moorer immediately stood it up. His man pulled out a
leather case, bit off the end of an expensive-looking cigar and lit it
with a Zippo.

"Morning, William. Morning, boys," he said, and inhaled
deeply. "Ah!" he announced as he blew out. "Breakfast." He held
out the case to William.

"Shit's bad for ya," Moorer grumbled. "Eat the lips right off
your face."

"Gotta go somehow," his man barked back.

"I'd like to hold the water in my mouth up until the last
minute," Moorer fired back, "not be sittin' in some chair with my
shit runnin' down all over the place."

"William Moorer, a big guy like you afraid of dying?"

"Nope. It's livin' scares the hell out of me. 'Specially when I
got to watch some fool waste it like we wastin' time talkin' this bull.
Let's go!"

"I don't know why I put up with you."

William cut in like a vaudeville partner. " 'Cause old as I am,
I'm the best caddy out here and even at my age damn near one of
the best players, and you wanna win that two-dollar Nassau you
been playin' for twenty years more than you wanna take a good
piss."

"Fuck you, William."

"And I love you too," William Moorer said, flashing a wry
smile. "Come on, boss." He scooped up two bags with one hand,
then placed a third on Sam Deacon's shoulder.

"Charlie!" Al barked.

Charlie jumped and was walking before he knew it.

"You and Figgs," Al told him. "It's Lang, Evans, Dr. Smith and Shaw. You'll carry Lang and Evans. They're having some breakfast, so relax."

Charlie headed to the shack where Jack stood in the doorway. "Got one, kid?" he asked.

"Lang," he said. "And Evans."

"Good loop. That's Randall's loop."

"Oh yeah?" Charlie said, and glanced down the bench. The men were restless, their eyes darting at him and then away, and Charlie knew what had upset them.

"They'll get over it," Jack said. "Some of these guys have been here a long time."

"What should I do?" Charlie asked.

"Nothing. Fuck 'em."

"What about Randall?"

"He ain't here," Jack said.

"What about when he gets back?"

"That's another matter."

A sharp, high-pitched voice said, "He's on a bender." Jimmy Figgs sat there holding his queen above the chessboard. "He won't be back until all the money's gone." He set the piece down. "Check."

"Fuck," Billy whispered. "I didn't see that."

"That's 'cause you're an idiot." Figgs looked up. "How long's he been gone, Jack? About three weeks I'd say."

"I don't know," Jack said.

"Not that that's anything new," Jimmy said. "Hell, he ain't the first caddy to blow every dime he has." He looked at Billy, who was laboring over his next move. "Come on, move, asshole, you're dead anyway."

"Fuck you, I'm thinkin'."

"About what? It can't be chess."

"Shut the fuck up," Billy said.

Figgs folded his arms. "Randall won't be back till he's flat broke." He bent over, lifted his coffee from the ground and took a sip. "Let's see, fifty-dollar hookers, three times a day. A case of beer, a fifth of top-shelf whiskey, crack, now that's gonna cost him."

"More ways than one," Spider chimed in.

"Plus a thirty-dollar room times the four or five assholes he's hangin' out with every day. I gotta tell you, you'd have to be a fuckin' accountant to even take a guess. Whaddya say we just ball-park it?" He took another sip of coffee. "I'll bet you that within two weeks his tired ass comes up that drive draggin' his fucked-up leg, limpin' and hackin' his lungs out without a dollar left or a pot to piss in." He then looked at Billy again. "Will you move a fuckin' piece? Whaddya think, Jack? You're his best buddy. Wanna bet? Hey, I got an idea. Let's get a pool!"

Jack laughed, then shook his head. "Randall's gonna be all right."

"Yeah," Jimmy said. "You're probably right. If bein' all right means lookin' like you're sixty when you're forty, havin' gout in both feet, and bein' a drunk and a crackhead, fuck, he's got it made."

"Back off," Jack said from his place in the doorway.

"Oh, now you're gonna get mad? A second ago you were laughin'."

"You go too far," Jack said. "It ain't none of your business anyway."

"I'm kinda surprised you ain't with him, to tell you the truth, Jack. Why's that?"

"Back off, asshole," Jack said.

Billy moved a pawn.

"That's your move?" Figgs said.

"Uh, yeah."

"Mate, asshole," he said, moving a bishop into place.

Still studying the board, Billy dug into his pocket and handed Jimmy a twenty. "Thank you very much," he said.

"Figgs," Al called out. "You'll go with Lang's group, with Charlie."

Jimmy Figgs looked at Charlie. "I hope you know what the fuck you're doin'."

"Lang asked for him," Jack said. "Don't ever remember him askin' for you."

"I used to pack for him all the time," Figgs said.

"When you could play."

"Fuck you. I don't need it."

"Right. Best fuckin' loop in the yard but you don't need it," Jack said. "You're a chump. You're all chumps. You ain't never been nowhere. You don't know fuckin' shit. And you ain't no player no more, either. Ain't no players here no more."

"Fuck you." Figgs stood up. He was bigger and stronger than Jack, younger too.

But Jack never budged as he stared him down. He smirked and shook his head. "What're you gonna do, huh?" he said.

Jimmy Figgs stormed past him into the shack and slammed the door behind him.

"Yeah," Jack yelled after him. "Good comeback. Let's make sure you and Randall have a little talk when he gets back."

"Can he play?" Charlie asked.

"We got five guys here who've had their pro cards at one time or another. He's one of 'em. Used to hit it long but he's just another par-shooter now. No balls." Jack kicked the door open and yelled back into the shack. "Never could putt!"

The place was suddenly quiet. The range was silent and the last group headed to the first tee. Men who did not get jobs during the rush either retired to the shack or went to get more food. Billy sat alone on the bench tapping his toe and looking to the clubhouse. Spider stood on number one with two bags.

Charlie wandered into the back lot. It was like a dream, thinking of playing again. It sent his heart racing and he took in a deep breath to try to slow it. He rubbed the inside of his arm as his thoughts jumped from "if" he'd play to "how" he'd play. When he closed his eyes, his body, independent of his will, began to move. His feet found their old stance, and the rocking motion, the easy pendulum of his swing, like springwater welling up softly to the surface, took over his body.

"Balance, Charlie, balance. The swing is built from the ground up." His father's voice rippled through his mind like waves lapping a riverbank.

"You all right?" someone asked. Charlie started out of his daydream to find Jack leaning against the shack lighting a cigarette. Then from behind a shrub he pulled out a tattered plastic shopping bag and an old beat-up club. When he dropped the bag a few balls rolled out and he scraped one before him and began bouncing it off the face of the club.

"You're gonna be here awhile, Pittsburgh," he said. The ball sounded off the face of the club. Click, click, click.

"I got a loop," Charlie said.

"That ain't what I mean," Jack said. One final click and he caught the ball on the face of the club, held it for a second, then let it drop. Charlie smiled at the old trick. He used to show off for his mother in their backyard, using the club like a ping-pong paddle, bouncing the ball high, then low, then catching it in his shirt pocket with a bow.

"Hot dog! Show-off!" she'd say, laughing, sitting on the back porch steps with his father, arm in arm, the three of them enjoying the warm summer evening together.

Jack offered Charlie the club. "Hit one," he said.

"I don't think—"

"Come on," he said, and looked to the first tee. "It's cool. We do it all the time."

Charlie immediately buried his right hand in his pocket and took hold of the club with his left. Jack felt a disproportionate strength move up the shaft, and let go.

Feeling the weight of it, suspiciously, as if it posed some danger, Charlie took the club back over his head one-handed and stopped there, inspected his position, then let it fall gracefully.

"Don't cup the wrist," his father said. "Keep it flat for consistency. The less movement the better."

One swing, then two and by the third time the club found a rhythm of its own, the shaft whirring as it split the air. Each time it tipped the ground, dust popped up and then quickly dissipated in the wind. He recalled sounds of his old neighborhood, the cars flying by on a nearby bridge that spanned the Allegheny River, rattling over the potholes and metal seams in the road, the radio broadcasting the nightly baseball game. The sun setting behind a wall of brightly colored clouds backlighting the pollution of steel mills. Most of all, his father's fluid, graceful swing, the few times they played, the miles walked together never more than a few yards apart, in the short grass and down the middle, knowing for the next few hours where they were going, whose turn it was and what direction they were heading.

"Shot, Dad."

"Putt, Charlie. Helluva putt."

Charlie swallowed the sharp stab in his throat, wiped his eyes and took the club with both hands, wiggling his fingers into position on the grip. He raised the club upright before him, the years whisked away by a magic wand. Two small steps and his feet were suddenly planted in the ground, as if they, like these giant eucalyptus trees hiding him from his past, had grown roots. He swung the club back above his head and stopped it there, at the top of his swing. Again he studied his hands and their position. Then his arms came down and, when his right elbow brushed his hip, he froze, wiggled his elbow in and out, then returned the club back to the top of his swing, all the time analyzing his movements.

Good place, Jack thought, parallel, perfect, right in the slot where it should be. Fuckin' perfect.

Charlie pulled the club through where the ball would be, tipped the dirt again, then up into a beautiful finish. Perfectly balanced on his left foot, he held the club for a second, feeling his weight. He toed a ball and it rolled into a ridge of hard-packed mud.

"That's a pretty tough lie, Pittsburgh," Jack said. "Why don't you move it over in the grass?"

"That wouldn't be golf."

"You got a point," Jack said. "You gotta play it where it lies."

He looked out over the practice range to the bordering trees and found his target. He settled, took the club back and then down with unexpected force, the shaft bending under the torque and snapping downward into the ball. A loud thud rang out like a muffled gunshot, a sound Jack had never heard before; an inordinate amount of dust and dirt flew and the ball zipped toward the trees on a low, hard trajectory. Following its flight, Jack expected it to descend, but instead the ball rose to another level and pierced the strong west wind, passing over the fence and rattling among the trees.

Jack did his best to hide his amazement. That's a good one-eighty, he thought. With a seven-iron. An old, shitty one at that. "Shot," he said coolly, then noticed that Charlie was paying him no mind.

Jack prided himself on reading people quickly and Charlie was obvious. At first glance he appeared worn out, damaged, cut deeply, with so little energy for confrontation that at times he had only enough to step aside. His manner was easy and gentle, and though he had a streak of street smarts he seemed reluctant to use them and clearly didn't like how they made him feel. But when he took hold of the club the change that swept over him was abrupt, disturbing. His mind churned, and Jack couldn't imagine a sadder or darker man. His energy was odd and dangerous, but only to himself. So Jack let a second or two go by. Charlie suddenly let the club drop to his side and hung his head.

"What's the matter, kid?" Jack said as he crushed out a smoke.

"I can't believe I can do this," he murmured.

"When was the last time you played?"

Charlie raised his head and Jack found it hard to hold his gaze, but he did. One thing he always had was a good bluff. "A long time ago," Charlie said. "Years."

"What happened?" Jack asked.

Charlie responded by rolling a ball to himself with the toe of the club. Jack kicked the plastic bag and sent more balls rolling to his feet. Charlie drove the second ball deeper into the eucalyptus trees, then another. Each time a cloud of dust exploded up from the ground and quickly blew away in the breeze. Again and again he swung with an angry force, the resonance echoing across the course, every shot traveling farther and farther, straighter and straighter, as if willed to do so.

"Left to right," Jack said, and the next ball did just that. "Knock it down," and that ball went on a clothesline, low and screaming, then ricocheted off the fence. "Right to left," Jack said, and Charlie hit a large sweeping hook.

"That ball hooked forty yards," Jack said.

"I always could hit a hook," Charlie said, genuinely pleased. Then he hit a high, fluttering draw that held up against the wind and landed softly in the grass short of the fence.

A stern voice broke his rhythm. "What the fuck is goin' on here?" someone yelled. It was Al. When he got to Charlie, he snatched the club from his hands. "What the hell do you think you're doin'? You can hit a few balls, but you have to be a little more discreet. What the hell's wrong with you, Jack?"

"I got carried away," Charlie said. "I'm sorry."

Unruffled, Jack waved Charlie off and stepped between him and Al. "I was just into it, Al. You should see this guy."

Clearly flustered and uncomfortable with his authority, Al said, "Well, I had to do something. You could hear it all over the place. It sounded like . . . I don't know what." He snuck a wary look at Charlie. "A group heard it when they were making the turn. They were pissed."

"They'll get over it," Jack said.

"They're the members."

"Yeah, yeah, I fuckin' know."

"Jesus, Charlie, for a new guy you're sure causing a stir," Al said.

"Why?" Jack asked. "What else did he do?"

"Well, Lang insists on him working for him, Evans too, and those guys are tough. Randall's the only one who's caddied for them in five years, and now they want Charlie."

"So they want him?" Jack said. "What's the problem?"

"I know. The member's always right. Whatever they want goes, that's the deal and always will be."

"It's their club," Jack said by rote.

"But let's just say there were a few people who thought they were in line for that loop."

"Figgs," Charlie said.

"Yes," Al admitted.

"You're gonna have to deal with Randall when he gets back," Jack said.

"Jesus, Charlie," Al whined.

"Sorry Al," Charlie said.

"Ah, you're just doing your job." He turned to Jack. "When do you think he's coming back?"

"I don't know," Jack said. "He called me on the phone in the shack on Thursday 'bout eight o'clock in the morning."

"Where was he?"

"I don't know, but there was a helluva party goin' on."

"Eight in the morning? Jesus. He's gonna die."

"It'll take a helluva lot to kill Randall," Jack said. "He's a tough motherfucker."

"So how much does he have left?"

"I don't know," Jack said.

"How can someone party like that?" Al asked.

"It's easy," Jack said, still laughing. "One look at Randall and it ain't that hard to believe."

When the three rounded the hedge, Daniel Lang was waiting there, his arms folded. Jimmy Figgs stood on the tee with his towel around his neck, leaning on two bags, Grant Evans, Dr. Smith, and David Shaw behind him, waiting too. The bench was clear and Charlie had no idea how long Lang had been standing there.

"Ready to go?" he asked.

"Tee it up," Charlie replied.

8

Like the day before, Charlie stood on the tee with Grant Evans' bag on his left shoulder, Daniel Lang's on his right, the last few painful years forgotten, at least for the moment, a bridge between when he could play and the present, finally traversed. He felt euphoric, restored to the game he loved.

From the first steps off the tee they all set into motion, falling into the familiar rhythms and moving along at a brisk pace, the caddies in skillful cadence with their players, quiet and out of sight when they needed to be, always in position and ready with information, factoring in wind, terrain and skill.

In search of an errant tee shot, Jimmy Figgs laid his bags in the fairway, veered down a steep hill and disappeared into the woods. Moments later he came strolling back into the daylight, a ball in each hand and a couple more bulging deep in his pocket. "O.B.," he hollered up to the fairway.

David Shaw's company had erected skyscrapers, leveled mountains and detoured great rivers around the world. He was tall and rangy, imposing at times, but at this moment he stood at the edge of the rough, like a cat not wanting to get its paws wet. "What?" he called, hand cupping his ear.

"O.B.," Figgs repeated. "Out of bounds."

"Shit," Shaw said. He pointed to his second tee shot and announced his position to the group. "I'm laying three here, damn it."

"Good start, partner," Evans said, then laid up his second to the par five with his usual left-to-right shot, a smooth swing and solid hit. Charlie was off at impact, following its flight until the ball vanished over the far hill.

"Shot," Lang said. He pulled out his three-wood, removed the headcover and flipped it to Charlie.

The fourth man, Dr. Alan Smith, "Schmitty," a short, pudgy and pleasant man, a ten handicap with thick lips and a bald head he hid with a sun-bleached cap, laid up with a fading five-wood and Shaw followed suit.

But not Lang. His unorthodox swing and old-fashioned waggle looked archaic, though by sheer athletic talent it all came together in the end; square contact was made, and the ball sailed over the crest of the hill. Jimmy Figgs pulled up beside Charlie. "That's on," he said. "So get out that piece of shit he calls a putter."

"He's pretty good with it," Charlie said.

"Yeah, he is," Jimmy admitted, and the two split up.

Charlie walked off the yardage, rested his bag on the ground and leaned on it, whistling.

"You seem to have caught on," Evans said as he strolled to his ball.

"It's a good day," Charlie said.

"Get laid last night?"

"Uh, no," Charlie replied, trying to sound as glib.

"What do I have?"

"One twenty-five."

Evans stuck his wedge close, and Charlie handed him his putter. "Good call," Evans said as he took off.

Schmitty's approach rolled just outside of Evans', and Shaw's farther away still.

"I'm five there," Shaw said, then tossed his divot back into place.

"What, are you proud of that?" Schmitty asked as he unwrapped a cigar.

"No, just being fair," Shaw answered. "I don't want anyone to think I'm putting for birdie."

Figgs handed him his putter. "Don't worry, Mr. Shaw," he said, and hustled away.

Shaw pointed. "What the fuck did he mean by that?"

Lang walked up and threw an arm around him. "We know, ol' buddy! That was a wonderful tee shot. Didn't we like it, partner?"

"Loved it," Schmitty answered.

"Fuck you, Daniel," Shaw said, and the three of them started toward the green like schoolboys heading down a country road for a dip.

Figgs pulled the pin and dropped it on the fringe. Shaw putted and hit it halfway to the hole. "I'll finish," he said.

"You're putting for seven," Schmitty said. "It's good."

"Pick it up," Lang said.

Shaw paused. "Don't I stroke here?"

"No," said Schmitty. "It's the eighteen handicap, the easiest fuckin' hole on the course."

"Nice try, partner," Evans said.

Schmitty placed his ball in front of his mark as Jimmy Figgs circled the putt studying the grain and slope, trying to find the line for the birdie putt.

"Please, gentlemen, today," Evans said.

"Fuck you, Grant," Schmitty said. "You can't rush genius. Don't you know that?"

"Here," Jimmy said, pointing to a spot with the butt of a club.

Schmitty addressed his putt. "Let's give you a run at that eagle, Danny boy."

"Are we playing aggregate score too?" Shaw asked, and Schmitty backed off his ball.

"Yes," Evans answered. "Fifty on the best ball, fifty on the second best, and a buck on you and your partner's aggregate score. The same fucking game we've been playing for twenty years."

"Don't let my putting get in the way of your conversation, guys," Schmitty said.

The putt came up a foot short. "What the fuck was that?" he growled through his cigar. "My partner's puttin' for a fuckin' eagle and I leave it short. Christ!" He went to tap in.

"That's good," Evans said, and Schmitty smacked his ball away.

"Christ," he spat again.

"Just where the hell are you, Danny?" Shaw asked.

Lang took a step closer and with his putter pointed to a coin five feet from the hole. "Got a good kick," he said.

"Jesus Christ," Shaw said to Evans, "I guess you better make that."

Grant Evans walked around his putt, took a second longer than his normal routine. He was a money man, stocks, a corporate raider, and a devil for details. He stroked the ball, his line and speed were good, and the putt found the middle of the cup.

"Look at him," Lang said, and a smile lit his face. "First hole and the sonofabitch is grindin' away!"

It was the most animated Lang had been and it was infectious and strange. The even keel he maintained was broken, consciously, with control, for effect and the result he wanted.

"Savin' my ass partner," Shaw said to Evans. "Great birdie."

Lang lined up his putt. The group settled. They were alive. The game was on and Charlie was right in the middle of it, his blood pumping as if he himself were putting for eagle.

"Be still," John MacLeod said.

"I am, Dad," Charlie argued.

"Like hell. You're looking over at the first tee when all your attention should be right here," he said, pointing to the ball in front of Charlie. "You're anything but still."

"Yes sir," Charlie said.

They stood facing each other on the practice green, putters in hand. "Not just your body, not just your hands. Up here." John tapped Charlie lightly on the forehead. "Your mind, clear it. Focus. Your eyes see nothing but the line to the cup. Your breath," he said, closing his eyes and inhaling as if he were taking in the fragrance of exotic flowers, and blew out slowly. "Be. Still."

When Charlie took a breath, his eyes fluttered. Even his father was surprised by the rapidity with which he could achieve such deep concentration, an ability he must have been born with. He was only nine years old.

"Now," John said.

Charlie bent over a clean white golf ball and set the putter behind it.

"Good," his father said. "Once you find the break, you'll see the line, then stroke the ball down that line."

Charlie pulled the club back easily and sent the ball rolling smoothly just left of the cup; it slowed a bit, took the break, and fell lazily in.

John shouldered his own bag. "That's it. Good stroke. Got it?"

"Got it," Charlie answered.

"I'll be back as soon as we're done." He pointed to the eighteenth green of the popular public course. "Look for me there."

It was a glorious day in late March. A brilliant sun blazed in the high blue sky, and no fewer than a dozen foursomes waited eagerly, itching to play now that winter had ended early.

Charlie watched him go. "Dad?"

His father turned sharply. "What? Something isn't clear?"

"Never mind," Charlie said, and bowed his head over another putt. A tear spilled over and rolled down his face, dripping off his chin and into the green grass.

"None of that," John said.

"I know." Charlie wiped his face. "Sorry. They're waiting for you."

"And I'll go when I'm ready."

One of the men on the first tee called out, "Come on, Mac. We gotta go!"

"Go ahead and hit," he shouted back, then walked over and squatted opposite his son. "Practice, Charlie, practice," he whispered. "I know you want to play, but that's not important."

"I know," Charlie said.

"Do you trust me?"

"Yes. Always."

"Then do as I say. You're already better than most. You believe me?" A bashful smile bloomed on Charlie's face. "You know that, don't you? When you see those guys hit it, don't you know you hit it better?" Charlie nodded. "Look at these people around you. They drop a few balls on the green, push 'em around and call it practice. They have no idea what it takes. None. But you do. That's what I'm giving you, son. That's all I have—your mother, you, and this game."

Charlie sighed. "Yes sir."

As his father's tee shot flew over the far hill, Charlie rolled in another putt. Two hours later, the foursome made the turn as Charlie, off in his own world, rolled ball after ball toward an overflowing cup.

"Hit for show, putt for dough, Charlie," one of them yelled as the group passed. But Charlie was hunched over a short putt that had all his attention.

The sun had set when his father came and stood beside the green with a six-pack. Charlie putted by moonlight.

"I can't see the hole," John said. "Let's go."

"I know where it is." Charlie rolled the ball into the dark corner of the green. It vanished, and a second later there was a rattle in a plastic cup.

"Great putt, Charlie," his father said, wobbling as he reached down for his bag.

Charlie stepped up quickly. "I got it," he said. His father waved him away. "Bullshit. The day I can't carry my bag . . ."

The two walked slowly through the parking lot toward the only car left. "How'd you play?" Charlie asked.

"Seventy-one."

"Good score for the first round of the year."

"Good enough for me," his father said. "Not you."

Lang's smile washed away. His concentration returned as he squatted behind a short, but quick, downhill putt.

"Lightning," Schmitty warned.

"Hmm," Daniel grunted in agreement. "How the hell a ball stays up here from two hundred and forty yards, I don't know." He took a stance. "A little right to left, Charlie?"

"Straight putt," Charlie said, and the whole group paused. Schmitty's cigar twitched back and forth between his teeth, Jimmy Figgs shifted his weight, Shaw pushed his sunglasses tighter on his nose and Grant Evans' eyes darted from Lang to Charlie.

"You can see that from over there?" Lang asked.

"Uh-huh," Charlie said. "It's straight."

Lang stroked it gently, giving it a good roll, and with every eye on it, the ball crept down the hill, never moving left or right, and on the last revolution dropped in the hole.

"Christ," Evans said. "Great putt. What a read."

"No shit," Schmitty snorted. "That ball has to move."

"Didn't," Lang said. "Not a bit."

The group started to the second tee.

"Stay here and spot," Figgs ordered Charlie, then took off down a steep hill, dodging and hiding inside the tree line while looking back to find each drive as it was hit.

"Ready golf," Lang snapped. "Whoever's ready, go."

Schmitty took his awkward swing and whacked a good drive. "Follow that, you sonsabitches," he said.

A moment later, Charlie led the group off the tee. Lang quickly caught up to him. "Helluva read back there," he said. "I didn't see it."

"I feel pretty good," Charlie said.

"Hittin' a few balls does that much for you?"

Caught off guard, Charlie couldn't tell if he was being reprimanded or complimented. "Is that all right?"

"Fine with me," Lang answered.

Again Charlie was left to wonder if he'd been accepted or warned. As the fairway turned steep, he felt his breath shorten and his patience wane.

"What do I have here?" Lang asked.

"I walked off twenty from the one-ninety trap. It's uphill and the wind's—"

"Playin' yardage, Charlie." Lang's tone turned cold. "You can keep all that other stuff to yourself. I know which way the wind's blowing and a monkey can walk off yardage. What's it going to play?"

"One eighty," Charlie said, trying to check his anger.

"What would you hit here, Charlie?"

"Five-iron," Charlie said. "If I were you I'd hit a five."

"I didn't ask you that."

Charlie shrugged. "I don't know. I haven't—"

"What, six? Think you can get a six there? You're not that big. I don't think you have enough ass."

"So what?" Charlie said. "Hogan was five nine, maybe, and he'd hit it by you all day long."

Lang suppressed a smile as he pulled a five-iron. "Seven? I'll kiss your ass you get a seven-iron there."

"Hit the five, but smooth it." Charlie picked up his bags. "Don't jump all over it."

"Is that what I do?" Lang asked. "Jump on my shots?"

Charlie couldn't believe the words had come out of his mouth. "No. I'm sorry."

"No, no. Tell me, is that what I do?"

Bewildered, Charlie set the bags back down. "Mr. Lang, I'm not a teacher."

"But you know. You can't hit a ball like that"—he pointed back toward the clubhouse—"and not know. I've been around this game too fuckin' long."

Evans yelled back down the fairway. "Are we taking a break or what?"

Lang waited for an answer.

"We gotta go," Charlie said.

"If you haven't guessed by now, I go when I'm ready."

A moment later, they followed his shot as it sailed toward the green.

"Shot," Charlie said, handing Lang his putter. Then as they climbed the hill, he began huffing and puffing.

Lang relented, "You a little tired?"

"Got to get my sorry ass in shape," Charlie said.

"Well, this'll do it." He put a hand on Charlie's shoulder. "It's about four miles around this track," he said. "You can work a lot of stuff in four miles. I've done it myself." They neared the green and paused as Shaw played out from a greenside bunker. Lang was once again poised and friendly; he'd gotten what he wanted, a bead on his new caddy. "I like to get to the point, Charlie," he said. "I hope we understand each other."

"I understand," Charlie said, before sucking in a deep breath to make it up the hill.

9

The players headed for the third tee, the caddies in the opposite direction, up a steep forty-yard hill through the rough. Jimmy and Charlie easily spotted the tee shots from well down the fairway, on the highest point on the course and a good two hundred yards in front of their foursome. The clouds and fog had cleared, the sun was out and Charlie decided to shed a layer of clothing. The last drive sailed off-line as he stuffed his sweater into Lang's bag.

"Got that one?" Figgs asked. "There's a big trap there. Lang's probably in it."

Charlie shouldered his bags once again.

"You must've caddied before," Jimmy said.

Charlie breathed heavily, trying to catch his wind. "Been a while. Jesus, that hill's steep."

"What've you been doing?" Figgs asked.

"Little a this, little a that."

"Hey, I'm sorry about before," Figgs said. "I'm just razzin' you a little. We got so many ducks showin' up here."

"Ducks?"

"Yeah. Assholes don't know what they're doing. Drunks and crackheads, just roll off the street, pick up a bag and make some money. They don't know shit about golf, don't have the slightest interest, then bitch when they don't get out. They fuck it up for everybody. Give caddies a bad name."

"I always thought the players were the ducks, the guys who don't pay."

"They're ducks too."

"Doesn't Al pick the caddies?" Charlie asked.

"He's another duck."

Charlie gained enough breath to laugh. "I guess nobody wants that job."

"Caddy master? No fuckin' way." Jimmy Figgs looked to the sky as he crossed the fairway. A calmness that did not seem possible passed over him. "And miss all this?"

Here, the world seemed to stop. Along the western edge of the property, a beautiful dense forest of soft pine trees formed a natural wall separating the course from the ocean and all things beyond. No structure could serve the purpose better. It was remarkably quiet. Just above the trees the blue sky melted into a gray tuft of fog, creeping and ominous, alive, weaving down and through the woods like giant melting fingers. A salty breeze snuck through, and Charlie regained his breath inhaling it.

With the bags off his shoulders he felt light, unencumbered, and here, between shots, he could take time and mark where he was. The players walked and chatted, the gentle breeze rustling their sweaters and pant legs. Across the fairway Figgs waited too, but it was peculiar. Grumpy and intense as he waited on the bench, or at a table playing cards or chess, he was as peaceful at this moment as a soul could be. His head came up and he took a deep breath, then closed his eyes and tilted his face to let the sun cover it with light and warmth. Still sunning himself, he said, "You got one fifty-two, Doc."

"Did you even look?" Schmitty asked.

"What's to see?"

"What a flake."

Figgs opened his eyes. "Yeah, one fifty-two."

"Is that all?" Schmitty asked.

"One fifty-two," Figgs said again.

"You don't think the wind—"

Jimmy came out of his trance and gave him an irritated look. "It's one fifty-two. On my mother's grave, and she's dead as a doornail."

"Believe it," Shaw said.

"I hate it when you're right," Schmitty said as he tossed his cigar to the ground and grabbed a club. "I'm gonna feather it in there, you fuckin' Irish bastards. Watch this!"

Figgs and Shaw headed toward the next ball.

"'Feather it in there,'" Shaw whispered. "He'll dump it in the front trap."

"Yep," Figgs said.

The breeze caught the weakly struck ball and sent it tumbling into the trap, buried it in the face of the bunker, barely visible in the sand. Figgs shook his head.

"You better play hard, Danny boy!" Shaw called out. "Your ten-handicap partner's over here feathering it in!"

"Are you sure it was only one fifty-two, Figgs? There's a lot of wind up there."

"Your ass," Shaw said. "Don't blame the fucking caddy. A man of your stature in the community. It's really pathetic."

"Don't let them rattle you, partner," Lang called back. "You get a stroke here!" His ball was sitting up nicely, but the face of the bunker was steep. He turned to Charlie. "Did you ever see a sixty-year-old man hit a nine-iron a hundred and fifty yards out of a bunker?"

"Tough," Charlie warned.

"Could you?"

Charlie smiled. "Maybe."

Daniel flushed the short iron, then hopped out of the trap to see the ball carry just beyond the pin.

"Helluva shot," Charlie said, and reached for the putter.

. . .

The round took three hours and forty minutes. "Didn't feel like that long," Charlie said.

"If it takes any longer people are just screwin' around," Daniel said, then handed Charlie his pay.

"Good job, Charlie," Grant Evans said, and passed him some cash. "I'll keep my bag here."

Lang tossed Charlie his keys. "Clean 'em up and put 'em in, will ya?" he said.

He hoisted both bags, dropped Evans' off at the back door of the pro shop, and was heading to the black Mercedes when he heard someone shout Daniel Lang's name. He turned to see a smartly dressed man, tall and slim with dark, wavy hair cut short and extremely neat, approach the group and shake Lang's hand.

"How are you, Stephen?" Daniel said.

"Hey, pro," Schmitty said.

"Dr. Smith," Stephen Ford said, and the conversation faded as Charlie quickly headed toward Daniel's car, his heart pounding, his mouth instantly dry. He struggled to find the right key, and when he clicked the trunk shut he kept his back turned, trying frantically to find Jimmy Figgs in the crowd of caddies and afternoon players.

"Charlie!" Lang called, motioning that he needed his keys back, and when Charlie broke into a slow jog he held up his hand. "That's all right, you don't need to run."

Charlie took a few steps more, feeling Stephen Ford's eyes on him, then stopped and tossed Lang his keys.

"So you're in town," Evans said. "How's the tour?"

Ford watched Charlie go into the shack and come out carrying a canvas duffle.

"You got a little break, don't you?" Shaw asked. "Going home for a while?"

Charlie passed by and into the parking lot. "Yeah, I'm playing in a charity event in Ohio, then heading home." He pointed at Charlie. "Who is that?"

"Do you know him?" Lang asked.

"I think I do."

"From where?"

"I'm not sure."

"His name's Charlie. I don't know—"

"MacLeod! Charlie MacLeod," Ford said.

"That's his last name?" Lang asked.

"Yeah. That's Charlie MacLeod."

"I'm lost," Shaw said.

"Me too," Lang said.

"He's from Pennsylvania, right? Pittsburgh?"

"I don't know," Lang said. "Back East somewhere. He just got here. Worked for me yesterday and today. Good caddy."

"Yeah, I'll bet he is," Ford said with a laugh. "Is he playing?"

Jimmy Figgs trotted up to Shaw and handed him his car keys. "Here you go, Mr. Shaw."

"I guess," Lang said. "I caught him hitting a few balls behind the shack."

"How'd he look?"

Lang hesitated.

"Good?" Ford asked.

Lang shook his head. "Good doesn't really describe it."

Ford smiled. "Did you ever see anything like that?" he said.

Lang shook his head again. "No. Never."

"We were teammates in high school."

"Really?"

"When he was fifteen I don't think there was a better amateur in the state. He was a caddy at Oakmont."

"Great course. Six U.S. Opens," Evans said. "Miller's sixty-three."

"The rain the night before helped out," Ford said. "I'm not taking anything away from Miller, but you could never fire at those pins like he did. The greens won't let you, not at Oakmont, not on Sunday. I know. I grew up there. Charlie too."

"But still the greatest round," Shaw said.

"Probably," Ford said. "Where'd he go?"

"Charlie?" Figgs said. "He took off."

"Maybe he didn't recognize you," Evans said.

"Oh, he recognized him," Lang said, gazing at Ford.

In the presence of such men, Stephen seemed to shrink. His eyes wavered as he tried to imagine what Lang was thinking. He grinned weakly.

"Is there anything you can tell us about him?" Lang asked.

"Charlie? I haven't seen him since I was a teenager."

Lang waited.

"Are we talking about golf?" Ford asked.

"We are," Lang said.

"I see." Stephen felt like a traitor giving up an innocent man. But his memories were still so vivid, so pure, that his enthusiasm overtook his caution. "The first time Charlie MacLeod played Oakmont he shot seventy-five. The first time he broke par, he shot sixty-four, from the back tees. With seven clubs. He'd just turned fifteen."

"Fuck you," Schmitty said.

"I'm tellin' you," Ford said. "Just me and him. I was the only one who saw it and I never told anyone, except my father."

"Why not?" Schmitty asked.

"Who'd believe him?" Lang said.

"I don't believe you now," Schmitty said. The men laughed briefly and then, like a board meeting being called to order, waited for Ford to speak. And he, relishing the attention, forgot who was present, their far-reaching influence and what lengths such men would go to for pride, money or vengeance.

"I dated a girl from his neighborhood. One night I'm picking her up, it was summertime, the sun's still up. As soon as I walk into her house I hear this *whoosh*, then *pow!* coming from the back-yard. I thought it was somebody building, hammering or something. I walk out back and in the next yard over there's this skinny kid wearing beat-up shorts and a T-shirt, pounding ball after ball at this old swing set. His father had taken the swings off and stretched old re-caps between the chains. The balls would hit them and just drop to the ground."

"My kind of playground," Schmitty said.

"Yeah. And his old man's sitting on the porch, and with each swing he takes a swig of beer and then corrects him. Now mind, I'm a scratch player by this time, I just came in second at states and I'm thinking, leave the kid alone, he's great, but not this guy. He whispers like he's in church chanting prayers on Sunday morning. And the kid's eatin' it up. He's taking every club in his bag and just striping the ball every time. Off bare dirt! You should've heard the sound."

Jimmy Figgs snuck a look at Daniel, who seemed to sense it but remained quiet. "So what happened?" Figgs asked.

"Well, my date comes down the steps, a half hour late, and this kid's still whaling away." Stephen shook his head. "He was so strong. I was twice his size and I'm getting tired just watching him. 'Hi, Charlie,' my girl says as she walks up to the fence. She says, 'You wanna meet Stephen? He's a good golfer. He plays at Oakmont! How about that?' Well, Charlie stops and says, 'Yeah, I know. Hi.' A nicer kid you couldn't meet. He starts to walk over but then his father says, 'Hey, what are you doin'?' and Charlie's whole face changes. He goes back and starts drilling these old balls again."

"Did you say anything to him?" Lang asked.

"No. You didn't say much to John MacLeod. He was an intimidating guy. I said, 'Good evening,' and started to leave. He walked over to the fence with a beer in his hand and said, 'Next summer this boy's coming to beat you.'"

"Was he loaded?" Lang asked.

"Yeah," Ford admitted. "He must have been. I met him again later. He was really nice, a gentleman. He did drink, a lot, but I'll tell you what. Charlie beat me. Bad. I was four years older and never had a chance." Stephen shook his head. "See, his father wouldn't let him play until he could move the ball left and right, hook and slice, fade and draw, with every club in his bag. No shit. He told him he didn't deserve to walk on a course until he could, and that Oakmont would be the first course he played."

"Could that sonofabitch do that?" Schmitty asked.

"John MacLeod was a player. He didn't have the means, but he made sure his son did."

"So Charlie beat you?" Lang said.

"Shit, I was just happy to be there. First time, we played on a Monday with our high school coach. Charlie knew the course pretty well from caddying. We played nine holes. He shot thirty-eight from the mid-tees and I shot thirty-nine. First time he ever plays on any course and he's two over on a U.S. Open track. He beat me for a dollar. A few months later, we went back to the championship tees and he shot the sixty-four."

"At Oakmont?" Evans said again.

"I never told anyone. Like Daniel said, who'd believe me? That fall he won states. I played my ass off, shot sixty-nine and came in second by six shots."

"What happened to him?" Evans asked.

As if shaken from a pleasant dream, Stephen answered quickly. "He got hurt. Right after states. Tore a muscle or something, in his elbow playin' with his dad." Stephen avoided their eyes while feigning concern, scanned the parking lot and the tunnel of trees. Charlie was long gone.

"I wish I could have talked to him," Ford said.

But Danny Lang knew a lie when he heard one. Grant Evans did too.

"That kind of injury was hard to fix then," Schmitty said. "Too bad. Christ."

Stephen forced a grin. "I guess."

"Your father's a doctor, isn't he?" Schmitty asked. "Damn good one, I hear."

"Yes, he is," Stephen said.

Even Schmitty, who spent his days cutting into arms and legs, shoulders and knees, could detect a pile of bullshit when it was heaped in front of him. With a look from Lang, he turned back to Ford, like a cat cornering a mouse. "Did your father work on him?"

Ford fabricated a look of surprise. "You know, I think he did. Yeah." He nodded as if the thought had just struck him. "Come to think of it, he did."

10

Charlie stood in the cool night air leaning against the railing in front of his room, one story up, incapable of sleep, mulling over and over again his reaction to seeing Stephen Ford. His nerves had calmed somewhat but he couldn't stop thinking how this random encounter had knocked him as low as he'd ever been. He had actually started to relax, to believe he could restart his life, but then, out of nowhere, the mere sight of someone he hadn't seen in years sent him spiraling down into a panic. He was certain of one thing: he'd never experienced such calamity, such doubt, until the very day he left Helen. Not until that beautiful, clear fall afternoon when he drove away for the last time did he know something was terribly wrong. And now this same feeling again.

His door was open, his bag packed and lying in the doorway, half in, half out. Where could he go? Out over the rooftops he could see the tops of bridges leading east, where he wasn't about to go. Under them the rough current of the bay swirled and pitched everything floating west and out to sea. The parking lot below was filled with cars, every room dark; only the glow of the office lights shone through the glass wall onto the front sidewalk. The VACANCY sign popped on and, knowing he couldn't fall asleep for hours, he decided to take a walk. He kicked his bag inside and closed the door.

In the street, sounds of traffic jarred him; a siren wailed nearby. The sidewalk was crowded, and the cold wind seemed to be coming from everywhere.

"How're you doing?" a gentle voice called out behind him. The front-desk girl, her red hair pulled back in a ponytail and a sweater draped over her shoulders, had cracked the office door open. "Aren't you cold?" she asked. "You look cold."

"A little," Charlie said. "I can't sleep."

"Well, I have to stay up." She smiled and waved Charlie in. "Talk to me."

The lobby was warm, the light low and soothing, the sounds of traffic muffled. "My mom comes in at six. Have a seat." In the corner was a worn, double-wide stuffed chair. "I'm Sarah."

"Charlie."

"I know," she said, tapping the registry.

"Right. Just the two of you? You and your mom?"

"Just me and my mom," Sarah answered as she slid back behind the counter. "My dad died. Cancer. Smoker," she said matter-of-factly.

"You didn't get along with him?"

"Of course," she answered, a bit puzzled. "He's my dad."

"I'm sorry," Charlie said politely. "It just came out a little easy."

Sarah shrugged. "He's been gone a long time. I grew up being the kid who said, 'Hi, I'm Sarah, my dad's dead, will you play with me?' You just get used to it after a while."

"Really?" Charlie said, trying to sound casual, but he choked. "My mom passed away . . ." he stopped and thought. "Almost a year ago now."

"I'm sorry. Your father?"

A scowl covered Charlie's face. "I haven't seen him for a long time," he said, and suddenly seemed worn out, so she let it go.

"Why don't you sit? It's a really comfortable chair."

Charlie sat on the edge of the deep, soft cushion.

"We've always lived here, and when I was a kid I was afraid to sleep upstairs alone so I slept down here, on that. If you can't fall asleep in that thing, it can't be done."

"It's comfortable," Charlie admitted. His heart slowed and he sighed. "Thanks."

"So, what do you wanna talk about?" she said. "I got four hours to kill, and I think I've drunk about a pot of coffee."

Charlie laughed and looked at her closely for the first time. She was young and pretty. Like an old-time movie star, he thought. Her light hazel eyes sparkled and a sensual, mischievous smirk curved the corners of her mouth. "Have you always worked here?" he asked.

"Long as I can remember. But a couple more months and I'm out. I'm free."

Her enthusiasm was infectious, and Charlie played along. "Free, huh? That sounds nice."

"Not a care in the world," she said. "I've saved some money and I'm going to travel."

"It's good to see other things," he said, but his heart wasn't in it.

"Of course it is," said Sarah. "Where are you going next?"

"Next?" he answered. "I don't know."

"No plans?"

"Not a one. I like it here, though. I even found a job." He shook his head. "It was going good."

"Was?"

Charlie slumped back into the chair, struggling to find a satisfactory answer, but then gave up. "I don't know."

"I think you should stay."

Sarah's words, stated with such conviction, sounded absurd. But holding out hope, he listened, even as he felt incapable of heeding them. "Why's that?" he asked.

"Well, you said you like it here, right?"

"I do," he admitted. "It's so different. The weather's great. It's like another country."

"Do you have to get back?"

"No," Charlie answered. "But I have a place there. A house and a car."

"You flew here?"

"No. Trains then a couple buses."

"And you don't miss your things?"

"I got tired of them," he said. "Let someone else drive, someone else make the decisions."

"Perfect. Then why leave?"

He wished he didn't, but in the light of such simple optimism he felt old, rigid. So he considered her as carefully as he did his words. "People travel, move or just leave for all sorts of reasons." He gazed through the glass wall at the busy street. "They change. Ambition. Or they get tired, scared."

"And you?"

He caught her reflection in the glass and she his. "Terrified," he said. "I didn't use to be, a few years ago, but I am now."

"You don't look it," she said. When Charlie turned, she met his light eyes. His boyish but lined face had a simple honesty, daunting but safe. She suppressed a chill. "What could you be afraid of?"

"Of meeting new people. Of seeing old ones."

"Are you scared right now? Of me?"

Again her abrupt simplicity took him by surprise. Relieved, he slumped back into the chair. "No, come to think of it, I'm not."

"I think you should give the place a chance."

Charlie took in a deep breath. "Maybe," he said, suddenly sleepy. "I'm here. I thought I was leaving, but I'm still here."

"Where else would you want to go?"

"That's what stopped me. Nowhere. I'm done in," he said. "I'm here." His eyes grew heavy and he nodded.

Sarah stole a look at him. She liked his angular face, his straight nose, his strong jaw. He folded his hands on his lap. "Working hands," Sarah said softly.

"What?" Charlie mumbled, falling deeper into comfort.

Her father was a welder in the shipyards, his body taut, his hands rough. "Nothing. Sleep."

"Do you mind?" Charlie said without lifting his head. "It's just so nice here."

"Not at all," she answered and opened her book. "I used to feel the same way."

He yawned and closed his eyes. "Could you wake me when you leave?"

"Sure," she said, and feigned reading.

His sadness was compelling. Beneath his grief lay a deep stillness and she wondered where he'd learned that. What else had he suffered?

"Thanks," Charlie said. "I got to get up, go to work."

11

Across the aisle, on the train, white towels draped over their shoulders, William Moorer and Sam Deacon were sitting together. Charlie hopped through the closing doors, sat down, tucked his bag behind his head and closed his eyes as the subway trundled out of a tunnel into the early-morning darkness. "You guys goin' to work?" Charlie asked.

"No, no," William said. "Out for our morning jog."

Charlie opened his eyes and smiled. "Is that right?"

"Gotta stay in shape, you know." He nodded at his friend. "Don't he look good?" Sam was a modest little man who looked even smaller sitting there, his deeply tanned skin pale compared to William's. "Wouldn't believe how old he is."

"Sh-sh-shut up," Sam said.

William rose from his seat, moving quickly, gracefully out of Sam's reach. "Eighty," he said.

Charlie stared at Sam, whose hair was gray only at the temples. "Get the hell out of here. Take your hat off."

Sam removed his hat to reveal a head full of thick, dark hair. Crow's-feet lined his eyes but his cheeks, jaw, and neck belonged on a much younger man. His dark eyes twinkled.

"Sixty," Charlie said. "And that's stretching it."

"Here," Sam said, holding out his hands. "These are old." His fingers were crooked and bent. "I-I can only hold it with these two," he said, wiggling his thumb and forefinger.

"He's talkin' about . . ." William grabbed at his crotch.

"That man's terrible," his friend said.

"No," Charlie said to Sam. "Still?"

"Well, yeah, sure," Sam said. "B-but I was talkin' about golf," and the three of them laughed.

"Got him a young girl now. Real sharp," William said.

"Eighty," Charlie repeated.

"Gives you something to look forward to," William said.

"You-you got a girl?" Sam asked.

Without meaning to, Charlie thought of Sarah. "No. But I've met someone."

"Oh," Sam said, but seemed puzzled.

"That's how they do it nowadays, Deacon," William explained. "They sniff around, do a little dance. See if it's safe."

"Oh," Sam said, pretending to understand.

"Not like me and you."

They all three laughed again.

"I-I thought I s-saw you out there loopin', didn't I?" Sam asked.

"Yeah. Twice. Danny Lang."

"That's R-Randall's loop."

"So I've been told," Charlie said. "He can have it whenever he gets back from wherever the hell he is."

"That ain't up to you," William said. "Lang wants to, he'll keep you."

Charlie sat up. "The hell it ain't. I don't need some crazy motherfucker getting on my ass about a loop."

"You got one thing right," William said. "He's crazy."

"L-Lang's a g-good loop," Sam said. "G-good man. L-looks out for the caddies."

"Shit," William said. "He's a member. If he wants you it's for somethin' nobody else can give him. Don't ever fuckin' forget that."

"True enough," Sam said.

"Minute you can't walk he won't know you."

Sam looked saddened by these facts but did not argue.

"Don't he know Stephen Ford?" William asked. "Saw him around yesterday. Him and Lang usually play together, but not yesterday."

"S-seems like you know h-h-him too," Sam said, looking at Charlie.

The train rattled along the tracks. The buildings became one-story houses and the sky grew wider as they moved farther from the city. "News travels fast," Charlie said.

"Shack's a small place. S-sometimes that's good. Nice little world. Somet-times that's bad."

"Yeah, I know Stephen." Charlie drew a breath. "A long time ago."

"Good p-player," Sam said.

"Lazy," William mumbled.

"T-t-true."

"That's him," Charlie said.

"Can h-h-hit it a mile."

"Big fuckin' deal," William said.

"I-I-I know," Sam replied. "Wh-wh-who do you think you're talkin' to?"

"You play, kid?" William asked.

"Well," Charlie said, "if I know Stephen, probably I did."

"You gonna play Monday?"

Suspicious, he eyed them both. "No," he said quietly, then turned to watch the rising sun.

"'S okay," William said. He looked to Sam, who waved him on. "You should play," William said as the train began to slow down.

Charlie grabbed his bag and stood. "Is this the stop?"

"Not if you wanna work," William said.

His hand on the overhead railing, Charlie stared through the open door debating if he should get off anyway. But then the train jolted forward, jarring him. "I'll just follow you guys for now." He took his seat. "I'm a little lost."

"Everybody gets lost, kid," William said. "Hell, the whole shack is lost. You fit right in."

"It's a g-great golf course," Sam said. "You should play it."

"I know it is," Charlie answered. "I don't have any sticks anyway. But most of all I don't want to."

"Y-you don't play th-this golf course," Sam said, "then you ain't no player."

"Who said I was?" Charlie's temper rose. "No disrespect, Mr. Deacon, but I won't be insulted into doing anything."

"I'm sorry. Th-th-that was stupid. I just heard y-you could p-p-play."

"Figures. Damn it! I never should've hit those balls. But really, Mr. Deacon."

"Sam."

"Okay, Sam. It was a long, long time ago."

"Just talk. It's a sh-shame, that's all."

"You got talent," William said, "you should play."

Charlie looked at him. "For what? Tell me."

"Fun," Sam said. "A little money."

"I don't think that's fun. I'm not sure it ever was. And I don't really need the money."

"Test yourself," William said. "Nothing like a little match to see where your head's at."

"I know exactly where my head is," Charlie said halfheartedly.

"And where might that be?" William asked.

"Right up my ass. It's been there for quite some time."

"So maybe it's time to pull it out."

"I don't think it works that way," Charlie answered.

"N-no, it doesn't," Sam interrupted. "F-fuck all that boo-boo-bootstraps b-b-b-bullshit."

When the train came to another stop, William shook his head. The automatic doors opened, but not a soul could be seen.

"He's a pretty good player," William said, pointing to Sam. "I wasn't bad myself."

"D-don't," Sam said.

"Okay," William said. Like a big kid playing a game, he bounded across the aisle next to Charlie.

"He don't w-wanna hear that old w-war story crap," Sam said.

The train pulled out of the station into the dawn, the harsh orange light revealing the lines on Sam Deacon's face. William nudged Charlie with an elbow, and it felt like a baseball bat poking him in the ribs. "He took Hogan twenty-two holes," he said. "Then beat him. Him." He pointed a finger. "That little motherfucker right there."

"G-gonna get warm today," Sam said, smiling as the sunlight played over his face.

"You livin' in San Francisco, motherfucker," William shouted. "It don't ever get warm, and don't change the subject!"

"Hogan?" Charlie said, and William pointed at Sam again.

"No, you're right," Sam said. "Glad I wore my t-t-turtleneck."

Charlie crossed the aisle and sat down next to him. "All right, no bullshit. You played Ben Hogan?"

"I did."

"It was the Monday match," William said. "Old man Blaney brought him out to teach us all a lesson. So the Deacon there had to get rough. Knocked it in from a hundred and thirty out on the twenty-second hole to win."

"Eagle?" Charlie said.

"Fuckin' eagle," William said, and Sam grinned and nodded his head in agreement.

Charlie sat forward. "What happened?" he asked.

"I caught him on a b-b-b-bad day. I got lucky."

William snorted. "Yeah, if shootin' sixty-six is what you call lucky. Kid, you lookin' at one of the best golfers ever lived."

"S-stop," Sam said.

"If he hadn't of fell in love, you never would've heard of Arnold Palmer."

"Please!" Sam protested.

"For years he beat everybody. The best in the West. They came from everywhere and we whupped 'em. New York, Texas, Chicago—we beat 'em all."

"When was this?" Charlie asked.

"Shit," William said. "Sam played till he was sixty."

"But the nerves g-go. Ask Hogan, he'd a t-t-told you. Can't putt anymore. Then you get old." Trouble clouded William Moorer's colossal face and Sam reached across the aisle to pat his friend on the knee. "But we did good. Had a helluva run."

"Bad read," William said to Charlie. "I gave him a bad read."

"I p-pulled it," Sam said, waving this off.

"The putt was good!" William boomed. "I know a good putt. Who you talkin' to? It broke."

Sam remained calm as ever. "So what? It was a long t-time ago."

"Still," William said, "we could've beat him too."

"It was time," Sam said. "I couldn't beat that boy."

"Not on his course. We'd of beat him here."

Sam shook his head. "It was time."

"Who?" Charlie asked.

"Young Jewish fella down in Los Angeles," William said. "Well, he was young then."

"Why'd you play him there?"

"No Jew ever set foot on this course 'cept to carry a bag, not back then. Only a few now."

"Right," Charlie said. "Wait a minute. You beat Hogan and this guy beat you?"

"Years apart, kid," William said, "but each one in their prime, I take my boy here, the Jew, then Hogan, 'specially when the money's out."

"Flat player, that kid," Deacon said. The two older men turned reverent and contemplative.

"Motherfuckin' player," William said.

"The guy in Los Angeles?" Charlie asked.

"Best putter I ever saw. And excuse me, but I could roll the rock pretty good m-m-myself."

"Mondays were special, kid." William put a forefinger to his lips. "But don't tell nobody."

"T-t-tour money got too big," Sam told Charlie.

"They'd come out for twenty," William said.

"N-no way. Not now," Sam answered. "Fifty, no less."

"That ain't the problem," William said to Charlie.

"No, that ain't the p-p-problem."

"What's the problem?" Charlie asked.

"The player," William said. "Figgs is the best in the yard right now and he's only scratch."

"That ain't good enough," Sam said.

"Not to beat a pro," Charlie said. "Well, a club pro, but not a tour player."

"Not that Jewish kid neither," William said. "Nowadays anybody gets any good they leave. Wanna take their shot at the big time. Can't blame 'em."

"Years ago you could m-make more right here," Sam said.

"They let the caddies bet?" Charlie asked.

"Hell, yeah!" William shouted. "We'd pool our money and match the member's bet, anybody's bet. Caddies bet with the members. Hell, money don't know where you come from. Fuckin' bet's a bet, money's money. If a caddy thought somebody could take a pro, they'd bet their last dollar. Shit, a caddy loves all that action. Shit! There ain't nothin' like it in the world. Well, maybe, you know . . ."

"He's the devil," Sam said.

"Didn't stutter that," Moorer said. "Did ya, motherfucker?"

"N-nope."

William's head rolled back for a booming laugh that echoed through the car. "Man, we used to skin 'em every week! Head pro'd bring in players from everywhere, members too, and they'd go away not knowin' what the fuck happened! Sayin' shit like, 'Fuckin' caddy just beat me out of all my fuckin' money. Damn!' We'd party like a sonofabitch all night and into Tuesday. No caddies on Tuesday! Have to tote your own fuckin' bag 'cause they all laid up at the Fairmont, passed out with hookers every-fuckin'-where! You never seen money disappear so fast! But we knew next Monday was comin', and if not that one, then the next. It was a thing. After a while the pros started beggin' to come in here and take their shot."

"And you beat 'em all," Charlie said.

"H-him too," Sam replied, pointing to William.

"We'd partner sometimes. But I ain't near the player that man there is."

"W-was," Sam said.

"Shit, he was so good the members started backin' off. All except old man Blaney. Motherfucker hated seein' a caddy winnin'. Hated caddies period. I could never figure out why. He paid like a fuckin' slot machine. But one day he brings in Hogan."

"How'd he know him?" Charlie asked.

"Hogan was invested in oil and Blaney runs one of the biggest oil companies in the world. Both from Texas. Anyway, Sam says 'So what?' and we played him. That day Hogan came, everybody stopped. All kinda members out here, elbow to elbow with caddies. We played him. I picked up the Deacon's bag and we played him, didn't we, Deacon?"

"Yes we did," Sam said.

"How come you didn't go out?" Charlie asked.

"On t-tour?" Sam asked, and William slumped back in his seat like someone had pushed him. "I was married then. She didn't want to do that. That ain't no life, n-not back then. No life for me anytime."

Charlie thought back to how simple his life had once been, how contented he was to work hard and come home to Helen. "Hogan was married," he said.

"He h-had to win. It ate at him," Sam said. "There are other things." He then leaned close to Charlie. "I made more here," he whispered, "and I saw my wife every day until the day she died."

William dabbed his eyes with his towel.

"N-now what the hell you cryin' for?"

"She the best damn woman ever walked this fuckin' earth," William said. "You one lucky sonofabitch."

Sam settled a peaceful gaze on Charlie. "Do you miss her?"

His placid manner, his insight, overwhelmed Charlie. So many times over the past years he'd needed someone to understand, but his friends all seemed in too much of a hurry or too frightened to comprehend his troubles.

"Easy to tell, huh?" Charlie said.

"Yeah," Sam said. "Can't hide that. Not around here. A lot of us, we seen it. Had it. I'm sorry." The train barreled along the tracks, picking up speed. "How long has it been?"

"Two years," Charlie said, then paused. "Two and a half."

"No one knows you like a wife," Sam said. "N-not even your mother. At least mine did."

"She knew me well," Charlie said.

"And then?"

"Then we were strangers."

Sam shook his head. "She's alive?"

"Yeah."

"My god, that's w-worse. I can't imagine living on this earth without Linda, to know she was somewhere but I c-c-couldn't see her." His voice trailed off. "No, not me. I couldn't have d-done that."

"I've thought about that too," Charlie said. "Not livin.'"

Deacon patted him on the knee. "You're stronger than you kn-know."

"It doesn't feel that way, Mr. Deacon."

"Believe it," Sam said. "You're sittin' here. You're aware. Still scared, I can see, but that's okay. You s-seen the worst of it."

"Maybe," Charlie said. "So you married again?"

"N-no. W-we just live together. It took a little while, b-b-but then I met Julie."

"You two of a kind," William said from across the aisle. Just then the train began to slow, and he stood up. "Let's go!"

Through the window Charlie saw other men with towels on their shoulders walking through the fog like ghosts in a cemetery bearing some great weight. They stepped off the train, crossed the wet street and headed up the long, narrow road to the clubhouse. The trees formed an arch overhead, dampness dripping from the leaves, and the fog rolled in over them. Charlie pulled out a second sweater from his duffle and pulled it on. "Gettin' colder," he said.

"Right when the sun comes up," William said. "Always does."

"But then it c-c-comes up, sure as hell," Sam said, "and everything's all right."

"What am I gonna do about Randall?" Charlie asked.

"One shot at a time, kid," William said. "One shot at a time."

12

It was unusual, to say the least, for caddies to meet with members outside the club. As much as they conversed over the game and however many hours they spent together—more, probably, than some spent with their wives and children—a wall stood between caddy and player, and it began the moment they stepped off the eighteenth green. But Daniel Lang had no problem with it. He'd done worse to get where he was. Needing a guy like Jack was no big deal, and need him he did.

Jack walked into a downtown bar, slid into a red leather booth, asked for a beer and waited for him to speak.

"So, how's our boy?" Lang asked.

"Looks good," Jack said. "I brought my old sticks in, leaned a seven-iron outside the shack."

"And he hits it?"

"Every day." The truth was that Charlie had been hesitant to even pick up the club again. But slowly he'd given in, and was now hitting balls daily. And once he began, almost instantly, his mood shifted; he seemed better, more certain with each swing. He'd spoken of a girl and was living in a hotel on Lombard Street. Everything was fine. So his reluctance was something Jack deemed unnecessary to mention. It was a thing of the past.

"And he's loopin'? Al's taking care of that?"

"Every day. There's a little grumblin' about it, new guy workin' so much, but fuck 'em."

Lang smiled, drifting off into his own thoughts. "Those cock-suckers will never know what hit 'em."

"When?" Jack asked.

"When will he be ready?" Lang asked.

"To play? Not very long," Jack said. "It's more of a mental thing for him. The physical part is there."

"What about the elbow? Does he need any attention?"

"He never mentions it. I see him rub it, but mostly out of habit. I don't think it matters."

"Do you think it just healed with time?"

"Yeah," Jack said. "I think not playin' helped. I don't know what he did for a livin' all those years."

"He worked in a foundry."

"Doin' what?"

"Shoveling sand, picking up shit." Lang shrugged. "I don't know."

"Must've made him strong," Jack said.

"He looks strong."

"You should see."

"What do you mean?"

"You'll see," Jack said as the waitress placed his beer in front of him. He began to dig into his pocket for money, but Lang waved him off.

He hated secrets. When the waitress left, Lang leaned toward Jack and said, in the coldest tone Jack would ever hear, "Don't fuck with me, you idiot." Then he sipped his own drink. "When I ask you a question, just answer me."

Jack swallowed hard and put his mug down on the dark wooden table between them. But one thing he'd learned is that when you're caught off-guard, at a disadvantage, it's best to be brief and better still to say nothing at all.

"So what did you mean?" Lang asked.

"You got no worries," Jack said.

"Good. 'Cause I'm talkin' about beatin' Siegal here, Jack. Not Jimmy Figgs, not Ford. This guy buried Ford. Closed him on fifteen. He's a money player. He's beaten everybody for years. The tour guys won't even come by. He's embarrassed them all."

"I know," Jack said.

"Yeah, I know you know, but—"

"You saw Charlie swing. You ever see anything like that?"

Lang was slow to admit it; he'd seen, played and hung out with great players his entire adult life. "No," he said, and sat back in the booth.

"What else did you dig up about him?"

"That's none of your business."

"Mr. Lang," Jack said. "I'm gonna put down a bundle. It's shit to you but every fuckin' thing to me."

"Money isn't everything, Jack," Lang said with a smirk. "It's just money."

"Then why bet at all?"

Lang raised his drink to his lips. "To win." He put his glass back on the table and spun it slowly. "I'll tell you this about our boy. Stephen Ford says he's one of a kind." Lang's face changed, imperceptibly to most, but not to Jack. He took his time, and Jack waited. "No one's been able to beat the fuckin' guy for years," he said.

"Siegal."

Lang nodded. "Yeah, that fat fuck."

"And he'll want to play here?"

"Yeah. Because he knows we'd never let him set foot on the grounds otherwise."

"It's not enough for him to win. He figures that's a given. He wants to rub your faces in it."

"Yep," Lang said. "He'll jump at the chance."

"That's good. It'll be to Charlie's advantage."

"Yeah."

"He's a Democrat, you know."

"Only with his morals," Lang said. "He votes with his wallet. They all do."

"Well, he's kinda like you guys then," Jack said, and couldn't help but smile.

Lang stared at him. "You always go one step too far, Jack. That's probably why you're just a fuckin' caddy."

Jack sensed his position strengthening. "Well," he said and took a sip, "I'm tryin' to remedy that."

Lang nodded. "You gonna make a bet with the Czar? You'll need a lot of money. The Czar doesn't do small shit."

"I got enough. I just need you to put it down for me. Other guys too."

"Oh, yeah," Lang said. "That's right. You and the Czar don't exactly talk these days."

"Not exactly."

"Would he even take your bet?"

"Let's just say I'd rather keep my distance," Jack said. "Are there gonna be any odds?" He sensed Lang's excitement as he weighed his answer.

"I think so. Nobody will put any money down on the other side if there isn't. No one thinks his boy can lose. The Czar doesn't think it's possible either. If I were him I'd be thinking the same thing." Lang grimaced, envy sweeping through him. "He still loves the action, even at his age. The fuck thinks he has the seventy-eight Steelers, the twenty-seven Yankees. I've never seen him so cocky," he spat. "But he doesn't know anything about our boy."

"Is there any chance he can find out?" Jack said.

"There's always a chance," Lang answered, "but the Czar's a New York Jew."

"They think Pittsburgh's another country," Jack said.

"Exactly. And Charlie's older too. That helps. Everybody's always looking for the next young kid, they think they know everybody. You know, the old 'If he's that good why ain't he out on the tour?' bullshit. There wasn't very much written about Charlie in the papers then, and what was would be hard to find. They'll check all the amateur tournaments for the past couple years. The lists at the qualifying schools for the PGA. He won't be anywhere."

"The Czar won't ask to play with him first?"

"No," Lang said. "It would be admitting he doesn't know what the fuck's going on. He can't afford that. He's supposed to know."

"Bad form," Jack said.

"Very bad. Besides, guys like Charlie and Siegal can shoot pretty much what they want. Even I might not be able to tell where they were throwing shots away." Lang took another drink, a bit of a buzz setting in. He loosened his tie and slouched in his seat. "Fuckin' guys like that, only a couple, maybe three, on the whole planet." He shook his head in disbelief. "They can put the ball above the hole or below it from a hundred and fifty yards closer than you or I could toss it from twenty. Push a putt, stroke it with dead hands and make it come up short, all kinds of shit you can't see. And the Jew's the best. Makes you think he's playing like shit, then the bets pile up and he beats your brains out. He can be playing lights out and be bitchin' the whole time until you want to strangle him. In the end, the fuck's taking all your money. This game, these guys, the difference is imperceptible. I mean, what are we talkin'? A fraction of an inch this way or that, an ounce of pressure with the hands, a split second. How big is a golf ball? How do you hit it just off-center with a three-iron? Shit, I don't know and I've been a scratch player my entire life. It wouldn't do the Czar any good. He's going to have to find out, and it'll have to be in a hurry and it has to cost him. He's got a reputation. That's how he makes his money. He's supposed to be on top of this shit. But he's getting old. Something's up. He's been out of sight more and more. I think we may have caught him. When Charlie's ready, we'll press him to set the date."

"So what do you think? Two-to-one? Three?" Jack said.

"Three would be a miracle. And the minimum's gonna be high. That would draw out a lot more money."

"More than when Deacon lost?"

"A helluva lot more. Fuck, inflation alone." Lang smiled.

"Pulled the putt, I heard," Jack said.

"Yep. Choked. It was a long time ago, but I remember. I was there and I couldn't believe it. Deacon was the best putter I ever saw."

"Next to Siegal."

"Maybe," Lang said.

"Charlie's got no choke in him," Jack said.

"Everybody's got a choke point."

"I don't think he'll even know anyone else is on the course. All that talkin' Siegal does won't work. All the jokes and that fuckin' laugh. Used to drive me nuts."

"How long have you been in San Francisco, Jack?"

"It's been a while now. I spent time in L.A., as you know, and then came up here."

"And you worked for the Czar. Caddied for him."

"Then Siegal. He was the man by then. Made a lot of money."

"Not all on the course," Lang said. "Greed'll get you, Jack."

"Sometimes, Mr. Lang, sometimes."

"Well, maybe we'll clip the Czar and you can get that money he stole back from you!" Lang laughed out loud.

"I hope so," Jack said, not nearly as amused.

Lang sobered quickly, leaning forward and placing his elbows on the table. "Don't let the money cloud your judgment, Jack. It's just money. What happened between you and the Czar, that's over. I need you to be clear about our boy. If for any reason you think he's going to fold, you let me know."

Jack shook his head slowly. "Charlie probably won't even look at him. It's like he ain't thinkin' at all, like he's gone, workin' off a memory."

"Good," Lang said. "That'll drive Siegal right up a tree. At the end of the day, there's a lot in it for you if you're right."

"And if he—"

Lang raised his hand like a cop stopping traffic. "Just pack your shit up and leave. There are plenty of states I never go to and don't give a shit about. Arkansas, West Virginia, China, pick one."

"Fair enough," Jack said as he drained his glass. "You know, it's kind of a shame. Hardly anybody's gonna get to see this."

"Kinda," Lang said sarcastically. "It's for those of us who can appreciate it."

"Two best players."

"Well, we really don't know about Charlie."

"I do," Jack said.

"I got a hunch too," Lang admitted.

"A hunch? You guys don't play hunches. I wouldn't even call it gambling."

"Gambling's for idiots."

"Winning," Jack said, like he was telling an old story.

"Yep," Lang said.

"Stack the deck."

"That's what losers call it."

"Not easy to do with the Czar," Jack said.

"He's a very smart man."

"The Czar and Siegal in one fell swoop."

"One swing," Lang said.

"The Czar still own him? Siegal? I just wanna know."

"Lifetime contract. He ain't allowed out of L.A. without the Czar knowing it."

"What a fuckin' life," Jack said.

"Don't feel sorry for that bastard." Lang finished his drink, now bleary-eyed and loose. "If he couldn't play he'd probably be in jail." He tossed some bills on the table. "We all have our limits, somewhere we want to go and can't. Out there"—he pointed through the window—"or up here," he said, tapping his temple with a forefinger.

"Not you," Jack said.

"Ha. I just stopped caring, Jack. Don't get the two confused."

"Not Charlie."

"Hell, Charlie's more boxed in than any of us," Lang said as he slid from the booth, stood up, and put his coat on. "That's what I'm counting on."

"How do you figure?"

"He's desperate," Lang said. "He's playing all the time, as soon as he wakes up, every day. In his head. I can see it when he's out there with me. I saw it the moment I met him." Envy filled his voice. "He's more alive now than he'll ever be. He just doesn't know it. He feels everything. His sight is keen, he feels the wind, his hands are ready. Fuck, I played my best golf after my first divorce. I played every day, got shacked up with a girl and thought everything was just hunky fuckin' dory. That's all I knew and all I wanted. What Charlie has—Deacon and Moorer, the club, the city, whatever fuckin' relief he's found—he won't risk that. Can't. He has to keep it, if only for now. He doesn't know that Moorer is a murderer and Deacon, well, he doesn't know what a choke he is, either. To him they're all angels, because that's what he needs them to be. He'd do anything to keep things as they are. He'll play his ass off. Hope," Lang said. "You remember what that was, Jack. Our boy is holding on to some good old-fashioned hope." Lang started to leave, then turned back. "So when he's ready, you'll make things clear to him."

"Yes," Jack said.

13

Jack had just fallen asleep when the familiar thud, resonant like a bass, sounded off the wall of the shack. Late in the day, the evening brought a colder chill. He peeked around the hedge just as Charlie struck another ball and sent it sailing. With each shot, his shape and stature seemed to change; his body became stronger, his face more somber, his hands mechanical as he took hold of the club, rolled yet another ball to his feet and took aim, then pulled the club back slowly.

"Perfect," Jack whispered. Charlie brought it down, the face of the club squarely to the ball, tearing a deep gash in the packed dirt. The sound went off, echoing out into the trees and fog; the ball fell over the fence, banging against a tree on the far side. Charlie slid another ball from the pile and repeated the move and another ball rifled off the tree a few feet from where the last one hit. The noise was too loud to be ignored, and Jack waited for Al to come from around the corner. A second later he did, waving for Jack to come help him. The two of them carried two big buckets each of range balls and placed them at Charlie's feet, then leaned back against the wall of the shack.

An hour passed and Al came and went, attending to his job, but Charlie never stopped; his right hand never leaving the club, ball after ball screaming out farther and straighter than the one before.

"You wanna drink, kid?" Jack asked. Charlie adjusted his stance and continued. Jack doubted if he'd been heard. Another hour and the last ball streaked over the fence.

"That's all the balls we have left," Al said. "We'll have to go over the fence and pick 'em up."

"That shouldn't be too hard," Jack said. "They're right by that tree, all three hundred of 'em."

The patch of dirt before Charlie was pocked with holes, the dead grass jutting out of the darker earth beneath like old wire. Small stones lay scattered in the direction Charlie had sent his shots. His pant cuffs were covered in dust, his white socks as dirty as the shoes he'd neglected to tie. Sweat shimmered on his neck and back. His hair was soaked, and steam rose from his head when he removed his wool hat. He grimaced as he flexed his hands. Light streaks of crimson ran to his wrists from blisters that had formed and broken. Jack tossed his clean towel over Charlie's shoulder.

"I'll get the First Aid," Al said.

"Better get you a glove," Jack said.

"I don't wear a glove," Charlie said wearily, and headed to the shack.

"Jesus," Al said. "You sure he's okay?"

"Yeah," Jack said. "Why?"

"'Cause it's been like that every day for weeks now," Al said. "Morning and night."

"He's fine," Jack told him.

Al held up his hands, surrendering. "Okay," he said, and Jack headed into the shack.

Charlie stood leaning on the bathroom sink, exhausted, cool water running over his hands.

"How you doin'?"

"All right," Charlie murmured.

"In the zone, huh?"

"Sort of."

"You gonna play Monday?"

"I don't have any sticks."

"I can get you a set," Jack said.

Charlie looked back over his shoulder, then turned away again. "No thanks."

"I got a putter in the locker."

"You can't putt, you can't play," Charlie mumbled.

"What's that?" Jack asked.

"Something I heard once."

"Truer words never spoke," Jack said. He backed off and took a seat on the couch. "I'll bet you can putt your ass off, Pittsburgh." Charlie had no reply. "I mean, you never really know until you see a guy out there. Golf is the weirdest thing. A tall, good-lookin' dude with a smooth swing and two thousand dollars' worth of clubs can be a duck. I knew a guy down South once, his name was Charlie too. That motherfucker didn't look like he could stand up, let alone play. Chubby around the middle, little hands and feet, pasty skin, bad beard, bad dresser, you fuckin' name it. Wore a straw hat, alcoholic to boot and threw a ball like a girl. Worked for him in a club championship; shot thirty-nine on the front and never blinked. Had a gin and tonic at the turn, shot thirty-one on the back side with a bogey—to win. Nine putts."

"You never know," Charlie agreed. He lifted his hands and wrapped them with the clean white towel.

"His putter looked like an old hunk of wood with a green plastic insert," Jack said. "Hadn't seen one before or since. Fifteen putts on the front nine, nine on the back. Six birdies, not one under fifteen feet. Fuckin' player. He'd get up on the first tee when all the bets were bein' made and say only one word."

"What was that?" Charlie asked.

For effect, Jack took out a smoke and fired it up before answering. "Whatever."

"You either can or you can't," Charlie said.

"That's how I know."

"Know what?" Charlie asked.

"That you can putt, that you're a player. Just the way you say that. You either can or you can't. I saw you hit, what, ten balls? And that told me something. But a million guys can get it to the green in regulation. Ain't that right? But if you can't roll the rock, you may as well stay home."

"Unless you're just out to have fun," Charlie said.

"Now that's where we're the same," Jack said.

Charlie collapsed on the couch. "Me and you the same? How?"

"We can't play *anything* for fun. It ain't in you. I see the change. With me it's money. But money ain't it for you. That's a shame, 'cause you can make a lot around here, if you're as good as I think you are. With you it's hard. You gotta go somewhere up here"—he pointed to his temple—"where you don't like to be. I figure you must not like how it makes you feel. You used to, but then you got soft. Or something happened. You fell in love, got burned. You were an optimist when life was good, but when you lost something that really counted, then you didn't know what the fuck to think. Life sucks, or something like that. I knew a guy once that went from scratch to a seven in three months. Wife had a baby. That's it. Well, anyway, it's always something like that."

"Something like that," Charlie said, wishing Jack would stop, but he didn't.

"It happened a long time ago and you kinda gave up. And the rest of your life just kinda, you know, happened. You trusted something else besides yourself and got burned again, maybe. You thought other people would do it for you, whatever the fuck it is we're supposed to learn on this fuckin' planet."

"Maybe" was all Charlie could muster.

"Well, man, there's only one thing you can do in this life. Take it back," Jack said, "and let it go. Nobody can hit it for you."

"It ain't that easy," Charlie said.

"How's your girl?"

"She's not my girl. We talk."

"Sleep with her?" Jack asked.

"Shut the fuck up."

"Look, after you fuck, you know a lot. Sometimes everything, if you're payin' attention."

"You ever lose anything, Jack? Anything you really cared about?"

"I loved my wife." His slick-talking demeanor subsided.

Charlie sat up. "Not as much as you loved whatever you were into, or you never would've left her. And that's why my wife left me. For no other reason. She was curious." Charlie threw the towel on the couch next to Jack.

"That's the way of the world, man," Jack said.

"Well, it ain't my way."

"So you're just gonna suffer?"

"How do you know all these things? You don't know me. I hit a ball! So what?"

"Come on!" Jack shouted, the energy of his words bringing him to his feet. "It's all over you. Christ! Anybody who knows anything can tell. Every motherfucker here knows. Sam Deacon does. He can look in your eye and tell. I saw you swing. And don't tell me anybody can hit it like that, please. It's like you don't belong over here," Jack said, pointing to the floor. "You belong over there." He pointed to the first tee. "Why do you think Lang's so interested?"

Charlie straightened. "Interested in what?"

"You. Your game. You think he feels sorry for you? Do you think he even likes you? Do you really think he gives a shit who caddies for him? If he didn't think you were a player, your ass would be ridin' the bench. He suspected something the first time you picked up his bag. He has a sense for shit. Then, after he saw you swing, he figures he has something special. A guy like that, something catches his eye, he watches it like one of those red-tailed hawks buzzin' around up there. He sits in a tree or circles above until the right moment."

"What does he want from me?"

"Look. A guy like Lang's already had just about every thrill there is on this earth. But one thing he can never be is as good as you. Hell, on some level he might even hate you. One thing's for sure. He's gonna ask you to play, and for a lot of money. And then you're gonna have to make a decision."

"I don't have to play."

"If you wanna work here, you do. If you wanna stay."

"Then I'll just go," Charlie said. "I'll caddy somewhere else."

"Not in this city, hell, maybe not in this fuckin' state."

"It can't be that important," Charlie said.

"Let me tell you something. Danny Lang decides what's important and what ain't."

Charlie felt a cold breeze blow through the shack. He shivered and felt sick to his stomach.

"You have any idea who you're fuckin' with? These guys here are the cream of the crop. Hell, man, presidents have belonged here! Fuckin' Clinton asked if he could play here. 'Hey, I'm just cruisin' by, like to check out your place,' he says with that hokey accent. Motherfuckers told him to get lost, go play where all the other fuckin' liberals play. Asshole Prince Ali Baba, or some shit, wanted to play. They said, 'Hey, we'll put out your oil-well fires; we'll build you your buildings and educate your fuckin' boys; we'll even make sure nobody invades your little kingdom. But we ain't fuckin' socializin' with you.' No, Pittsburgh. Danny boy didn't get where he's at by takin' no for an answer."

"What does he want?" Charlie asked.

"Simple. He wants you to play," Jack said. "And I'd be willing to bet you couldn't throw a match. It's not in you. You ain't wired for it. You got too much respect for the game. Whoever taught you did a bang-up job." Jack motioned for Charlie to follow. "Come here. Let's settle this."

When they reached the other side of the dirt lot, Jack stopped. "The deal's all on you, man. I'm sorry. I don't know exactly who the fuck you are, but they sure as hell do."

"I know what happened," Charlie said. "Stephen."

"Right. This Ford guy said something and until they find out different, you're it. And if they can make a few bucks or have some fun, then you better get ready to go along."

"What are you talking about?" Charlie asked.

"The Monday match. I think they're gonna resurrect it."

"Oh."

"You know what I'm talkin' about?"

"Yeah."

Jack was immediately suspicious. "How?"

"Moorer. Deacon."

Jack took a quick look around to make sure they were alone.

"You should stay away from William Moorer."

"Why's that?" Charlie asked.

"Lang don't like him. Crazy."

"Crazier than who?" Charlie said. "Who's sane around here? Point to someone—please."

"He's done time, I can tell you that much. Seven years."

"Bullshit," Charlie said. "For what?"

"Killed a guy. Blew his temper. One punch was all and the guy died," Jack said. "Dead before he hit the ground."

"Maybe it was self-defense."

"Whatever, kid. I'm just warnin' you. That's who he is."

"Should I stay away from Deacon too?" Charlie asked. "What's he done?"

Jack shrugged. "Nothin'. Salt of the earth."

"Fuck you," Charlie said, and started for the shack.

"You think you can work here if you don't play? Lang won't let that happen. He'll hate you. He'll run you out. You'll sit on that bench till you're broke."

"Did he tell you that?" Charlie asked.

"He didn't have to. A lot of caddies'll feel the same way."

"Why should they care?"

"You don't know why?"

"No. Tell me."

"'Cause they want to see it too. It's all they want to see. Look around. Come here," he said, and they walked across the lot to the end of the hedge, where the front nine spread out before them.

"Look at 'em," Jack said. "There ain't one of 'em wouldn't want to be where you are right now. In their minds, they're all players. Some can hit it a mile. Others can make a ball dance, knock it down, turn it both ways, make it run, make it sit like a dog. But they can't make a three-footer for a buck. Jimmy Figgs can putt like a bandit but can't hit it out of his own shadow anymore. Booze. Christ, Billy can play his ass off, but he's damn near an idiot. William Moorer could do it, Deacon was one of the best I ever saw and I didn't see him play till he was sixty-odd years old. Struck it better then than when he was a kid. But he's old, and so is Moorer. They're past it. They all got somethin' or had somethin', but now they don't. Everyone but you. You got it. That's plain." Jack pulled out a joint from his pack of smokes. "And Pittsburgh," he said as he fired up, "I don't mean to get left out, either. You got to know a caddy loves the action. For most of us it's all that's left, and quite frankly I'm convinced that's all there ever was."

"And the money," Charlie said.

"That *is* the action," Jack said.

"I'll just leave, then. Fuck this place and all of you."

"And go where? Home? Pittsburgh? What the fuck's back there? Ain't you tired of runnin'? Of doin' everything else besides what you were put on this earth to do? What about Moorer? What about Deacon? What about that girl? You don't give a shit?"

"I just met them. I'll get over it."

"It's funny, Pittsburgh." Jack took a toke. "It takes a lifetime to get to know someone, but if it's right only about a second to give a shit. Ain't that a motherfucker?"

"Look, I haven't played since I was fifteen," Charlie cried. "You have no idea what it takes to play like that. The amount of practice. How tired you get. But I do. I remember what it costs! It cost me everything!"

"Then why'd you pick up that club at all?"

"The first time I held one, when I was with Lang, I didn't think I could swing. I hurt my elbow really bad—years ago. I had no reason to believe I could."

"And then?"

Charlie sighed. "I knew it was back. The swing, the game, the memories, everything; like it's always been there, waiting for me."

"So?" Jack said.

Exasperated, Charlie drew in as much breath as he could. "So what about all that time in between? All those years—what could've been, what should've been. I don't know what to do with it."

"Play," Jack said.

"That's your fucking answer? Just play like nothing ever happened?"

"It's over," Jack said.

"But *I* ain't over it," Charlie snapped. "I don't know how I can play with this shit in my head. When I was a kid I didn't know any better." Then he spoke as if by rote. "You got to be clear. You have to be focused. It has to be the only thing in your head."

"That's how you did it."

"That's how I was taught, and it was fucked-up."

Jack had been waiting for this moment. "By who? What fuckin' genius taught you this game?"

Charlie felt like a traitor. "My father."

"Uh-huh," Jack said, shaking his head.

"It didn't have to be like that. One thing at a time, the same way every time, and then you'll hit the shot—every time."

"He'd want you to play," Jack said.

"It's just a game."

"Keep tellin' yourself that. Tell it to Sam Deacon. To Palmer, Trevino, and Player. And Hogan too, after that bus wreck that nearly killed him. Sure, tell it to your father and tell that to yourself, but don't fuckin' tell it to me."

Charlie's eyes went dark, but Jack stared right back, took another toke, blowing smoke rings as he exhaled. "Boy, what fathers do to sons."

"He didn't mean to," Charlie said. "It's the only way he knew."

"He taught you well. You still have time."

Charlie bent over, hands to knees. "I don't know."

Jack crouched beside him. "Look. There's a lot of fuckin' things I don't know and I don't want to. But I do know one thing. If you wait for everything to make sense, you're gonna wait forever. If you're waitin' to feel like you used to, just lay down right now and don't ever get up. It ain't like that. There are some things on this earth that ain't for knowin'. That's a fact." Jack licked his fingers and snuffed the joint between them. "But this I know. This place was made for you. All you gotta do is play."

"I haven't played since I was fifteen."

"I've been watchin'. I'll bet you're better than ever."

Charlie straightened up and looked out over the course. Players and caddies dotted the hills and valleys, white flags waving in the stiff breeze, and he could see half a dozen swings at once. Sam Deacon was coming over the crest on nine. After his player struck his approach he took a few steps, the bag still on his shoulder, scooped up the divot with an iron, carried it back and plopped it into place, tamping it down so neatly that no one could tell that the piece of earth had been uprooted. Walking slowly after his player, he cleaned the dirty club with a towel that seemed affixed permanently to his shoulder, then twirled the iron like a baton and slid it back into the bag like he was sheathing a sword.

Perfect, Charlie thought. He nodded toward Sam Deacon. "I just want to caddy. I just want to walk out there, have a few laughs, get my money and go home, have a few beers and something to eat. It's really all I ever wanted, to be like my father. He was a steelworker until there wasn't any work left. He just worked and came home. That's all I want. And now this." He shook his head.

"What would he want?"

Charlie's jaw tightened. "I don't know. If you ever run into him, go ahead and ask him."

"He'd want you to play," Jack said. "Christ, every father wants his son to play." Now he pointed at Sam. "What do you think he wants you to do?"

The reasoning was sound, and Charlie, some part of him, gave in. He glanced around this place that had so quickly become home. He looked forward to another midnight talk with Sarah. He wanted to see her face, hear her voice, register her sense, be calmed by her, be covered in her.

He headed to the shack, reached behind the bushes and pulled out the old seven-iron. "I can't beat anybody with one club."

Jack sprang across the lot. "I got an old set of Wilsons, one-iron through wedge. I'll get a driver and some—"

"Just give me the blades for now," Charlie said. "If I can't hit the one-iron, then I can't play. I won't play. Find me a sand wedge, fifty-six degrees."

"No problem," Jack said. "'Course Lang'll buy you anything you want."

"I don't need it. And a putter." Charlie's voice dropped to a whisper. "Make it soft and flat. No loft, no offset. Straight up and down. Bull's-eye would do fine."

"I'm on it," Jack said.

Charlie gathered his things, stuffed his towel in his bag, then changed his shirt. "I was going to ask who I was playing, but I guess I already know."

"Siegal," Jack said.

"Do you know him? Ever seen him play?"

"Used to pack for the fat fuck."

"That's why I'm talking to you, isn't it? That's how these guys operate. If you have something they want—"

"It's their world, Pittsburgh. We're just rentin' it."

"And the minute you don't—"

"You're out. Waitin' on the bench." He paused. "Forever. So there's only one thing to do."

"Yeah?" Charlie said.

"Play while you can."

14

J ack was leaning against the wall talking on the payphone, and
when Charlie waltzed in and tried the bathroom door, he waved
him away. Then the door handle clicked and Spider, in green from
head to toe, came stumbling out.

"Hey, Spider," Charlie said.

Spider put his hand out to brace himself against the wall, took
one giant step then stood tall. "There," he said, straightened his
collar and walked slowly out of the shack.

Jack hung up the phone. "I got your sticks," he said.

"Is he okay?"

"Yeah, why?"

"Nothing. I don't want to know." Charlie closed the bathroom
door behind him and ran warm water over his sore hands. In a
couple of weeks' time the blisters had completely healed. He
poked one on the heel of his left hand. "Club's too much in my
hand," he mumbled. "Gotta grip with the fingers." He raised his
hands to the mirror and studied his imaginary grip, remembering
the first time his father showed him how to place his hands on the
club.

"Do you want to know the secret?" he'd asked.

"Yes," Charlie said into the mirror.

His father spread his hands, big, calloused, and rough, with
deep lines crossing the palms. "This is the key," he said, wiggling

the fore- and middle fingers of his left hand, the third and middle fingers of his right. "These are the secret, and the others are just along for the ride. The pinky on the right lies over the forefinger on your left. And your left-hand thumb—keep it short, don't lay it down flat. That's your grip, right there in those fingers."

"It feels weird," Charlie said.

"Get used to it," his father said. "No right-hand thumb, no pinky on the left; if you get a blister there, on the heel of your hand, your grip pressure's wrong." His father adjusted his fingers. "That's it!" he said. "Now hit it with both hands, Charlie, and don't hold back."

In his reflection, Charlie took his hands back and above his shoulder to check where they were at the top of his swing. "Good," he said. Then he slowly started his swing, his eyes fixed on the mirror. He made the first move and his hands cocked as his lower body began to turn toward the target and his right elbow dropped toward his side, catching up with the hip. "From here you've got to be quick," his father said. "Hips are already firing, so catch up now and let your hands go!"

Charlie let his hands come down in a slow-motion version of his swing. "Good," he said, then, "Pow!" and he saw the ball in flight, straight and soaring.

"That's it," his father said.

He was about to open the door when he heard voices from the other side.

"Yeah, I got it," Jack said, "but you ain't gettin' it. No fuckin' way. You made me promise. I promised. You ain't gettin' it."

"Forget that bullshit! I want my fuckin' money!" a gigantic voice screamed.

"Can't do it, Randall," Jack said. "You're just gonna piss it away on crack and fifty-dollar hookers."

"Oh! But you won't piss it away," Randall said. "No, you'll blow it all in one shot! Bet it on a horse or a fuckin' football game when you get some bullshit tip! So give me my motherfuckin' money!"

"No," Jack said, and Charlie could hear the springs of the couch creak as he sat down.

"Jack, we been buddies a long time, but I'll beat it outta your ass!"

"That's no way to get what you want," Jack said. "Besides, you don't know where it is and you need me to get it."

"AAAaaah!" Randall screamed, and it sounded like he'd been stabbed.

Charlie opened the door and froze. Sprawled on the floor was Randall, tearing at his filthy, tattered clothes, kicking and thrashing his feet, the soles of his cowboy boots all but worn away, the black leather shafts sagging practically to his ankles. Charlie could barely make out a faded pair of jeans beneath ripped orange sweatpants. With at least four shirts of mismatched colors, he looked like a rodeo clown, the bull and the dung having gotten the best of him. He continued ripping off layer after layer until he'd exposed a densely tattooed, thickly muscled torso.

But all this was nothing compared to his face. His coal-black beard, impossibly tangled with bits of food and grass, looked more like hay than hair. His face was skeletal, with deep hollows in his cheeks, his nose as straight as a Greek god's. His eyes were small and sunken, but even in this wasted state, Charlie could see the blue in them. Then he sprang to his feet with surprising speed and agility and Charlie readied himself for an attack.

"What the fuck are you starin' at, cocksucker!" Randall screamed.

"He's new," Jack said, resting comfortably on the couch. He was tapping the ash off his cigarette into the palm of his hand, then letting it drift to the floor. "Helluva player," he said.

Strangely, this information seemed to soothe Randall. But only for a moment. "Big fuckin' deal!" he exploded. "A million motherfuckers can hit it. Christ, I can hit it." He raised his arm and pointed at Charlie. "This is my fuckin' shack, motherfucker! Player or no player, to me you're just another fuckin' duck. Remember that! I don't know where the hell you come from, but I been here twenty years and I ain't goin' nowhere. No matter where I am or where I'm sleepin', whether it's at the Warsaw"—and then he lifted his huge, thick arm and pointed toward the course—"or out in that fuckin' bush, this is still my fuckin' shack."

"The bush?" Charlie whispered to Jack.

"Yeah! The bush! The fuckin' weeds!" Randall roared, taking a step toward Charlie. "Out there, asshole! Behind number one or four or along eight. That's where motherfuckers end up around here! In the fuckin' bush! You can't pack, you're out! And let me tell you, it's a cold motherfucker out there, I don't care what fuckin' state you're in." He stopped to catch his breath, suddenly on the verge of passing out. He shook violently from head to toe, his knees buckling and swaying. He reached for the wall and found it a foot too far away.

"Fuckin' bush is a cold motherfucker, 'specially when all you got is . . ."—his breath slowed and his eyes rolled wildly in their sockets—"is a piece of fuckin' plastic to roll up in." Suddenly he was on the edge of tears. It was then that Charlie noticed a clear tarpaulin, rolled up with a string tied around it, lying on the table. Randall staggered to one of the ratty overstuffed chairs and collapsed. "Motherfuckin' coons walkin' over you in the middle of the night," he mumbled, struggling to stay awake. "Fuckin', fuckin' . . . what are those things? Weaselly lookin', you know, maybe possums, hey, I don't give a shit, but those motherfuckers crawl up and take a sniff, the scavenging beady-eyed white cocksuckers. Shit," he huffed, and expired into a coma-like sleep.

Jack tossed his cigarette on the floor and tramped on it, pulling the butt away from the paper and tossing it in the ashtray. "That's it for now," he said.

"So that's Randall, huh?" Charlie said.

"The one and only," Jack answered.

"I've seen him before."

"Where?"

"Along seventeen. My first loop. Scared the shit out of me." He thought back to Lang and Evans arguing on the tee and how they'd quit after nine holes. "Is he likely to kill me when he sobers up?"

"He won't even know you. He's a lot of talk. Crack, booze, you name it. Always goin' up, comin' down. Flyin' or crashin'. But don't get me wrong. He's a bad motherfucker."

"He can't always be like this," Charlie said.

"Lately, yeah, he is. He was a biker, on the road for years. He dumped his bike outside the gate and they scraped him off the road and hauled him in here. Weighed about two-twenty, bad as hell. Look at him. He's about one-eighty now and shrinkin' by the minute. He's got fucked-up knees, diabetes and gout. Could get well, Dr. Smith'd fix him up, but he's scared of doctors. Thinks once they start cuttin' they won't never stop. It bummed him out. Thought his loopin' days were over."

"So he drank it," Charlie said.

"You can't take a guy's hope."

"No, you can't."

"If a caddy can't walk, he ain't a caddy."

"No."

"So you walk till you can't walk no more."

"I guess so," Charlie said. "What else you gonna do?"

"What else you gonna do."

"It's no different than anything else. Walking. Living. Same fuckin' thing."

"Figured he might as well have a good time."

"I don't blame him a bit," Charlie said.

Jack opened his locker.

"There you go," he said. "One set of Staffs blades circa nine-teen seventy-six. Stiff shafts. New grips. One-iron through the wedge. One fifty-six-degree sand wedge and one putter, no loft. Let me know if you want to change the grip on it. It's pretty old."

"Why don't you give him his money?" Charlie asked.

"That's none of your business, Pittsburgh." Jack lit another cigarette and pulled the clubs out of the locker in a new black cloth bag. There was no writing on the sides, no name brand logo. It had a stand and stood lightly and easily on the wood floor of the shack.

"I didn't know you could get one without all that shit on it," Charlie said.

"They special-order 'em here," Jack answered. "Go ahead. They're yours."

"I'll pay you."

"That's all right, I'll get my money back and then some."

"I'll pay you," Charlie repeated as he pulled out a club and felt the weight of it.

"How are they? Like your old ones?"

"Yeah," Charlie said as he held out the club and gave it a twirl. He put it back and looked at Randall.

"He'd kill himself," Jack told him. "Look what he did to himself in a month."

"He wasn't like that a month ago?"

"Fuck, no!" Jack motioned for Charlie to follow him outside, so he grabbed the clubs and they sat down on the bench together. The morning had cleared and the sun was warm, all the caddies out playing. Figgs and Billy were coming down nine approaching their drives.

"He went through twenty grand in a month."

"What, he saved it and then blew it?"

"No," Jack said. "In case you haven't guessed by now, caddies don't save much."

"Well then how in the hell . . ." Charlie stopped, quickly figuring he didn't really want to know how a guy like Randall or Jack might stumble onto so much money. He held up a hand. "Never mind."

"Evans, Lang, they all begged him to give them the money, they'd do him a favor and invest it for him. He kept sayin' he was going to, but then he disappeared. What a fuckin' asshole."

"So you gave those guys what was left?" Charlie said.

Jack took a drag off his cigarette and blew out the smoke. "Yeah, they got it."

"Well then he shouldn't have anything to worry about. If he's around to spend it, that is."

"That's up to him," Jack said. He watched as Charlie took a club from the bag and began swinging it gently. "How do you feel? Ready to play a little?"

"I'm going to practice," Charlie said, shouldering his bag.

"You can hit balls on the side of the range if you want," Jack said.

Charlie walked to the practice green and started collecting range balls that had been left out. Jack followed and soon filled two shopping bags, then set them down on the fringe. "Here you go," he said.

Charlie slid the sand wedge from his bag and looked at the bottom of the club.

"It's fifty-six," Jack said, "just what you said."

Charlie's hands fidgeted on the grip, and Jack, as if he were watching a magician, tried to catch him in the act.

"What's the secret?" he finally asked.

"Watch," Charlie answered.

Once satisfied with his grip, he took a few easy swings. At the top of his backswing the club was perpendicular to the ground, seemingly weightless as the sun glared off its steel shaft. His jaw and lips were tight, the black of his pupils enlarged and flooded, blotting out any color. He craned his neck, loosening the muscles, and his whole body seemed to lengthen, his shoulders grew bigger and his hands, still and solid, looked like old iron. They held the club easily, but Jack wouldn't have bet a dime that he could pull it from Charlie's grip. He doubted if anybody could. Charlie looked strong and immovable, his head unwavering, his feet planted into the ground as if they'd sprung from that patch of earth. His eyes were cold, unforgiving and removed, seeing nothing, looking for nothing.

Rage, Jack thought as Charlie scooped a ball toward him. Pissed off.

A moment later Charlie brought the club back waist-high or so, dropped the head smoothly and the ball shot out onto the green. Then again and again, Charlie never once looking up. He wasn't chipping toward a hole, an area, anyplace in particular, just focusing every ounce of his attention in front of him. Each and every time the club came back to the same height and the ball flew the same short distance—too hard, seemingly—and hopped once before the spin of the ball would make it check up, halt for a moment, then roll a few feet to a stop. Ball after ball shot sharply from the rough, carried just onto the green, then came to rest as if it were tired.

That's so hard to do, Jack thought, and he makes it look easy.

Charlie pulled balls gently from the green with the toe of his wedge, spreading them out and then began taking small steps that pushed them deep into the thick rough. Then he started again. With full swings the buried balls shot from the thick grass like they were being chopped out of the ground, soaring high to land softly on the green, roll a bit and stop dead.

"Fifty, sixty balls there," Jack said as one after another followed the path of those before.

The greenskeeper and ground crews passed by clad in rubber boots and floppy hats, holding rakes or weed-whackers or shovels, on wet, muddy golf carts. An hour or so later they walked or drove by again and saw him still there. Caddies playing up number nine and going off ten, carrying their bags and gently waving a club or eating a candy bar, stared at him. Jack sat smoking one cigarette after another, sneaking sips of beer in a paper bag, dozing in the warm sun, jerking awake from time to time only to find Charlie in a different place but with the same results. Somewhere on the green was a circle of balls not more than three feet wide, twenty or thirty in each grouping. Foursomes and twosomes of caddies teed off and later made the turn onto the back nine, each time seeing the same thing: Charlie swinging yet again, and a ball flying a short distance, landing softly and trickling to where it seemed to belong, as if returning home.

Hours passed. Charlie stayed, while workers and players came and went. Some stopped to watch but after a minute or so ran out of patience, the sight at once tedious, incomprehensible and unsettling.

Then the players were gone and the groundspeople too, all of them hungry and thirsty. As Charlie hacked ball after ball out of the rough, they arrived home to whatever comfort awaited them, some telling friends and loved ones of the strange thing they'd seen at work that day. The sun began its descent as Charlie gathered the balls once again and threw them into a sand trap as men and women sat out on their porches anticipating the cool night air. The club thumped the sand; children played until dusk, laughing and crying, running, swinging and climbing and rolling until called in by their mothers, cleaned up and put to bed. The ball fell lazily onto the green. The sun set, the stars came out and couples settled into their own time speaking quietly and smiling. In the moonlight, another splash of sand. And like a ticklish feather, the image of a ghostlike man roaming the edges of the practice green played in their minds. One man laughed uneasily and shook his head. "I ain't never seen anything like it," he thought out loud, "in all my years around this game."

A chill rattled his body and stood him up, the sweat on his neck and back drying in the cool night air. He arched his back and surveyed the grounds. It was eerily quiet, and Charlie loved it. Sarah crossed his mind and a knot in his gut, one he didn't even know was there, loosened.

Light from the clubhouse gathered and with the moonlight illuminated the white flags on nine and eighteen as they snapped and waved in the wind. Charlie replaced the club, slung the bag over his shoulder and walked toward where Jack sat in the grass, his back against the clubhouse, drinking a beer, the red glare beneath the ash lighting his face like a dying ember in a campsite fire.

"That's the secret?" Jack asked.

"Yeah," Charlie said. "I'll need to put these in your locker. I don't have one."

"It's open," Jack said. "Just lock it up. You need a beer or somethin'?"

"No thanks." Charlie trudged toward the light of the shack, then emerged moments later, his canvas duffle slung over his shoulder, and vanished into the darkness, heading for the city with Sarah on his mind.

Daniel Lang stood in a large picture window hovering above the eighteenth green. He held his glass out to Jack as if toasting some great event, then downed the last of his drink.

When Jack got back to the shack, he took hold of the door handle, then stopped. "I'm lockin' you in, cocksucker," he said.

"Better than that fuckin' bush," Randall moaned.

"Al gets here at six o'clock," Jack said, "in case you forgot. Try not to scare the shit out of him."

Randall was so drunk he didn't hear the door open, but he sure as hell felt it when somebody grabbed him by the arm. So he balled his hand into a fist and swung, feeling his knuckles crash into his assailant's ribs as a voice cried out. Then other hands grabbed hold of him and the weight of he didn't know how many men pressed down on him. Tasting his own blood, he screamed, then felt a cool, damp cloth pressed tightly over his mouth and nose.

"Strong sonofabitch," a man said above his head.

"Well," another said, "he told us he was."

"Yeah, but . . ." And the voice faded as Randall fell into unconsciousness.

15

They met nightly. Charlie practiced, and in the early evening would lie down in his room, tired but comfortable, released from the strain by the repetition of work. Later, as the evening slowed and the hotel filled, he'd join Sarah and they'd talk or sit quietly, she with her book and he with his thoughts of playing. Charlie would doze from time to time, then wake, and they would pick up where they'd left off. For the last few nights, though, he was more serious, restless, his spirits dim. Sarah wondered what he must have been like years ago, a young man who had yet to lose a thing.

"Did you get a loop today?" Sarah asked.

"Yeah," Charlie said. "I got out about noon."

"You waited all that time?"

"That's the trade-off. Sometimes you have to wait. But you go to work when you want and leave when you want."

"They don't care?"

"Not really," Charlie said. "It's understood."

"What is?"

"That a caddy will just up and leave. That's why he's a caddy."

She picked up her book, thumbed through the pages. "So you're thinking of leaving?"

"Sarah," he said. She looked up. "I'm sorry. I'm here. I like it here. I meant caddies in general."

Satisfied for now and glad of his company, she closed her book. "So you have to sit and wait?"

"On a bench."

"Like a baseball bench?" Sarah said. "My dad and I used to go to Giants games."

"Yeah, that's where the caddies sit. There and in the shack."

"I get the picture. Now I'll be able to see you."

"See me?"

"I have a clearer picture now. You sipping coffee on this bench in the fog—you know, a picture."

His mind drifted through images of Helen sitting at home, above the city, alone and without him, and he tried to recall her soothing voice but could not. He felt sad but relieved, the pang blunted, the memory fading.

"What else, Charlie?" Sarah said. "Tell me."

"It's a great place," he said. "There aren't any flowers. No man-made lakes with colored blue water, nothing like that. It's just a golf course where everybody knows the rules, knows the deal. There's so much order in that." He sounded almost desperate. "Do you know how rare that is, Sarah? To find something you know will always be the same; that it'll be there as promised and never taken away, for as long as you live?"

"It doesn't sound real," Sarah said.

"Maybe not." Then Charlie recalled Sam Deacon strolling up the ninth fairway, and a smile spread across his face.

"What?" Sarah asked.

"Walking the course, working, it's a great feeling."

"Sounds nice, being out in the fresh air."

"And the best part is you *have* to take a caddy," Charlie said. "And you have to walk. No carts."

"What do the older guys do?"

"They walk," Charlie said. "Jay Blaney's ninety-one. His caddy's seventy. They walk. Sam Deacon is eighty and he still carries a bag."

"A little stroll through paradise," she said.

"Yeah," Charlie said. "For a couple of hours you know just where you're going. Guaranteed."

"So you're like a coach."

"Sometimes. If that's what they want. Sometimes you're just a mule, carrying bags up a hill. It depends on the player. Some members know the course. Some don't care. Some just want reassurance. Others want you to spell everything out and hold their hand. They're all different, and a good caddy adapts, he knows."

"Like a good waiter."

"Exactly. And when you have a good player who trusts you, there's nothing like it." Charlie sat up, his eyes lighting up like a young boy. "You have this hook-up. You're both on the same page. He's asking you how far a shot's going to play, which is different from just the yardage. Anybody can walk off yardage. You have the wind, maybe in your face, maybe behind. It might be uphill, downhill, the ball below your feet or above, and each factor affects the shot. Then there's the size of the green and what part of it you're playing to—the front, middle, back? All that on every shot, and you always have to know. 'Speak when spoken to,' that's the rule. But if they ask, you'd better know. You have to understand your player's game. Do you want to take a seven-iron from a hundred and fifty-five and hit it high so the wind holds it up and it comes down softly, or a six and knock it down, keep it low, so it bores through the wind? Do you want to draw the ball right to left, or take it in left to right? And every player hits each club a different distance. On top of that, you have to read the greens."

"And say which way the ball will turn?"

Charlie nodded. "That's where you make your money."

"Why's that?"

"Because the putter's the only club you use on every hole. It can make up for a world of sin. Some guys can do it, some can't. But if you can't putt, you can't play."

"Play at all?"

"Play well," Charlie said. "Really well."

A playful smile lit up her face. "Can you play?"

His confession came slowly, fearfully. "I used to. God could I play." A cool, waking chill swept through his body. "When I was a kid, in high school, with my dad." He rose, rolled up his right sleeve and laid his arm on the counter between them, closing his fingers into a fist and stretching them open again. Sarah gasped ever so slightly, then reached out—and it was the strangest reaction Charlie had ever gotten. The scar was jagged and fleshy, thick and zig-zagging from the inside of his elbow halfway to his armpit. When he wiggled his fingers, the muscle beneath his skin moved, but the scar, like some dead thing, remained still. Sarah rolled his sleeve farther back, tears welling in her eyes. "May I?"

Charlie nodded. "It used to look worse."

She stroked the scar. "Christ, you got that from swinging a golf club?"

"The tendon, here, the medial collateral," he said drily, clinically, pointing to the spot. "Completely torn, almost. They reattached it but for years I couldn't bend it."

"Does it hurt?"

"Not anymore. I just couldn't bend it, so I couldn't play."

"And now?"

"I can." He said this as simply as if he were saying his name.

"And all those years?"

His eyes, as if reading, scoured those memories. He bent his arm and winced, feeling the phantom flash of searing pain again and the cool rain falling on his sunburned skin. "Without golf I was lost. We were all pretty lost." He didn't seem to know what to say next.

Sarah waited, silently, patiently, for him to explain what had happened and to fill the chasm between them.

Charlie placed his other elbow on the counter and his hands came together with an exactness, a precision, as if he had a firm hold of something. He repeated it, his fingers meeting in the same place, and when it was complete his two hands seemed like one.

"It's the most important thing: how to hold the club. To have a good grip's only the first step, but God help you if you ever lose it or forget it. You don't know where the ball's going and you could end up anywhere. In the woods, the water or just lost. My dad taught me to play," he said, rocking his hands in a short, side-to-side motion. After a few times he opened them and laid them palms up on the counter, begging Sarah to rest hers there. She found them rougher than his sad blue eyes suggested. Then she kissed him and he her.

"Tell me," she whispered.

Charlie drew in a breath, preparing a story he hadn't once told in fifteen years of marriage, never in his life. "The first day I caddied I was twelve. I was so little they weren't going to let me. But my dad told them I could do it and he had a way of convincing people. So I carried these big leather bags and walked every day up and down those hills. I got pretty good at it." He took in another deep breath. "On Mondays caddies play for free—that's the tradition—but my dad said no. 'This,' he said, 'is a *great* golf course and I won't have my son hacking it up, not knowing what he's doing. Caddy. I'll let you know when you can play.' And he wouldn't let me play anywhere else, either, not until I was good enough to play there."

"That sounds pretty rough," Sarah said.

"Maybe," Charlie said. "I didn't know any better then."

"And now?"

In judgment of his father, Charlie could only shrug. "I practiced every day and when I was fourteen I played. I tried out for my high school golf team, and after a few swings the coach told me I was on the team. I was a freshman and I traveled with the seniors to play all over Pennsylvania, Ohio and West Virginia. I never lost a match. I beat everybody. Later that year I stood on the same tees that Hogan and Palmer and Miller used, all the great players, and I shot sixty-four at Oakmont Country Club. By number twelve the guy I was playing with was walking along watching me. We never told anybody."

"Why not?"

"Because a fifteen-year-old shooting sixty-four at Oakmont, that's like a kid pitching a no-hitter in the World Series. It's impossible. Only one player ever shot a better round on that course."

"Was it a fluke?" Sarah asked.

Charlie shook his head. "You see, all the time I wasn't allowed to play, I was practicing, learning. I really can't remember anything else. I don't know why, and I still wonder, but it's all I wanted. I thought it was easy. I finished the season and won the state title. The next day my father and I went to play."

The rain pattered on the leaves of a maple tree; his ball deep in the wet rough beneath it. But he had a clear shot to the green. "You all right over there?" his father called out from the middle of the fairway.

A wall of fog pressed the window of the lobby, the muted white headlights of cars rolled by the hotel.

"And you hurt your arm?" Sarah asked.

"Yeah."

"And then you couldn't play."

"Right," Charlie said.

"But now you can?"

"I think probably better," Charlie said. "I'm stronger, a lot stronger."

"So you have another chance."

"Yes."

"But it's hard," Sarah said. "I can see on your face that it's hard."

He opened his hands.

"Callouses? From practicing?"

Charlie nodded.

"They look like they hurt."

"They did," Charlie said, catching her eye. "Not now."

"It's serious stuff, isn't it?"

"It's the only way I know how to do it."

"I've noticed the change," Sarah said. "You've seemed a little distant this last week."

"The guys I work for, they want me to play. I have to."

"Have to? Why?"

"If I want to stay. If I want to work."

"I don't understand."

"They call the shots. Especially this guy I work for."

"Can't you do something else?" Sarah asked.

"Before I got here I could've done anything, gone anywhere. I was ready to."

"And now?"

"I want to play."

"But it's hard."

"Yeah."

Sarah leaned on the counter and kissed him lightly on the cheek. "You look tired."

"I am."

"What time do you have to be at work?"

"Never."

Sarah smiled. "Right. Lucky you."

"Lucky me."

She kissed him again. "Do you want me to come up? When I'm done?"

"I do, I really do. There's so much I don't know. It's hard for me to ask."

"You don't have to," she said. "I already did."

16

Monday soon became the only day in the week; the other six were just preparation. So when Charlie walked onto the course it revealed no fewer than a dozen caddies of the twenty or so allowed to work at this esteemed club, now ready to compete themselves at the game they all lived for. Bags circled the first and tenth tees. Some practiced putting while others swung clubs trying to loosen up their bent bodies. Sam Deacon was there and William Moorer too, both having patiently waited the last couple of weeks for Charlie to show. They'd seen him practicing and let him be, satisfied in knowing he would come when he was ready.

Henry and Spider were playing together. Billy waited for Figgs. Jack lurked in the background, watching it all, waiting for Charlie too. As the minutes passed, the sense of putting your money where your mouth was became palpable. It grabbed hold of Charlie and brought him back to Oakmont, where the older guys, caddies and members alike, would bet on every last shot and putt, every swing meaning money. They would argue about the bet, the strokes, and who was playing with whom. Once matters were settled, the first player would sink a tee into the ground and they'd play all day.

As Charlie waded through the group, conversations began to slow and everyone eyed him warily, waiting to find out who he was playing and to see him tee off.

They'd all heard so many stories over the years. About some guy who could hit it a mile, about somebody shooting sixty-five from the championship tees or eagling from the fairway to win. Day in and day out they saw wads of cash being bet and lost, a guy without a cent in his pocket hitting it stiff when he had to or a millionaire yipping a three-footer for a buck. Collectively they'd seen and heard of how on Mondays past, great players teed it up just steps from where they stood and shot sixty-five or sixty-six. They had been around the tournaments, caddied on the tours, played in events all over California and the country. They watched on television each weekend and checked the papers each morning to see who was high on the money list or struggling to make it to the next week. Caddies hear and see it all until, over the years, nothing is new, nothing can surprise them, and they have their questions that dispel the bullshit.

"That's good for eighteen, but can he put four rounds together?"

"Can he take the fuckin' heat? No? Well then, fuck him. He can sit right next to me on this fuckin' bench."

"What was the bet? That ain't no money."

"Where'd he play? Well shit, that ain't no fuckin' golf course! Hell, I shot sixty-five at that dog track—drunk!"

Familiar with such scrutiny, Charlie laid his bag on the ground, then squatted to wait. The bickering stopped, but no one teed off or even moved until Jimmy Figgs' old BMW creaked and lumbered into the parking lot. Seconds later, Figgs came packing his bag, as alert and focused as a gunslinger. Gone were the friendships and conversations, along with any consideration. This was Monday.

"Game's on," William Moorer said. "Oh shit."

"Who wants a game?" Figgs called, and Charlie stood up. "Twenties?" Figgs barked. "You wanna play for twenties?"

Charlie reached into his pocket—to count his money, Figgs presumed—then pulled out a ball and said, "Okay."

"How about fifties?" Figgs said, and Jack moved off the wall of the shack toward the first tee. Spider dropped his putter on his bag and joined him.

"Sure," Charlie said, and the others came forward and lined the first tee.

"Is that the bet?" Figgs snapped. "Fifty on the front, fifty on the back, hundred on the eighteen?"

Charlie pulled his one-iron. Figgs eyed it and tried to smile, even as his own hand went into his pocket. "If you get two down, you're pressed, another bet starts."

"Automatic press," Charlie said.

"Skins too? Five—no, ten-dollar skins, birdies double."

"Carry-overs?"

"Of course." Figgs pulled his driver from his bag. "Billy!" he shouted. "You're caddying today." He turned to Charlie and snapped, "MacLeod, I don't need to explain that we pay on the eighteenth green. I don't have to tell you that, do I?"

Charlie tossed a tee into the air and when it came down it pointed at Jimmy Figgs. "You're up," he said, then bent over to roll up his trouser cuffs one turn.

William Moorer stepped forward and pulled Charlie's bag off the ground. "No charge, kid," he said.

Figgs sent his ball down the middle of the fairway.

Charlie wiped his hands on the towel draped around William's neck, tossed his ball to the ground and with his one-iron toed it around until he was satisfied with the lie. He backed away, drew in a breath and blew it out, the last of the cold morning air forming inches from his lips. His mind raced back over the years and his concentration narrowed, everyone around him witnessing the change. To them he seemed to grow taller, but Charlie's world was rapidly shrinking down to a single thought and image: his father alongside him, and the ball now sitting inert on the clipped grass.

"Tempo, Charlie," he heard in his mind. "Tempo."

Billy coughed. Henry shifted from foot to foot. Spider, dressed in purple, was as awake as he'd been in years. The sun spilled brightly into the still morning, the fog off in the distance wisped aside as if ordered.

Charlie worked his fingers along the grip. He came to address, glanced down the fairway and drew back the club. The shaft came parallel to the ground, the steel flashed in the early-morning light, then vanished. The sound exploded and echoed across the property. A divot the size of a half-dollar popped into the air and the ball went screaming down the fairway. The men struggled to catch up, searching the sky where the ball ought to be, but then it landed yards beyond Figgs' drive, bright white against green grass, hopped once and bounded over the far hill.

One by one they turned—their shock buried behind sunglasses, low brims and poker faces—to see Charlie, frozen like a statue, hands finished high above his head, peering down the fairway, his lips moving as if in some inaudible conversation. He nodded when he got the right answer, then held out the club for his caddy.

Still stunned, William took the club. "Uh, shot, kid."

"Sh-shot," Deacon said as Charlie strode off the tee, his two friends close behind, smiling and giggling. "I'm-a throw my clubs in the fuckin' ocean," William whispered.

Back on the tee Jimmy Figgs stood shell-shocked.

"I think you're away," Jack said.

"Fifty yards away," Spider mumbled.

"Shut the fuck up," Figgs snapped before starting slowly down the fairway.

"You been around, Spider," Jack said. "You ever see anything like that?"

Spider placed a fresh toothpick in his mouth. "Never. Fifteen years on the tour, all the years here. Hell, I been stoned on my ass and never dreamed I'd see somethin' like that."

"It's like it ain't real," Jack said.

"What? The shot or him?"

Jack dropped his guard. "You noticed that, huh?"

"I'm fuckin' high, not blind," Spider said.

"What do you make of it?"

"The change? The mood?"

"Yeah. What's your take?"

"A little spooky. Knew a dude years ago, white dude wasn't very big. Motherfucker useta play hoops with. Kevin O, we called him. Irish kid. Could shoot the fuckin' lights out, I mean from downtown. Thirty feet? No problem." Spider sauntered away, firing up a joint and cupping it with his hand. "Now that ain't nothin' new for a white guy. But this honky had hops. Wasn't six feet tall and could dunk without takin' a step. Brothers couldn't believe it. I mean he could flat fly, and this is back in the late sixties. Had black hair down to his shoulders, light blue eyes and the whitest skin you ever saw." Spider dragged and sniffed. "But here was the deal. Motherfucker'd take off with that ball, he'd scream like a motherfucker, like he been stabbed. All day long he'd play and never get tired, talkin' shit and laughin' and killin' everybody and then all of a sudden screamin' like he was gonna die. I mean everybody screams now, but not then. Hell, that was how you got your ass kicked. Scared the shit out of me. Nobody could call him out. He was the strangest, meanest mothorfucker I ever saw." Spider pointed down the fairway. "Charlie quiet, but he remind me of him."

"Did you want him on your team?"

"Fuck, yeah," Spider answered. "I sure as hell didn't wanna play against him."

"Where'd he go?"

"Just gone. Can't really say when. Lived right next door to me, the only white guy in the neighborhood. Dudes like that just disappear. Burn up. Burn out. One day they gone and you wonder if they was ever there in the first place. Even existed. They're like pure, you know? Fine." Spider took a deep toke and handed the joint to Jack. "Me and you, we don't know nothin' 'bout that. Can only look at it, try to grasp it, enjoy 'em while they still here. 'Cause one day he be gone for sure and we sittin' around sayin' shit like"—and he gestured ahead at Charlie—"'Did that motherfucker really do that?'" Spider's smile showed his too-white false teeth. "And we can say, 'Yeah, motherfucker. I was there.'"

Jack blew out the smoke. "Charlie ain't bad to be around."

"How long's he been playin'?"

Jack thought about it. "Not very long. We don't need him to play forever. Just one time." Jack pointed ahead. "Like that."

"Look," Spider said, "it's a matter of trust. You better be sure when he plays the Jew, that the dude comes like that."

"He always does. Every time I seen him practice, every time he takes that club in his hands."

"Well, long as you're all right with it."

"What about you?" Jack asked Spider, handing back the joint.

"Oh, I might put a little down."

From the middle of the fairway, Figgs hooked his ball badly into the left rough.

"He's toast," Jack said.

"Done," Spider agreed, snuffed out the joint and pocketed it. "Stick a fork in his ass."

Charlie hit a mid-iron onto the green of the par five.

"I ain't never seen anybody there off the tee."

"With a fuckin' one-iron," Jack said. "Nobody hits a one-iron anymore."

"I beg to differ, motherfucker," Spider said. "I beg to differ."

17

Figgs quit after nine, having had enough, paid what he owed and went home, but Charlie played on. William carried his bag while Sam shuffled quietly along with his own clubs, hitting a shot here and there, watching.

On twelve, Charlie hit his approach close to the pin.

"Shot," William said, shaking his head.

Charlie threw down another ball. The second was lower, straighter and just as close, and he pulled out another ball and did it again; then again and again, each shot landing on the green until the pin was surrounded.

"What are you tr-tryin' to do? Make it?" Sam joked. But each shot seemed to pull Charlie farther and farther away, down into a dangerous funk.

The thirteenth hole was a sharp dogleg right. Charlie removed his one-iron and hit another low shot that bored through the wind and came to rest in the middle of the fairway.

"You got about one-twenty left," William said.

"I'll bet you can get it close to the f-front of the g-green," Sam said, pointing to a grove of pines down the right side of the fairway. "Maybe drive it."

"Old man Blaney wanted those trees cut down, he hit 'em so many times," William said. "Over there so often he said he should pay rent or buy a house over there. The sonofabitch probably get buried right there. Hit one too many and just fall over."

Charlie grinned. "Will you miss him when he's gone?"

"Oh yeah," William said. "Pays like a slot machine."

All three men laughed.

"There!" William said. "I was beginnin' to wonder if you had any teeth left."

"I know," Charlie said, shaking his head.

"Try and relax. You got a lot of golf ahead of you. Nobody's gonna take that away."

A doubtful look swept across Charlie's face.

"Here," Sam said, pulling his driver and handing it to Charlie. "Let's work. Take it over those trees, and bring it back into the fairway."

"Two seventy carry over the valley," William said. "'Bout three to the front edge."

The club was steel-shafted and had a persimmon head. The first drive clipped a branch but he teed up another and sent it well over the trees.

"Th-that's the shot," Sam said. "Damn, that's right in front, maybe on."

Holding the club before him, feeling the weight of it, Charlie said, "It's like my old one."

"You can borrow it," Sam said.

Charlie nodded and they resumed their walk.

"I know neither one of you gonna like it," William said, "but you'd get another twenty yards with one of the new drivers. Light graphite shaft, metal head. And the mis-hits go straighter."

"What mis-hits?" Sam said.

"You know I'm right, Sam."

He nodded as if giving in to death itself. "I h-hate to admit it, Ch-Charlie, but you should look into it."

"I know," Charlie answered. "But I can feel the ball with this one, right up the shaft into my arms. And the sound of that metal, Christ."

"You can bet Siegal's got one," William warned. "That boy can't hit it with you, not by a long shot. But this new shit'll get him closer. And your length's a big advantage. You got to take every inch you can get, long as you can keep it in the fairway."

"Out with the old, huh?" Charlie asked.

"You got a problem with that, don'tcha?"

Again the mood threatened to become stagnant, contemplative, and Sam slapped his hands together to snap them out of it. "Let's play," he said.

From a hundred and twenty yards Charlie played his first ball, high and soft, tight to the pin.

"Three feet," Sam said. "Damn."

Charlie smiled, his spirits rising, and rifled the club back into the bag and pulled out another.

"That was a pitching wedge," William whispered to Sam, tossing down another ball.

Charlie hit a high cut, the ball sliced forty yards, landed softly, took the contour of the green and rolled up to the pin.

"Seven-iron," William said as Charlie took yet another club.

The third ball was a low, hard punch shot that skipped once and stopped dead next to the pin.

"N-n-now you're just sh-showin' off."

"Fuckin' five-iron," William said, laughing. "Hell with it. Keep the fuckin' driver. Keep 'em all. Do whatever you want."

The balls were so close to the hole that Sam kicked them away to different parts of the green and tossed a few more balls into other areas, and William started working with Charlie.

"Here," he said, bending over to point at a spot. "Downhill, so watch your speed." They putted for an hour, a few groups played through, then they played the rest of the back nine, Charlie occasionally catching Sam golfing his own ball down the middle and on the short grass.

As they approached the clubhouse, music and laughter rolled out over the course, the caddies' day coming to an end. But Charlie headed back to number one.

"Wh-where's he goin'?" Sam said.

Charlie sunk a tee in the ground, pulled out the driver and unleashed a huge shot down the right side. He was shouldering his bag when Sam approached the tee.

"No," Sam said, holding out a hand for the bag. "Th-that's enough."

Charlie looked down the fairway.

"L-leave it," Sam said. "You got a girl. Go home. T-talk to her. Rest. Eat some good food."

Again, Charlie looked down the fairway.

"I mean it," Sam said. "You can't play like this, c-can't live like this. It ain't healthy."

"The match," Charlie said.

"You ain't gonna w-win it today."

William Moorer and Jack were standing by the shack, nose-to-nose, when Charlie and Sam rounded the hedge. William was hot and Jack, even though hopelessly outmatched, was staring him down like a terrier.

"I'll give it to him," Jack hissed, then reached into his back pocket. Between his long, bony fingers, an envelope flashed in the dusk. He handed it to Charlie even as he stared William down. "There, see? I found it taped to the payphone." He looked at Charlie. "It's a wire."

"Didn't read it, didja?" William said.

"It's sealed," Jack said. "It's sealed, ain't it Charlie?"

"It's sealed," Charlie said.

Jack glared back at William. "So fuck you."

Holding the envelope, Charlie suddenly felt his heart pounding. Who knew he was here? Not Helen. And if not her, who could possibly know?

"Go ahead," Sam said. "We're here."

So he opened it and read.

Charlie,

I'm sorry to tell you this in a note, but I was afraid you might not return my call. I'm home visiting. I'm so sorry to tell you but your father has passed away. Ernie, the old grounds-keeper at Oakmont, read the obituary and put it together. He remembered what a great player you were. They are waiting to hear from you. I'm so sorry I got you into this mess.

Stephen

"What's up, kid?" William asked.

Charlie handed him the note, then sat down slowly on the bench.

The three men read the wire, their separate thoughts parading through their heads. When finished, they were surprised to find Charlie calmer than they'd ever seen him, even tranquil.

"It's a tough thing, losin' your old man," Jack said.

"It's been coming. I've had a long time to think about it."

"Don't make it any easier," William said.

Charlie stared up at them. "Yes, it does."

Sam took a seat beside him. "When was the last time you saw him?"

"Not since I was a kid," Charlie said. "We were playing one day. I pushed my drive right, under a tree. It'd been raining and the grass was wet, lying over the ball. I was tired but he wanted to play, and so did I. Could hit any shot I wanted, right? You know what that's like, Sam."

"I do," he said.

Charlie patted his elbow. "I blew this out and he never

stopped blaming himself. But it wasn't his fault. It wasn't anybody's fault." Charlie scooped up his canvas duffle and started walking.

"Where you headin'?" Jack asked.

"Going home," Charlie said.

"Home home?" he asked.

"Yeah."

"Comin' back, ain't ya?" Jack asked as Charlie passed from the last sunlight into shade.

18

As evening came, the sun seemed to drop from the sky in an instant. Light from the clubhouse bar cast a long rectangular box across the tenth tee, turning the rich green grass gray. Sinatra's voice floated through small outbursts of muffled laughter. The wind barely moved the blond hair on Danny Lang's head.

"Partyin'?" Jack said.

"Yeah," Lang said with a smirk.

Jack looked a little longer at Lang than he normally would. He had a story to keep straight. Charlie was as good as gone, but he wasn't about to tell ol' Danny-boy a god-damn thing. No way. He might call the whole show off and Jack wasn't settling for that. He was a little surprised, and in fact relieved, to see Lang loaded. Redness rimmed his watered eyes, and he wobbled slightly as he turned to acknowledge his buddies.

"They got a pretty good poker game goin' on," Lang said. "Schmitty's kickin' the shit out of 'em."

Jack's face was illuminated briefly as he lit a cigarette.

"That shit'll kill you," Lang said, then wondered why he'd said anything at all. He was in control, as always, and he'd worked his ass off his whole life to make sure of it, sitting elbow-to-elbow with presidents, princes and kings, dealing with world-moving decisions. So it rattled him a little when he got such a deadpan act from Jack.

"Kills ya real slow from what I hear," Jack answered, then exhaled a gray cloud. "But we all got our vices and you're bound to die. Every one of us, and it's gonna hurt no matter what."

"Yeah," Lang said. Cockiness was what he liked about Jack, his brash, foolish bravery that belied his situation. Even with nothing in his pocket, no single thing or friend in the world, he had a bluff or some line of bullshit good enough to make you wonder, to put a doubt in your head, if only for a moment. And that might be enough to beat you at whatever game you might be playing. Lang knew the only difference between this caddy and most of his own friends was that Jack wasn't born with a seat at the table. At this moment, regretting that Jack was even involved with the bet, Lang debated how to cut him out. He was smart, maybe too smart. But he couldn't. Jack was the only one who honestly knew their opponent, who'd been inside the ropes, and that kind of information was invaluable. Jack not only had stood shoulder-to-shoulder with Siegal but also, by coincidence and sheer luck, had discovered Charlie. So he'd have to take Jack's shit until everything was in place. And though Danny hated waiting in line, he'd do whatever it took to get what he wanted.

Charlie is the most revered man on these premises, Lang thought, and he doesn't even know it. There were players and then there were players. And so far as he could tell, Charlie was *the* player. No matter what Danny Lang did or how much money he made or how hard he practiced, he could never be what Charlie so completely was, seemingly since birth. No, Danny's world was endless, boundless and ultimately unattainable. You can never own the whole thing. Someone was always trying to get what was his and he to take what was theirs, be it money, land, or position. Position. He could never have that feeling, like Charlie, the total command. There would always be something missing, and compared to Charlie and Siegal, he was just poking the ball around.

Standing in the dark, he saw himself, slovenly, lonely and teetering like some drunken bum, discussing strategy with a man he wouldn't let enter his house or walk his dog. And for now he stood behind him, of all people!

Jack looked out over the course, forever smoking, to a flock of stars in the west. "What a night," he said.

"Yeah," Lang said. "What happened with Figgs and Charlie?"

It was all Danny wanted to talk about, but Jack quickly decided to keep him waiting and let him stew. As his mouth went to form the answer, he laughed, bent over from the waist and threw his cigarette to the ground. "I can't smoke and laugh at the same time. I get the hiccups."

Adrenaline rushed through Lang's head and sobered him slightly. He was being played, and despised it. So he waited for Jack to finish his act, decided to eat a little more shit, took a breath and stuffed his hands in his pockets.

"Sorry," Jack said a few seconds later. "But you should've seen the look on Figgs' face comin' up nine! He was so pissed off he pulled his bag from Billy's shoulder, threw twenty bucks at him and kicked him in the ass!"

Lang forced a smile. "So Charlie beat him?"

Jack picked up his cigarette. "Yeah," he said. "Charlie shot thirty-two on the front side. Four under. With a bogey. Moorer said he must've hit a sprinkler head on number three. His tee shot took a crazy bounce up into the grass and they couldn't find the ball. He still made five. Figgs lucked in a thirty-footer for bogey. That was the only hole he didn't lose."

"What'd he do on eight?"

"He almost holed out. Gimme two. The guy's a machine."

"Did they play for anything?"

"Caddies don't play unless there's a bet. Charlie took him for about two fifty."

"They only played nine?" Lang asked.

"Figgs'd had enough," Jack said. "Charlie would have bet anything he wanted, gone back to the first tee, anything, it wouldn't matter to him, but Figgs didn't want to. He could've made another bet, but he was done. He could never beat Charlie."

"So the money doesn't bother him?"

"He doesn't care one way or the other."

"How's his head?" Lang asked.

Jack measured his words as he thought of where Charlie might be at this second, at his hotel by now, maybe on a plane. "I told you before. He's kinda strange when he plays. Doesn't talk at all, just mumbles to himself. Spider thinks it's good, that if he showed up happy-go-lucky then you'd have to worry. Some guys gotta get in a zone, you know?"

"You can't talk to him?"

"You can talk all you want," Jack said. "Charlie ain't hearin' nothin'."

"What about Moorer? Didn't he want yardages?"

"Plays by feel. Looks at his target and pulls a club. Moorer said not a word passed between them. He'd hand him his putter and Charlie would knock it in the hole."

"Does he still think he misread that putt?" Lang asked.

The question threw Jack, his heart jumping as he wondered if Lang had thrown him a curve. But Jack was on his game too. "Who? Moorer? When Deacon played Siegal? I don't know."

"Deacon pulled it."

"I wasn't there," Jack said, regaining his calm now that he realized Lang was simply on a rambling high. He suspected nothing.

"He choked. Best putter in the world and he choked."

"Shit happens under pressure. Sam's a nice guy. Too bad."

"Fucked up," Lang said. "Changed his life."

"Maybe he wanted it to change it," Jack said.

"What do you mean?"

"From what I hear he makes that putt in his sleep. Still."

Lang straightened. "So what do you think happened?"

"Like I said, I don't know. Maybe he got tired of the shit. Whatever happened, I think he did the right thing."

"And what might that be?" Lang pressed.

"How the fuck would I know? The guy has a nice life. No cares. Look at him. Eighty and he looks sixty. Had a great wife who understood him, now this new girl. No bills. Eats well. Sleeps like a baby. He can still take a piss and travels where he wants, which is nowhere. He's the freest man on earth. Everybody loves the motherfucker. Hell, I love him and I hate everybody."

This was something Lang couldn't fathom. "But he could've played on the tour."

"He's a player still. That mantle never leaves you. Palmer's still a player and he can't break eighty. Larry Siegal will always be a player. Those that know, know. The Deacon's a player. Charlie's a player. Probably the best."

Lang nodded. "Lotta fuckin' money," he said. "Everyone wants in."

Jack, having pulled it off, decided to have some fun. "Lotta ego flyin' around, huh? Everyone pullin' their dicks out? A lot of anti-Semitic, fuck-you gentile money bein' laid down."

Lang grinned. "Yeah, and it's all on your word, Jack. How's that make you feel?"

"I ain't worried. Just have my money ready."

"Randall's money, you mean," Lang said.

"He'll get it back with interest."

"Tough guy. I wouldn't fuck with him."

"Never fuck with a man who's got nothin' to lose," Jack said.

"So if Randall lost that money—"

"He'd tear apart the first motherfucker he saw and everybody else between them and me. That's where he's at."

The thought sent a chill through Danny Lang. His high was evaporating and the cold night air snapped at his face. Part of him wanted out of the whole thing, but he realized then and there that all his money and property, all the influence and prestige he'd acquired over the years, added up to nothing. He needed the action. He had no more than Jack, a little less than Charlie, and nothing compared to Sam Deacon. He was caught like a drunk sitting in front of a drink, his body shaking and lips dry. There was no stopping now.

"So I'll set the match," he said.

Jack nodded, then threw a curve of his own. "How's Randall doin'?"

"He'll be all right," Lang answered.

"Can I ask you one thing?"

"Sure."

"Why are you doin' that? Takin' care of him? Why Randall?"

Lang almost lied but decided the truth was better. "I don't know," he said whimsically. "I just felt like it."

"Just like that?" Jack asked.

"Just like that."

"And tomorrow?"

"We'll see."

"Whaddya gonna do?" Jack asked.

The conversation was over. "Take the jet to L.A. in the morning," Lang said. "These things have to be done face-to-face."

19

Charlie opened the note and read it again just to make sure. Then Sarah read it.

"I have to go," he said.

She stood in the open doorway to Charlie's room as he hurriedly gathered his things. "I'm going to have to fly. I don't know how much time I have," he said, then reached into the drawer, grabbed a wad of money and carelessly stuffed it into his pocket. He reached in deeper, took out another handful, and threw it in his canvas duffle.

"You won that playing golf?"

"Some of it," he answered, as if giving the time of day.

In an instant all he had was packed up once again. He stood before her as he had arrived, bag shouldered, disheveled as ever, hat in hand. But the melancholia and exhaustion had vanished. His presence was now straight and boundless, a change that would serve him well as he moved purposefully forward to a private place where it seemed she couldn't follow. Their time together was dwindling, her feelings turning hopeless and sad. What had been gained? Nothing. Not one thing, not a single moment standing out in time and place. Eventually, everything would be laid low. She struggled against her feelings by trying to recall faraway places she'd hoped to visit, but found her desire faded and wanting. She'd witnessed souls coming and going her whole life, it was her business, people checking in and out, her own father a frail memory confined to childhood. So however uncomfortable her acceptance of transience and longing, for Charlie's sake, she would dismiss whatever fears lay within her.

But the cold night wind swept through the room to weaken her and test her; the curtains blew out, then fell back again. She found herself thinking how nice it would be to hold on to him, to persuade him to stay with her and keep warm for just a moment longer. Then a new hurt seeped in, threatening to take over. Why must it always be this way? Why did he have to leave? Why now, and why can't I go?

He approached the door and she stepped aside. In a hurry just a moment ago, Charlie now took her hand and a slower, more pleasing air radiated from him. His voice rose in his throat and she kissed him before he could speak, then he was gone.

The door clicked quietly shut and the room settled. The curtains hung perfectly and a terrible loneliness overtook her.

20

I t wasn't so bad when Charlie didn't show up on Tuesday for work; Tuesdays can be slow, and many caddies take the day off. It really wasn't all that bad that he wasn't seen on Wednesday or even Thursday. But Friday's another thing. There's always the possibility of getting around twice, more big-money games were played and the tips were bigger. So when Charlie was nowhere around by twelve o'clock, well, everyone started getting a little nervous.

"He's comin' back?" Al asked. He was a little more twitchy than usual, and his voice had taken on a shivering quality. "I put money on him. H-he's going to show up, ain't he? He didn't take off?"

"Al, relax," Jack said. "You know that's how Deacon started. Nice guy, but do you wanna sound like that?"

"He hasn't practiced since Monday," Al argued. "That's weird."

"Not *here*," Jack said. "He hasn't practiced *here*! He's ready, for Christ's sake. Maybe the guy needs a little fuckin' space! Christ, I know I do." He pushed away from the wall of the shack and strolled into the back lot. Balls from the range flew weakly overhead, all falling well short of the fence. Jack recalled Charlie hitting that first ball and how it banged off the tree on the far side.

First ball he hit in twenty-five years, Jack thought. Christ. Once he was alone, a scowl steadily grew on his face as he thought of where Charlie was and all the things that could possibly go wrong. How little he, or any of them, knew Charlie, especially given the fortune Lang was surely betting. "No fuckin' doubt about that," Jack mumbled as he moved to the far end of the dirt lot. But why would he? It was practically outside Lang's nature to trust anybody. Besides the little information Stephen Ford had passed, nobody knew a thing about Charlie. None of them even knew where he was staying. And who was this girl he was hanging out with? Women can mess you up faster than anything.

They'd all been so taken with his game that they hadn't bothered to find out. They'd gone on feel alone and, at best, a shadowy past. He seemed so normal until he took that club in his hands, Jack thought, lighting a cigarette. So straight. Jack cursed himself at even thinking of Charlie in the past tense. Greedy, every one of us motherfuckers, he thought, and greed will get you.

At least Lang was in Los Angeles, and not here busting his balls. Right about now he'd be offering to host the match here, and Siegal and the Czar would jump at the chance. To win here, two Jews among all these racist motherfuckers—that would be glorious.

The game would be straightforward, match play. Simple. But the stakes were something Jack couldn't fathom. He knew how much he was betting. Everything.

Jack wondered again where Charlie was and how he was taking his father's death; how much was on the line, and how good Siegal was.

"Whatcha thinkin' about?" a voice called from the opening in the hedge. William Moorer was eyeing Jack. He knew who Jack used to hang out with, that he'd been Siegal's caddy, working in L.A. and in Vegas, and of course he knew of the Czar's reputation. Bad man, William thought. Jack'd had it, then fucked it all up. William didn't know the specifics but he figured Jack hadn't done enough to get himself killed, just banished for life from the entire city of Los Angeles. That takes some doin', he thought as Jack strolled toward him. With thirteen, fifteen million motherfuckers down there, how could anybody even find him? Well, William told himself, the Czar sure could.

And Jack hadn't been out of San Francisco since. He'd done some time, but so had William, so that wasn't anything to hold against him. After Jack paid his debt he landed at this club; William couldn't remember exactly when. It was like he'd always been here and could be gone at any second.

And there was Randall. He and Jack were tight. As bad a man as William was, he didn't want to try kickin' Randall's ass. Not at my age, he thought. Even half dead, Randall'd tear a big piece off anybody who messed with him, win or lose.

So to keep the peace he had to cooperate with Jack until the match was over. For one thing, he'd laid a bunch of money down. But beyond that he and Sam liked Charlie, and in the end, not only to protect his interests, he'd do what needed to be done, with Jack and Lang and Randall too.

"We got somethin' to talk about?" Jack said.

"Yeah," William said. "I got a call this morning."

"Where?" Jack asked

William pointed over his shoulder to the shack. "Early," he said. "East Coast time."

21

He's fuckin' *gone*?" Daniel Lang said. "Do you know where I just got off a plane from?"

"I know where you were," Jack said.

"And you know what I was doing too, you asshole. The money's down. The word is out."

"He's back East," Jack said. "It was an emergency. His old man died."

"How do you know that?"

Trying to protect all parties, Jack kept it brief. "He got a wire."

"When did you find out?"

Jack gave it his best lie. "Tuesday, the day after we talked."

"And he got home?"

"Yeah. Moorer got the call in the shack."

"He asked for Moorer?"

"Yeah."

"I don't trust him."

"Charlie?"

"Moorer."

"Charlie trusts him."

"Why?" Lang said.

"He feels safe with him. Him and Deacon both. They speak the same language. They look out for him. Maybe want the kid to find a little peace."

Lang took a threatening step toward him. "I don't give a shit about his fuckin' happiness. I couldn't care less. I'm talking about whether or not he'll show up. And if he does, can he play? Will he win?"

"Don't worry, Charlie's perfect for Siegal. I already told you that."

"Then get his ass back here!"

"Want to fly me to Pittsburgh to kidnap him?" Jack shook his head. "He'll be back."

"How can you be so sure?"

"He's honest, for one thing. Not that any of us know much about that." Jack pondered his next words. He felt like a traitor. He too had come to admire Charlie. "And for all the reasons you said, Danny. He ain't sure, but he thinks, maybe, he got his life back. A place to fuckin' be. And it's here, not there. He'll figure that out once he gets there. Plus the girl. He'll come back."

"A girl," Lang said. "This guy could be set, win more money than he ever dreamed of, have whatever the hell he wants, just by playing a game. That's not enough to bring him back."

"You oughta be glad," Jack said, then thought Lang was about to take a swing at him. He'd never seen him lose his temper so completely. He'd cut other members down with a look and chewed Al out on occasion, but always in private. He's scared, Jack thought.

Thankfully, Lang backed off. "We don't have a lot of time," he said.

"When's the match?"

"Two weeks."

"He's ready," Jack told him.

"Okay. But tell Moorer that if he calls again, he'd better let him know the score. My money . . ." He hesitated, then whispered, "Other people's money. My reputation. Your money too, Jack. Randall's money. All of it. So make sure Moorer tells him. Get him to understand. Tell him whatever it takes. Say he can do whatever he wants after the match, no hard feelings, no matter what happens."

"That's a fuckin' lie," Jack mumbled.

Lang nearly exploded again. "What do you care? You gettin' moral on me?"

"Not me. Never happen."

"Well then, how's this? Tell Moorer I'll shit-can every last one of you."

"You ready to do that?"

"What do you think this is, some fuckin' union? I'll clear this yard in a minute! Tell Moorer to tell Charlie that! If he doesn't show up, none of his buddies will ever find work again. Not Moorer, not Deacon, not anybody, including you."

Jack shrugged. "Got it," he said.

"We get one day, Monday, to practice as much as Charlie wants. The next morning, that Tuesday, we play the match."

"You mean Siegal gets a day to see the course."

"No, Charlie gets to see theirs. We're playing there."

Jack was astonished. His heart raced and he couldn't feel his feet. "Why the fuck would you agree to that?"

"Odds," Lang said. "The Czar gave me three to one."

"Christ!" Jack snapped. "He's never seen the course! The grasses are different! There's Poa annua, kikuyu! For Christ's sake, Charlie's never played on that! The greens are the weirdest things you ever saw. Up looks down, down looks flat, they're tiny and slope in every fuckin' direction! Nobody knows those greens like Siegal!"

"You do," Lang said.

"What?" Jack suddenly felt the wind go out of him.

"Yeah," Lang said. "Pack your bags. In two weeks we're going to L.A. I got special dispensation from the Czar. He wants to see you."

Jack's mouth went dry. "Me?"

"Not face-to-face, from a distance. He thought it'd be nice to see how you're doing."

It took a moment or two, but Jack regained his composure. "He always was thoughtful."

"That's the only reason I'd agree to play there. That fat bastard gets to play his home course, and the Czar thought that would surprise me, but I was way ahead of him. He about shit when I said your name. But he played it cool and agreed. Evidently he doesn't respect your abilities."

"Fuck," Jack said and reached for his smokes. "Okay, so the Czar gets home field and you get the odds and me."

"Not to mention Charlie," Lang said. "I know the odds, and I know you. You wouldn't have packed for Siegal without knowing what the fuck you're doing."

"I remember the place."

"Great place, great course."

"Little slice of heaven."

"Well, now you get to go back," Lang said. "Like a fallen fuckin' angel."

"Yeah," Jack said.

"If Moorer does his thing, you get to do yours."

Jack tamped the fresh pack on the palm of his hand. "I'll be very clear."

22

The man who greeted Charlie had large, wrinkled hands, gray hair, and an old, shiny black suit hanging from his thick, towering frame. His face was kind and he spoke softly but firmly in a soothing manner, casting his eyes over Charlie with the patience that comes with seeing so much pain over the years. He'd buried many, including members of his own family, and seemed to be patiently waiting for his own end. It was his business.

Waiting to see his father, Charlie wondered what lay ahead. He was alone, the last person alive in his family. His thoughts were spiraling away when the man spoke in a gentle, deep voice.

"I remember your father, Mr. MacLeod," he said.

"Charlie, please," he said, extending his hand.

"Thomas Riley," the man said.

"How did you know my father, Mr. Riley?"

"We went to the same high school. He was older than me."

"But you remember him?"

"Oh, yes. He was quite popular. Good athlete." He flashed a friendly, devilish grin. The change in his demeanor, the sudden playfulness, relaxed Charlie. Mr. Riley leaned in close to Charlie and whispered, "Quite the ladies' man. And mischievous. We all wanted to be like him when we grew up."

"That's great," Charlie said. "I wanted to be like him too."

"And I also think I remember you," Riley said, as if he was putting Charlie on.

"Maybe. We lived right down the street," he said, pointing in the direction of his old home.

"And when I received your father's remaining possessions, I was sure of it." Mr. Riley held up an old manila envelope and opened the door for Charlie. "Ready?"

Charlie nodded. He tucked the envelope under his arm and stepped into a room where John MacLeod—covered in a white sheet to the neck—lay on a cold metal table. It took Charlie by surprise.

"There's no casket, since he's being cremated," Riley said.

"And I'm the only one coming."

"It's how he wanted it."

Charlie wiped his blurry eyes as he stepped close to his father, and took a deep breath to steady himself. "That's him," he whispered.

"Yes," Riley said again.

"He looks so small." Charlie's throat tightened. "He always looked so big to me."

"A child's perception."

"What did he die of?"

"Heart attack, very quick. A copy of the medical report is in the folder. Since you hadn't seen him for so long, I wanted to give you as much information about him as I could. It may help. Fill in some blanks over the years."

Charlie's eyes were riveted on his father as Mr. Riley gently pulled the folder from beneath his arm and opened it. "Let's see here," he said. "He lived in Rye, New York, and traveled back and forth to Florida."

"He always hated the winter," Charlie said. "Couldn't play."

"Golf."

"Yes," Charlie said. "How did you know?"

Mr. Riley held out a beat-up scorecard, white with faded green lettering, and handed it to him.

"Seventy-one," Charlie said.

Mr. Riley's eyes brightened. "That's pretty good, isn't it?"

One by one he handed over scorecards from golf courses in New York and Florida, as well as the Carolinas.

"These were his low rounds, I bet," Charlie said. "Sixty-eight, sixty-nine—wow, a sixty-five."

"I guess he was really good," Riley said.

"He was a player," Charlie said, flipping through newspaper clippings from the *Pittsburgh Post-Gazette* and photographs of Charlie holding the state-title trophy, practicing in the backyard, with Stephen at Oakmont.

"You played? Very well too, I see. You look so young."

"Fourteen, fifteen," Charlie said.

"Did you win it every year?" Mr. Riley joked.

"No. Where was he, Mr. Riley?"

"He was found in his car in South Carolina. The police said that people saw him swimming in the ocean just minutes before, somewhere around Wilmington. People he worked with in Rye said he was on his way south for the winter. I guess he just stopped off for a swim."

"Is that why he's so dark?" Charlie asked. "He must've fallen asleep in the sun."

"He spent a lot of time in the sun anyway," Mr. Riley said. "He has a few surgical scars on his temples, probably a bit of skin cancer from exposure. But all in all he looks great for a man in his late seventies. Thin. Very strong."

"What did he do?" Charlie asked.

Mr. Riley's large, heavy eyes opened wider than Charlie thought possible. "Why, he worked at a golf course, Charlie. I was told he worked in Rye all summer, then moved to Naples, Florida, for the winter. He was a caddy."

Charlie was stunned. "That's what the caddies at Oakmont used to do. Just before winter they'd take off for Florida. I wonder if he ever ran into them."

"That I don't know."

"Thank you. Thank you for this." Charlie held up the old folder, then stepped closer to examine the lines the sun and wind had carved into his father's face. His gray hair was cut short and neat. "It's a shame you can't see his eyes," Charlie said. "He had beautiful blue eyes."

"I'll leave you alone," Mr. Riley said, and closed the dark wood doors behind him.

Under the thin branch of a maple tree, in full autumn colors of red and yellow, Charlie stooped low to see if he had a shot. Water dripped on his neck and arms, and branches scraped against him, but all his energy was focused on the ball.

"Do you have a shot?" his father asked.

In a week the leaves would fall and the tree would be bare. Against a golden hillside under bulging black clouds, Charlie came to address. Low, cut shot, he told himself, feeling the weight of a five-iron in his hands. A little left-to-right. He could hardly contain his excitement about showing his father what he could do. He was one day removed from winning the state championship.

John MacLeod also beamed as his son methodically executed what he'd been taught—step by step, like a violinist or mathematician, doctor or carpenter—Charlie's future was laid out before him. He'd seen to that, having given his son a map, a detailed set of beliefs. The least superstitious man in the world, he believed in hard work and faith, not luck. When opportunity meets hard work, that's luck, he told Charlie any number of times. "Luck's what people believe after they've lost their faith." And the bad luck awaiting them, he added, was called fate.

What he taught was true. There, there is the proof, he thought, even as he felt his son parting from him, transcending the sum of his knowledge.

Charlie took aim at the dew-covered green, then looked down at his ball. The rain started coming harder. He was set to hit, but instead stepped away.

"What's wrong?" his father called out.

Charlie shook his head, re-addressed his ball quickly and set himself to swing. John was surprised by his sudden lack of patience. But his accomplishments were so vivid, and being with him so comforting, that he decided this once to just let his son play. But his stomach tightened as Charlie drew the club back above his head. The silhouette confirmed that he was about to make a good hard move to the ball, something John had always believed in: be aggressive and *will* the ball. Now, for the first time, he wished he hadn't taught Charlie this lesson. Something was wrong but it was intangible, nothing he could see or identify. So he hesitated, his cry of warning dying in his throat.

The club came down and ripped into the deep rough, then suddenly stopped. The ball rolled out weakly. The head of the club had struck something, and the ferocity of his swing sent Charlie's hands jerking beyond the point of impact, his right elbow contorting sickeningly. His father dropped his bag and ran across the fairway. The pain rushed up Charlie's arm, and he'd heard a snap. From twenty yards away, John swore he'd heard something too. A hot rush flowed from Charlie's elbow to his armpit, and when he finally let go of the club, it stood there on its own, buried beneath the root of the tree. Charlie was white with fear.

It took two hours to fight the morning traffic back into town and the hospital. His arm was badly swollen, but another two hours crawled by before a doctor put an ice pack on it. By dinnertime, a second doctor arrived to examine him.

"How'd it happen?" he asked.

"We were golfing," his father said. "He swung and hit the root of a tree."

"Well, you won't be doing any golfing for quite a while," he said, and Charlie wasn't surprised.

The doctor pulled John aside and spoke in a whisper. "I'll be honest. This is bad. The tendon's torn if not detached. You'll need a specialist, and a damn good one, just to get normal use of the arm back. Let me see who I can call."

That evening there was a sharp rap on the front door, and Maureen MacLeod opened it to see a stranger standing there in a black cashmere overcoat, a red silk scarf draped around his neck. "Yes?" she said.

"I'm Dr. Harold Ford."

"Stephen's father, of course," Maureen said. "Come in, please."

"I got a call from a colleague. He said something about a boy hurting his arm playing golf, and unfortunately Charlie's name came up." He stepped inside, removed his coat and handed it to her. "Thank you, my dear." He smiled thinly and sighed. "Oh my. I haven't made a house call in years, not since the good old days." He looked about impatiently. "Well, where is he?"

"Upstairs, with my husband. I'll get them."

Ford hardly recognized the frightened, weary boy who appeared in the living room. Just the day before he'd looked so alive, marching up the eighteenth fairway alongside Stephen, silent, certain, and victorious.

"I didn't realize what a little guy you are," Ford said, and John and Maureen stood side by side helplessly as he extended Charlie's arm slowly. "This may hurt, son," he said. But it was John who winced, and Maureen kissed her husband on the cheek to comfort him.

As he moved Charlie's arm this way and that to check mobility, he waited for his patient to grimace or cry out, but Charlie remained silent. The boy's threshold for pain was unusually high. This explained a lot about what he'd achieved, but the doctor was not about to say so.

"Yes, I see this all the time," he said. He rested Charlie's arm on his lap, then pulled a prescription pad from his coat pocket and began scribbling. "We push these kids too hard, place unfair expectations on them, and they end up getting hurt. They're boys, not men." He stood up. "Your playing days are over, son," he said. "I'll have to operate, reattach what I can, and you have to concentrate on just getting some use out of that arm."

"I can't pay you," John mumbled.

He handed the prescription to Maureen and smiled again. "We'll work something out," he said.

Maureen gave him his coat and walked him to the front door. "Thank you," she said.

"Your husband doesn't seem very appreciative," he said.

"John's got a lot of pride, and things at work are a little tough right now. And this, well, he doesn't know what to do."

"I don't suppose so," Dr. Ford said. "But he'd better figure something out."

Some months later, in the spring, as the days turned warm and hopeful, Maureen came home from work to find Charlie, his arm still in a sling, sitting at the kitchen table, red-eyed and sullen.

He handed her an opened envelope and walked slowly upstairs to his room.

My dear Maureen,
I pushed too hard. I can't look at him. Not now, not this way.
I'm sorry.
    Love always,

                                                                                John

23

Dr. Harold Ford, like Stephen, had been handsome in his youth, but as he aged he drank and ate too much and it showed. His lips had practically vanished from consistent pursing and his shoulders were perpetually slumped. First and foremost a doctor, he expected people to jump without delay when he spoke, behavior that carried over into every facet of his life dedicated to the accumulation of money and power. He had come from old West Virginia coal money, a background he would never admit, and they in turn gladly rejected him. He prospered early in his practice, his reputation tied to the fact that he'd been entrusted to operate on a Pittsburgh Steelers quarterback. Never mind that the player was cut the next year; everyone blamed it on his arm, and Dr. Ford had worked on his knee. The fact that such a young doctor had been given this responsibility was all that mattered and on that, with some good public-relations work, he'd built his practice. But in the late sixties, a talented and dedicated doctor came out of one of the universities to dominate his field, both locally and nationally, and this would forever grate on a bitter Harold Ford. Forced to take a back seat, he resorted to talking old men and women from the country club into knee and hip surgery long before the technology could promise much success, only a good deal of pain. He strongly intimated they'd be hopping around like new until their dying day or else, if they spurned his advice, be faced with the gravest of consequences. The small fortune he amassed, though, was not enough.

Attempting to increase his wealth by investing, he failed miserably. He wanted a place with his own table so people could notice and envy him, but the three restaurants he'd bankrolled each failed within a year.

He invested in the stock market on tips—not research—and lost even more money. Still, people continued to pile into his operating room, and this bankrolled his lifestyle. And he was lucky. At his lowest point his mother died, and he inherited millions that bailed him out, though not for long.

His father, a bear of a man who'd commanded services—if not the loyalty or affection—of thousands of working men, despised his only child all along. "Knees! Elbows! Shoulders! How fucking stupid is that?" he yelled when deep in his senility. "Is this what I paid for?"

Dr. Ford was dressed in his black cashmere topcoat, leaning against a shiny black BMW like a teenager on a Friday night date, his hair dyed too dark, cut too perfectly. He looked conspicuous amongst the everyday people passing by the run-down backdrop of an auto store, a laundry and a mini-mart. A short old lady in a washed-out flower-print housedress, a black babushka draped over her head, walked by rolling her eyes.

Then he looked up and saw Charlie standing in front of the funeral home, staring across the street at him. He gestured for Charlie to stay put and crossed the street.

"How are you doing, Charlie?" he asked, his hands still in his pockets.

Charlie stared at him. "What are you doing here, Doctor Ford?"

This caught Ford off-guard. His eyes narrowed. "I was sorry to hear about your father."

"Thanks," Charlie said.

"And I heard you ran into Stephen."

"No. He ran into me. I wasn't looking for him."

"I understand," he said. "Charlie, you look upset. Did you have something you wanted to say to me?"

Charlie's anger welled up, but he held his temper. "No, Dr. Ford," he said. "But if I did, I'd be right."

"Well, I'm standing right here," Dr. Ford said. His cocky nature made Charlie sick, but just then the door to the funeral parlor opened and Mr. Riley slipped through and waved. Charlie returned the greeting and held up the envelope. The old man smiled and waved again and began his walk home.

With newfound patience, Charlie turned back to Dr. Ford. "Is there a reason you came here? It couldn't be for my father."

"I see. All right, then." He glanced over at his car. "I am here," he said, sticking out his chin, "to see if you're going to play that match."

"I don't know. My father just died."

"Yes, yes, son," he said. "These things happen. What can you do?"

Charlie smiled. "Do you have a bet down, or are you waiting to hear the odds?"

"I have something down."

"But that isn't your biggest concern."

"It concerns me. It's not a little bit of money." Again he looked at his car. "But no, you're right." He weighed his words carefully. "Stephen is home for now, until Pebble."

"He gets invited every year, doesn't he?" Charlie said.

"Well, he didn't earn it, that's for sure," Dr. Ford said. "Thank God it's an invitational."

"And he knows all those guys," Charlie said.

"Yes."

"He's got his card, though," Charlie said. "Still gets to play, still has the life."

The day was wearing on. The sun was drawing close to the hillsides, and the streetlights snapped on. A bus rolled by packed with people going home. Some read, others dozed with their necks uncomfortably contorted, while others still gazed out the windows, looking forward to dinner and a good sleep after a long, hard day.

"Yes. I suppose he does," Ford said. "But for how much longer?"

"How much longer what?" Charlie asked.

"How much longer will he play?"

"If he'd practice a little, for a long time. Senior tour and everything."

"Well, there's not much chance of that."

Charlie grew impatient. "Right. How much money, golf, travel, sunshine and partying can one man take?"

"It's not all that great, Charlie."

"It's more than he deserves and way more than some people got, thanks to you."

"Don't blame me!" Ford shot back. "Your father—"

Charlie took a step closer. "I wouldn't say anything about my father if I were you," he hissed, then gathered himself. "Stephen was always lazy, and he still is. There are guys out there with nothing, beating their brains out with half his ability, no money, who'd give anything to be in his place."

"He's spoiled."

"He has exactly what he started with. Talent and you."

Ford shrugged. "Yes, he has me."

"And you don't want him," Charlie said. "I see."

"I don't think you do."

"Then what? Just say it, for Christ's sake."

"Lang's his sponsor. And Lang made this match, this bet, because of Stephen's word. That idiot never learned to keep his mouth shut."

"He's had no consequences," Charlie said. "You always made sure of that."

"Enough moral lessons. If you lose, Stephen will lose his sponsorship and Lang will see to it that he doesn't get another one."

"Why don't you sponsor him?" Charlie asked, and when the blood ran out of the doctor's face he tried to imagine how someone could've gone through so much money. Looking into his troubled eyes, Charlie recalled conversations between Lang, Grant Evans, and Shaw that suggested that Lang himself had risked and lost a fortune before gaining an even larger one, and that the extremely wealthy had done just that more than once. They were the richest, the most powerful people in the world not because of the money, but because they had the key: the knowledge and the talent to get even more. Whereas Ford was inept, incapable of protecting or regaining a fortune he hadn't earned to begin with.

"A lot of people lost money in the damn market lately," he said.

"I have an idea where it is," Charlie mumbled.

"Huh?"

"Never mind. Does Stephen know?"

"No."

"Well then, he better start practicing."

"He's not that good."

"How nice of you to say," Charlie said. "Couldn't you get him a job at Oakmont or one of the other clubs around here?"

"No, I can't," Ford answered, and Charlie was struck by how different he looked from the imposing, arrogant man he remembered seeing at Oakmont back when he and Stephen were just kids.

"Stephen had the misfortune of seeing what he was up against a long time ago," Ford said. "You. So he quit. He still plays, but he did quit. People do that, you know. When they see how easy it is for some, they give up. If they can't ever be that good, why try?"

"It wasn't easy for me," Charlie said. "I worked hard. I missed a lot. I can't even remember being a kid."

"Your father worked you."

"Yes, he did. But he was a worker himself. He left me that."

"I gave that boy too much," Ford confessed. "I guess I just wanted to hear from you that you'll win."

"I don't even know if I'm going to play."

"The arm?" Ford pointed at Charlie's right arm.

"That's fine," Charlie said, "no thanks to you."

"I did what I could, son, believe me."

"I don't, but that doesn't matter, not now."

"Then why wouldn't you play?" Ford asked. "It's everything every one of us wants. Why in God's name would you not play?"

"It's complicated. I'm not sure I want it. Or everything that goes with it."

"Why the hell not?"

"I've seen some other things that are a little less complicated."

"I can't imagine what those would be."

"I'm not surprised," Charlie said.

"To walk into any club, to be known as a player. The world at your feet."

"It's not like that. Not for me."

"You know you're not getting any younger," Ford said. "What else are you going to do? You have no education. No skills other than golf."

"Save your breath," Charlie said. "You did your best to hurt me a long time ago."

"I did not do that on purpose," Ford shouted. "And I will *not* be talked to in this manner by the punk kid of some ex–mill hunk! I did *everything* for my son just as your father did for you. I wanted him to be the best and, God damn it, you took that away from him." He looked once again to his car, raised his arm and snapped a wave. "Well, maybe this will get you to play." The passenger-side door opened, and Stephen trotted across the busy street.

"Tell him," Ford said to him, and like a soldier Stephen stepped forward. "I'll be in the car."

"Hello, Stephen," Charlie said, and the two shook hands. "I'm sorry I ran out on you that day. Thanks for the note." He gestured toward the funeral home. "I don't think they ever could've found me."

"Look, Charlie," Stephen said, "I could get in a lot of trouble. I guess they found out who sent that wire. Lang called me here at the club. He knew you were here and asked me, told me, to check up on you."

"This guy's something else."

"He's in deep, Charlie. So am I."

"What do you mean?"

"This thing got out of hand," he said. "Between the Czar and Lang, it just got out of hand."

"But that's not the worst of it."

"It's bad enough, but Lang's my sponsor, Charlie. He pays my way. I'm too old to get new ones, and he treats me well. But he started this whole thing back up because I told him about you." Stephen paced back and forth on the sidewalk. "I never thought anyone would try to clip Siegal again."

"This guy, they call him the Czar, what about him?"

"Ben Miller's dangerous, Charlie, a bad man."

"Says who?"

"Everybody," Stephen said. "He owns Larry Siegal, Charlie—without his say-so Siegal can't do anything. He hardly leaves L.A."

"Look, Stephen, what do you want me to do?"

"The match has been set."

"When?" Charlie asked.

"Tuesday after next. You get to see the course one day and then play the next."

Unruffled, Charlie said, "So I'll go there. That makes it a little tougher. And what if I don't?"

"Don't make me tell you, Charlie. It's shit. It's really shit."

"Lang can't do a thing to me," Charlie said. "He's not above the law."

"Think about who he is above, Charlie."

"He'd do that?"

"Every one of them. Moorer, Deacon, Spider, they don't have any rights. They never did."

"Do they know this?"

"I don't see how they could."

"So they'd never know," Charlie said.

"They'd put it together, but there's nothing they could do. One by one, they'd each get fired for no reason or just ride the bench until they left on their own."

"After all those years, a guy won't even get an explanation."

"They're caddies, Charlie. They all know it could end at any time. That's the trade-off for coming and going as you please. They don't want to look any further than the next few hours."

"I know," Charlie said.

Stephen glanced at the car. "But why do you want to caddy, Charlie? You have all this talent, and now you're well. Why not play?"

"You already said it," Charlie answered. "Caddying's simple. Carry two bags, get paid, go home and lie down with someone. Get up if you want to. Go when you feel like it. Don't worry about anything but today. I don't have to think about tomorrow."

"Or yesterday," Stephen said.

Charlie sucked in all the air he could and blew it out. "It's hard to trust. I feel numb except—"

"Except when you have that stick in your hands," Stephen said. "I know."

Charlie nodded. "Or that bag on my back." Then Sarah crossed his mind. "There are other things too, Stephen."

"These people don't care about that stuff, Charlie. Not when it comes down to money. Oh, they might help out from time to time or lend them money or even throw them some, but don't ever think they care much beyond that."

"I don't know if I can," Charlie said. "The divorce, Stephen, it took a lot out of me."

"And now this," Stephen said, nodding toward the funeral home.

"I knew this was coming," Charlie sighed. "I had time to work on it, years to get ready. I guess I did."

Stephen paused, and Charlie remembered why he'd liked him back when they were young. "Maybe, in time, Charlie, you'll feel the same way about your wife."

In the few hours he'd been home, she had yet to cross his mind. Indeed, even as the taxi crossed the bridge and downtown came into view, all he could think about was his father and the task at hand, and then he'd stood over him, remembering their times together. "Maybe," Charlie said, and smiled. "Did you ever see my dad play?"

"No," Stephen said.

"He was long. Man, he was straight." Charlie sliced the air with a rigid hand. "Could putt his ass off."

"But you're better," Stephen said.

Charlie summoned all his courage. "Maybe," he said. "I just need a little more time."

24

The day was cold and crisp, with winter coming on. Charlie stood over a small square hole cut in the ground as a preacher he didn't know whispered the last words over his father's remains. Next to his mother's grave, the small box looked absurd. Did his father somehow intuit that his wife of forty-eight years had died and, upon realizing this, lay himself down too? Charlie had heard of such things, and having missed Helen so badly he could believe it. His parents had never divorced.

Not quite a year ago, Charlie, bouquet of roses in hand, stood dressed in his best suit and overcoat before his mother's grave. Maureen had many friends, husbands and wives from work wrapped in each other's arms around her grave, their heads bowed reverently, as Charlie cursed his misplaced thoughts. As leaves drifted across the vast lawn and fell into the hole where his mother lay, he could think only of Helen. His neck tingled wildly and lights blinked in his eyes. He felt the wet grass on his knee, then a stranger's hand on his shoulder.

"She promised," he hissed. "She was supposed to be here."

Long after the ceremony was over, while two young, strong men started shoveling in the remaining dirt, Charlie stood over the casket, determined to give his mother one solitary thought. The foreman, a wrinkled and weatherbeaten man, leaned on an old red pickup truck, smoking. "Son?" he said.

Charlie pulled a shovel from the mound of dirt, drove it deep into the pile, threw the dirt into the hole and heard it land on the metal casket with a hollow thud. He removed his coat and handed it to the old man. With the second shovelful, his nerves began to settle; dirt was dirt and metal was metal. A short time later, drenched in sweat, he slid his arms inside his overcoat.

Charlie now hovered above a small square cut into the dark earth. The same red pickup arrived and the same old man climbed out and trudged up to the grave with a shovel over his shoulder. "You been here too often, too soon, son," he said.

Charlie extended his hand, and the man handed him the shovel. One scoop of soft dirt, then two, three, and four, with a quick pat to finish the job, then he walked a few blocks to his home, opened up the front door and fell asleep in his living-room chair. He woke sometime in the night, cried like an abandoned child and, when the sun came up, fell into a deeper sleep.

Mid-morning he woke up under a tattered old afghan his mother had made. Sometime in the night he must've pulled it over himself. The sun shone through the front window and felt warm on Charlie's feet, and he was as comfortable as he could be.

How easy it would be to get his old job back. Life was simple here. He had friends, though they were Helen's friends too. Still, this was home, wasn't it? Or maybe he could caddy somewhere else, where nobody would know him. But could he, for the rest of his life, not play, even for five-dollar Nassaus on Mondays? Who wants to play with somebody they can never beat? Inevitably questions would be raised and he'd have to move on, at least until he no longer could play, when perhaps he would find some peace.

And he missed Sarah. He wanted to know how and what she was doing. He'd left so soon, and there was so much he wanted to tell her.

His past was all around him—his house, possessions, pictures on the walls, furniture—even the din of traffic drumming in his ear—but he now realized he liked and missed *this* place, not the one he'd shared for so many years with Helen. While he was gone, he'd missed this room and these things.

And I have them, he thought, and a smile lit his face. Again he thought of Sarah. He wanted to be honest with her. She hadn't asked for promises. He'd known her for such a short time, but Jack was right. It takes only a second to know. But would he always hold something back? And how much did he have left? His best years had been taken and Sarah, though it was all she knew, was getting what was left over. This made him feel old, even as they were in the first rush of love. His marriage had always been like that, the romance, the newness, the playfulness never subsiding. He and Helen had been like children, spending every cent they made, never saving a thing, both of them physical and passionate. The last morning they spent together they made love. And then it was over; gone in the manner it had existed, suddenly, impatiently.

25

Charlie awoke the next morning and climbed the attic stairs. In the corner, lying there as if wounded, was what he was looking for: in a white cloth bag with the faded red logo of his high school inscribed on the side, his old sticks.

He took to the road late that afternoon.

The Boulevard of the Allies starts just above Monongahela River, four wide lanes running between the Press building and the Pittsburgh Plate and Glass towers, which catch and reflect the sunlight as if through a prism. In a few blocks the avenue turns uphill dramatically, passing the county prison on the right and a university on its left and east, so from their cells the prisoners can see pretty girls walking to class.

As Charlie ascended, the hillside across the river began to reveal itself. In a few moments he would spot a small white house, secluded in the rich green hillside, and once again imagine Helen alone, curled up on their couch reading, their yellow tabby in the crook of her arm, her long blond hair falling serenely over her shoulders. For a year, seven days a week, he'd drive by late at night hoping that he was still in her thoughts, pleading that by some miracle she would feel his presence, change her mind and rescue him from this nightmare. Sometimes he would pull over and stare out across the river valley, praying to a god he'd long ago lost faith in, and when no answer came he would curse and leave.

As the road rose higher above the river, he wondered if all that was a dream because those days, once so startling and vivid, now seemed surreal and gray, only the road new and exciting. The traffic was light, and he slowed down to glance at the little white house on the opposite hillside. The rivers were a muddy gray, the water still and stagnant, empty and lifeless.

He grew anxious, imagining mountains and deserts, great forests, faraway places in every direction and how much he'd yet to see. Ahead, a road sign announced 376 EAST, an interstate that would lead to Philadelphia and from there who knew where. The East Coast is a tangle of roads. Anyone lacking in purpose could head for New York and easily end up in Connecticut or Long Island or Rhode Island.

But a few miles past 376 East was another exit. Charlie pulled off the boulevard, navigating the roads as though he'd never left, rolled down a steep hill and drove alongside the water. Once the river was behind him and gone, he turned through the hills and was fast approaching Route 70. From there he felt he could go anywhere. On the ramp, the smallest amount of faith turned him west, where the road's much straighter, the exits are miles apart, and there's plenty of time for a not-so-young man to awake from a dream.

26

Charlie drove for three days and much of the nights too—across the plains, through Texas and New Mexico, over mountains and a desert and finally to Interstate 10. The last time he looked at a map he was somewhere near Albuquerque. Twenty miles from Los Angeles traffic thickened, but the speeds increased; when a tractor-trailer roared by he realized he was driving much too slowly. So he turned down the radio, inclined his seat and put both hands on the wheel, welcoming the change of pace. To the north, the city rose like a vision in the desert, sprawling, low and blunt for miles in every direction, the hazy sun dulling the edges of cleanly cut skyscrapers, glass and brick towers fading into the hills behind them. Charlie squinted as a thousand windows reflected bright light across the smoggy miles, the small wooden houses lining the highway stretching as one to the undefined horizon. Everything looked flimsy, the whole landscape hard to believe.

The interstate narrowed and then ran along the ocean, cool air suddenly rushing through the car. The sun was warm, the sea smells thick and briny, and a surge of energy passed through Charlie as he sped north on the two-lane highway. A single-story, cedar-covered motel sat snuggled in the sand, its red electric sign reading BREAK-FAST, and Charlie thought it might be a good place to stay. Judging from his map, the golf course was minutes away. So he pulled in.

The tiny restaurant was practically empty, the only patron a sunburned young man with shaggy blond hair to his shoulders, still half asleep but gobbling his breakfast. Old planks creaked beneath Charlie's feet as he entered. A dark wooden bar ran the length of the room, and beyond it a porch hung out over the sand with a short staircase leading down to the beach. The fresh aroma of coffee and bacon masked the scent of last night's alcohol. A pretty girl, thin and pale, escorted him to a corner table and shoved open the large, peeling windows to let in the light and the breeze.

"Coffee?"

"Please." The waves crashed, muffling the din of traffic like the sound of light applause, and a soothing quiet enveloped him. Surfers bobbed in an erratic line looking for a ride as couples walked lazily up and down the shore. These homes had none of the grandeur of houses back East. There was no foundation, nothing to dig into, with only sand beneath them. What would hold in place when the storm hit? When that time came these people would have to run.

Framed on the opposite wall was an old map of the area before the millions had arrived. With a pointed finger he followed a long street winding east and then south until it dead-ended in a plot of land about half the size of Charlie's palm. He recognized the name written in tiny script.

Twenty-five hundred miles and twenty-five years later, Charlie found what he was looking for. Then he looked around and headed for the payphone at the end of the bar.

The phone rang forever. Finally, somebody picked it up but said nothing.

"Hello," Charlie said.

"Huh?"

"Give me the fuckin' phone," Jack screamed in the background.

"Thanks, Spider," Charlie said.

"No problem."

The phone bumped against the wall, then Jack spoke. "Where are you?"

"Malibu," Charlie answered.

"Thank God," Jack said.

"The match is Tuesday?"

"Yeah," Jack said, and for the first time Charlie heard a strain in his voice.

"Are you okay?" Charlie asked.

"Yeah. I'll meet you there Monday. Lang says we can play all day."

"William coming?" Charlie asked.

"Moorer?" Jack said. "Fuck, no! He don't know that course like I do. I'm your caddy."

Charlie smiled. "Fine, but I still want him here. And Sam too."

"Wait a minute. What's up?"

"Nothing. I'd just feel better if they were here. I mean, Siegal's going to have people, right?"

"A few," Jack said.

"Well then," Charlie said.

"I'll ask Lang."

"If you have any problems, tell him to talk to me."

"I'll work it out," Jack said. "Just moral support, eh?"

"Yeah. Don't get so paranoid."

"It's my best quality."

"See you Monday."

"What are you gonna do till then?"

"Take a swim and sleep the rest of the day. Caddy tomorrow."

"You're gonna work?"

"See you Monday." Charlie hung up, waited for the dial tone, then made another call.

27

The gate was eight feet tall and made of iron, guarded on two sides by large men, one black and the other Latino, who couldn't seem to care less who entered. Before Charlie could even roll down his window, the gate opened and he drove through.

The morning air was cool, a light fog clearing as the sun rose. Charlie coasted past the Mercedes and the BMWs and Porsches, row after row of shining sedans and coupes. In the corner of the lot, an old black man with a clean white towel over a shoulder walked slowly toward the course. Charlie tossed his own towel around his neck and followed. A cement walkway emptied onto a large patio lined with dozens of green-and-white electric golf carts.

"Christ," Charlie muttered as he passed by them.

A sprawling, glaring-white building housed the clubhouse, pro shop and restaurant. A young Latino boy heaved golf bags through a giant glassless window onto a wide stainless-steel sill, and a tall, stoop-shouldered, gray-haired man carried them to two long metal racks situated between the tenth and first tees. Players crowded a large practice green as Charlie strolled up to the starter's window.

"Where's the caddy master?" he asked.

A large square-headed man leaned forward and in a grating nasal voice said, "We don't have one. You a caddy?"

Charlie jiggled his towel.

"Sure, why not?" The man tossed a clipboard through the small opening. "Print your name there and then take a seat." With his thumb he pointed in the direction Charlie had come from.

The shack was a large, brightly lit room attached to the side of the building. The sun burned through the glass walls, leaving the room airless and stifling. The place was spotless, the black linoleum floor buffed to a shine, not a scrap of litter in sight. Shining new vending machines lining the walls filled the room with a steady, droning hum.

A crowd of Latino men waited both inside and out, outfitted in white jumpsuits with green plastic nametags clipped to their chests. They all wore identical green caps bearing the name of the club on the front. On the back of each uniform, CADDY was stamped in bold green letters, just in case, Charlie thought, some idiot got confused.

They sat around white Formica tables, eating breakfast and drinking coffee and watching the morning news on a television perched high in one corner. At one table, three white men quietly played gin. A tall, skinny Asian kid, dreadfully out of place, sat by himself outside on the bench smoking and craning his neck to see what was going on between the tees. The lone black caddy moved through a doorway in the rear of the room, and again Charlie followed him.

This interim room was filled with neat rows of lockers, each with a man's name printed on the door. The bathroom had three stalls, a white tile floor, pristine white walls and three basins with soap and sunscreen dispensers and paper towels mounted above them. Even the garbage cans looked clean.

Finally a loudspeaker clicked on, feedback screeched and the nasal voice called names one by one or two by two, and the men dashed like they were sprinting to first base trying to beat out a ground ball. One was a bit slower, and quickly got told about it.

"Is José there?" the voice blared. "You're on one, José! The tee's in the ground!"

Players milled on the practice green, and caddies ate and mumbled amongst themselves, their eyes fixed on the railing of bags. As more of them were called up, Charlie estimated his chances of working were good. Suddenly the loudspeaker blared, "New guy! Get up here! I need a single!"

Charlie headed around the corner and was within sight of the starter's booth when the voice shrieked again. "The new guy, Charlie! Did he leave?" On the practice green, a few heads bobbed up and down like cows in a pasture, one old man adjusted his hearing aid, but no one objected to the braying. Charlie walked up and stuck his face in the window.

"I don't know where you're from," the starter said, "but I hope you move faster out there."

"Why? They're playing golf, aren't they?"

"What?"

"Nothing," Charlie said.

"Take that bag right there and go to one. And if you want to caddy here you got one week to get a uniform and hat."

"Okay," Charlie said.

"Here." The man tossed a plastic nametag—CHARLES— through the window.

"Thanks," Charlie said politely, picked up the tag, turned and slipped it into his pocket.

A small dark-blue bag stood by itself on the first tee and looked as if it should. Old and worn, it had no identifying tags or brand names, just the name of the club sewn on the side. The whole set was immaculate and in order, the irons old but refinished and regrooved. The metal woods were new.

Pretending to clean the clubs, Charlie pulled one out and heard a sharp rap on the window, the starter waving him around to the opening.

"Now don't say a word to this guy."

"Why would I?" Charlie said.

"Huh? Well, some guys talk too much . . ."

"They should know better."

"Just find the ball and lean the bag. It'll be in the middle all day. He doesn't need anything."

"Doesn't he have a steady guy?"

"If he did, you wouldn't be caddying for him, would you? He hates everybody. He'll hate you too, by the second hole."

Number one was a dogleg left—short and tight, lined by pines and eucalyptus on both sides. Two men pulled up in a cart and sat waiting for the third. Charlie sized up the hole, estimating the landing area to be no wider than thirty yards. He'd hit an iron to the corner and a wedge to the green.

But when his player pulled a driver he thought again. Big and fat, he had pasty skin, thin lips, a thick, wide nose, and a sour look hanging on his face. He wore no hat, his long hair sticking out in every direction. But he had a swagger in his step and even though he was overweight by eighty pounds, Charlie guessed he'd once been quick, maybe still was, his plaid Bermuda shorts revealing thickly muscled legs. His move to the ball was athletic, graceful and powerful, his considerable skill unmistakable. Startled, Charlie snuck a quick glance at him, then remembering his duty, quickly spotted the ball as it flew the corner, caught a down-slope, and kicked left toward the green.

"Shot, Larry," one of the men said, and Charlie's suspicion was confirmed. The swing was too good, his nature true to what little he'd heard of him. It was Larry Siegal and Charlie couldn't believe his luck.

Siegal pulled a sand wedge from his bag, lit a cigarette, and offered Charlie the pack. Charlie shook his head and his player seemed to appreciate the silence.

The two men he was playing with rode a cart and kept their

distance. Neither even looked at Charlie. After they played their approaches, Siegal hit his wedge from seventy-five yards to within two feet of the hole, and one of them walked onto the green and batted it away. "Nice birdie, Sieg," he said.

"You're both down one," Siegal replied.

Charlie picked up the ball, cleaned it, and now daring a closer look, tossed it to his man.

"Thank you," Siegal said coldly, then took his driver again, lit another cigarette and walked back to the next tee.

The hole came back so Charlie stayed where he was, standing in the wet rough, bag on his shoulder, anxious and ready. Siegal's tee shot sailed down the fairway, Charlie marched after it, and even though the match didn't start until Tuesday, the game was on.

28

Charlie did as the starter told him. He said nothing and leaned the bag, took each club back only when it was handed to him and walked a comfortable distance ahead of his player, always waiting for him at the ball with the yardage computed and the wind gauged. He was now, for the first time in twenty-five years, firmly in his element, everything making perfect sense. And he and Siegal were strangers, but also strangely hand-in-glove.

As early as the first hole he started figuring what clubs he'd hit and how he would attack this course. He casually stepped off yardages to where his own tee shots might land, and then the approach shots, discreetly estimating the width of fairways and walking off the depth and width of each green. He carried an extra scorecard on which, when alone, he quickly scribbled notes. While the three players relied on the yardage markers, Charlie looked around for natural markers— trees, traps, hills—that would help him keep a sense of where he was on the course. He'd play as he always did, by feel. He registered that in certain areas the rough was more a weed than a grass, thick and gnarled, laid over in tangles, its roots tenacious enough to choke out the lighter growth.

"Fucking kikuyu," one of the cart guys whined as his ball flew weakly back into the fairway. "Why's this shit so high?"

"That's why they call it 'rough,'" Siegal whispered just loud enough for Charlie to hear. Through nine holes he'd played every shot from the fairway.

The back nine was much harder, tighter and longer. It ran around the edges of the course, with out-of-bounds always on the right. Here Charlie noticed something peculiar about the greens. On the front nine they received an approach shot nicely, all sloping back-to-front. On the back they were canted in different directions and were all much smaller. On the tenth, Siegal's putt grabbed his attention. From about fifteen feet, it looked uphill and straight, but the ball rolled much faster than he would've guessed and broke sharply at the hole, falling in on the high side. Charlie looked up to see Siegal smiling at him, just as pleased with himself as one could be. "Local knowledge!" he said, and laughed as he snatched the ball from the hole. After Charlie replaced the flag, he looked again, but the putt still looked dead straight with no break at all.

The same was true on number eleven. A putt that looked left-to-right, surely breaking down the hill, if anything moved a little the other way, and Charlie quickly scanned the green for other such spots.

Here's where the pin will be on Tuesday, he thought, then thought again, quickly running through the entire front nine trying to recall all the pin placements. He looked back at number ten and then this pin. No, he figured, this is exactly how it will play.

Indeed, the whole course was set up as it would be for the match. Tomorrow, when Charlie played his practice round, the pins would be accessible, on easy parts of the green, then changed overnight. He smiled at the gamesmanship, and would expect no less from Lang if the match were being played in San Francisco. As Siegal pulled another birdie out of the hole, Charlie tried to hold back a smile.

"Do you play?" Siegal asked.

"A little."

"Well, caddies here play on Mondays," he said. "You should take advantage of it. It's a fairly nice course."

"I think I will," Charlie said.

"See you in the fairway," Siegal replied, lit another cigarette and sniffed as the sun rose to warm the mid-morning.

A mild east wind had been dominating, but on the fourteenth hole it picked up and now came out of the west, off the ocean, and Charlie set the bag down in the fairway and calculated that from here he'd hit an eight-iron into the green.

Siegal pulled out a seven-iron and then, feeling the wind in his face, switched to a six. Trees lined the left rough that sloped away into a thick forest of pines. The hole narrowed to the width of the tiny green, out-of-bounds looming closely on the right. The pin was placed in the front of a green that sloped severely back-to-front, with a steep-faced bunker guarding the left side. A high draw was the shot, Charlie knew. Throw it up in the wind and bring it down soft.

Siegal's six-iron ballooned in the stiff breeze, landed in the middle of the green and stayed twenty feet above the hole. "Shit," he spat, slamming his iron back into the bag and jerking out the putter.

After lagging the ball down the steep slope he tapped in for par. Larry Siegal had played it safe.

Midway through the back, he seemed to lose interest, bogeying fifteen with a sloppy approach shot and a careless three-putt, and after a poor drive on sixteen, he stomped off the tee like a spoiled child. It was a par five though, and he nearly birdied it anyway but the putt lipped out.

"Good putt," one of the others said. "Good putts go in," Siegal said, batting his ball off the green.

He hit a mid-iron on the par-three seventeenth green, the pin tucked left behind a small, steep bunker. He anticipated the ball spinning back, but it stayed above the hole. "Fuck," he spat.

He wasted little time on the steep downhill putt and muttered, "Sit down, you bitch," as it slid by the hole. But he rammed a six-footer coming back like it was a foot away and saved his par, then grabbed his driver from the bag, tore the head-cover off and threw it at Charlie's feet. "I'll meet you way the fuck down there," he said.

Eighteen was a huge par five, five hundred and eighty-five yards. For the first two hundred and sixty the fairway was wide, though in the next thirty yards the landing area narrowed and then emptied into a wide, deep barranca spanned by a small bridge. Towering trees blocked out the sun on the left side, which the fairway sloped toward, but on the right side a huge mound would push any ball short of it even farther right, leaving the player with a blind second shot. Beyond the mound and the ditch, the fairway widened again.

Siegal's ball rifled off the face of his driver, but even with the new technology it rolled weakly up to the barranca and trickled in. Charlie heard him yell out his dissatisfaction from the tee, then watched the other two come up short but in the fairway. He started to move when he heard another hit, then turned to see Siegal's second ball come to rest just short of the ditch. He came waltzing off the tee, his mood suddenly bright, holding a cigarette European-style in his left hand and twirling the driver in his right like the leader of a marching band. Charlie rested the bag by the ball and gazed over the barranca at the fairway that narrowed to a tiny green guarded by mounds and sand, the pin tucked lethally in the front, no more than five or six paces beyond the steep edges of a small, murky pond.

·   ·   ·

Larry Siegal paid Charlie more for one bag than he'd ever gotten for two. "Nice job," he said. "You oughta teach these other morons how to caddy."

Once off the course he seemed to lack purpose, awkward again, tipping from side to side as he walked, like a cork in rough water. Scores of people walked up wanting to greet him; he spoke to none of them. But outside the clubhouse, he stopped to chat with a man who was a head taller and broad, walking with a cane. Round, dark sunglasses covered his eyes. His bald brown head gleamed in the sunlight, bobbing up and down in agreement, his face wrinkled and specked from years in the California sun. White slacks were pulled up over his pot belly like any other old man, and a white linen shirt hung loosely past his waist. A cigar as long as his large hand was clinched tightly between his teeth. The Czar ended his short meeting with Siegal by kindly patting his player's rear end.

His feet a bit sore and his back tight, Charlie indulged himself with a hot bath and lay there thinking of Siegal. His eyes suddenly opened wide.

"Play the course, Charlie," he heard his father say, "not the man. Play the course, one shot at a time. See it. Imagine it. Then do it. Beat the course and you'll beat the man."

So as the hot water soothed his body, Charlie pictured himself standing on the first tee, set up perfectly and drawing back his one-iron.

Later that night he headed down to the restaurant. "This way," the hostess said brightly, and when he got to the corner table, Sarah was sitting there. "Have a great dinner," the hostess said, then smiled and walked away.

"So you got my message?" Charlie said. He leaned over, kissed Sarah, inhaled her smell, and sighed.

She sighed in return. "I got a few days off."

"Why didn't you come to the room?"

"You left in such a hurry."

"I know," Charlie said. "I'm sorry. I had all these things I wanted to tell him."

"And you got to say them."

Charlie shook his head. "When I saw how small he was, how old, how long it's been, none of that mattered. It was so plain, right there in front of me. He was laid out on this table, no coffin, no makeup. He laid himself down and was done. And so was I."

"You look different, Charlie."

"Really? How?"

"I don't know. Just different."

"That's because we haven't seen each other."

"I don't think so," Sarah said. "You look confident."

"I think I'll play well."

"I hope so," Sarah said. "And then what?"

A look of surprise sprang to his face. "I really hadn't thought about it."

His singularity of mind only brightened her spirits. "Because I have things I want to do."

"Yes, I know you do."

"And you look like . . ." She feigned a smile. "You look like you're not sure of anything but the game."

"It takes most of what I have."

"To play."

"Yes."

"That's what you look like," she said.

"And you're wondering if there's room for anything else."

"I'm not wondering."

"Then why are you here?"

"Not everybody can be sensible. You know, always do what's good for them, now can they?"

"Lord knows I haven't."

She took his hands, and Charlie braced himself.

"All those years you were with Helen, you never thought about playing?"

"No. I was hurt, injured. Done. I don't even know when my arm completely healed."

"Did you see her, when you were home?"

He'd missed her directness and loved it. "Well, that's honest. But no."

"Did you think about it?" she said.

"I thought about you," Charlie said. "I wanted you."

"Good," she said, beaming at him.

She too had her eye on the ball, knew the task at hand and what was most important, for her, for Charlie, for the both of them.

"So," she said, "When you play, will you think about him?"

"I will. I can't help it. But I'll play my own game."

"You a player?" she growled.

This caught him off-guard and he laughed. "Christ, you sound like William Moorer." Her bright hazel eyes lit up. "Yes, I am," he said.

"You're ready, Charlie. I don't know a thing about golf, but you're ready."

They had a drink, and Charlie told her about the endless plains of Oklahoma and Texas and the preachers on AM radio. "I didn't have enough music," he said, shaking his head. He mentioned spotting a little nine-hole course just off the highway in New Mexico and playing with an old man he let beat him for a dollar. Grizzled and toothless, he laughed every time Charlie intentionally shanked a shot or pushed a putt, screeching, "You better practice up, boy!"

Charlie told her he'd slept in his car one night and how he'd awakened, freezing, at the rim of the Grand Canyon as the sun lit the eastern sky and set fire to the rock walls on the far side. And later that day it was a hundred and thirteen degrees when he stopped near the town of Needles and a biker dressed in black leather appeared out of the desert horizon, filled his helmet at the tap and took a drink, then dumped the water on his head and it ran down his back onto the scorching pavement, sending steam rising up all around him.

The ocean crashed while they talked, the sun flared on the horizon and they watched it go down together.

29

The place was quiet and lazy, empty but for one caddy sitting alone on the bench. Charlie trudged past the shack and two more caddies, an older Latino man and the same black caddy he'd followed in the day before, came out, dressed in khakis and polo shirts, ready to play. A young Latino boy was ready to play too, loading two bags onto a cart while the black caddy strapped his bag onto his own cart. When they finished, all three sat on the cold vinyl seats and waited.

The starter from the day before was again in the window, the white from a powdered doughnut circling his mouth and a newspaper spread out before him. With undisguised apathy he checked the clock on the wall behind him. It was two minutes to seven. Unsatisfied, he turned back to the counter and flipped the page of his paper.

Charlie dropped his old bag on the first tee. The starter methodically set his doughnut down, wiped his lips with the back of his hand and, still chewing, pulled the microphone toward himself with a burst of feedback. He scowled when he recognized that it was a caddy with one day on the job who was breaking the rules. He tapped the microphone to make sure it was good and loud. "Where do you think you're goin'?" he blurted.

Charlie sprang up to the opening and leaned his arm heavily onto the sill. "Hold on," he said, glancing over at the Latino man and his son, the boy's deep brown eyes fixed on him, seemingly fearing for Charlie's life. Charlie winked at him. "How you doing this morning?"

"Very well, sir."

"You guys need a fourth?" Charlie asked, and they all pointed at the booth. "I believe I'm a guest of Ben Miller's," Charlie told the starter, who went pale.

"Oh," he said, fumbling for the list before him.

"And Mr. Siegal too, I guess." Charlie pointed to the threesome. "I'll play with them if you don't mind."

The man grabbed the microphone.

"Please, don't," Charlie said, and turned to the threesome. "May I join you?"

"Fine," the black man said.

"I'll take a caddy." Charlie pointed to the older man on the bench. He wore an old Dodgers hat and his uniform was clean and white. White, oily sunscreen streaked his reddened nose and cheeks, the sun gleaming off him as he walked up.

"Clark," the caddy said.

"Charlie."

As they shook hands, Charlie noticed scars on the back of Clark's hand. The sun had also taken a few pieces from his right cheek and the bridge of his nose.

"You caddy here awhile?"

"Fall of sixty-eight."

"Where you from?" Charlie reached inside a box of tees mounted on the wall. "You got a ball?"

"Detroit. Here you go," he said, handing Charlie a used ball. "The Tigers won the World Series, so I left."

"Why's that?"

"Things goin' the way they were, I figured that's as good as it was gonna get."

"You played it right," Charlie said. "You want to pack for me today?"

"Sure," Clark said, and they moved toward the first tee. "Did you clear it with him?"

Charlie looked over to the window and pointed to Clark, and the starter nodded. "I think we're cleared," Charlie said.

"What an asshole," Clark whispered, then picked up Charlie's bag and began to clean the clubs. "Nice sticks," he said, pulling one out and gauging its weight. "I always liked Staffs. Couldn't hit 'em, but sure liked 'em. Grips need changing."

"I have another set coming," Charlie said. "I'll get them at the turn."

Clark wet his towel and rubbed the grip roughly as Charlie unzipped a pocket of his bag. Dust from his attic blew out, the familiar smell wafting past his nose. He dug deeper, found a quarter to mark his ball and slipped it into his pocket.

The father of the young boy extended his hand. "Arturo," he said, and they shook hands.

"Charlie."

"Do you wish to play the black tees?" he asked.

"If I could," Charlie answered, and the young boy's eyes lit up.

"Grady," the old black man said, still seated in his cart sipping coffee. He grunted and stood up, pulled the head cover from his driver and slowly walked to the tee. "Black tees. Sure, why not? I ain't been back there in a long time. Forgot what it looks like."

The boy stepped forward. "Adrian," he said, and shook Charlie's hand too.

"Charlie."

"What's the game?" Arturo asked, and the common language was struck. "Nassau?"

"Fives," Grady said.

"Fine," Charlie said. "Three ways?"

"Front, back, eighteen," Grady said.

"Automatic press," the boy said.

"What's your handicap?" Charlie asked. "I don't want to get hustled."

"He's a ten," Arturo said.

"What's yours?" the boy asked.

"I don't have one," Charlie said. "But I'll give you three a side. Let's hit it."

The boy played first and snapped a hook into the dogleg left. But he watched carefully to see where it rolled to, wiped off his driver and placed it back in his bag, then waited.

"Got it?" his father asked.

"Yes," he answered.

Grady sent his ball down the right side and picked his tee off the ground. "It'll play."

Arturo was athletic and strong, especially for a man his age. His balance was perfect and the ball soared down the middle, hit and took off rolling.

"Shot," Charlie said as he put a tee in the ground. He took hold of the club softly, his stance relaxed and natural. But the violence and pace of Charlie's swing took them all by surprise. The club met the ball and collectively they tried to follow the flight of it. When it came down on the other side of the trees, they all looked back to Charlie, stunned.

"You flew it over those trees," Clark said. "I've never seen anybody do that. Seen people turn the corner and run it up, but never over."

"With a driver," Grady said. "Not an iron."

The boy jumped out of the cart and pointed at Charlie. "You're him!" he said. "You're playing tomorrow!"

"Let's go," Charlie said.

"No bet!"

"Let's just play," Charlie said, smiling, as they walked off the tee.

Grady pulled up in his cart. "Don't you wanna go by yourself?"

"No," Charlie said. "I'd appreciate the company."

Clark shouldered the bag and quickly caught up. "Look, I . . ." he started.

"Don't worry," Charlie said. "I know. I'm the enemy. You don't have to say a word. Just hold the bag."

"Okay, I guess."

"I just want to get going. I have my own caddy coming later."

"Jack," Clark said, but the worry was still set on his face.

"Yeah. You know him?"

"I remember," Clark answered. "They're a rough bunch here."

"Yeah, so I hear."

Grady hit his approach shot.

"There isn't much you can do in this part of the city without them knowing about it. Not on a golf course."

Charlie smiled. "Look, don't worry. Just hold the bag. I won't ask you a thing."

"All right. Thank you," Clark said.

Adrian chipped out through the trees and into the fairway.

"Smart play!" Charlie said, and the boy waved back.

Arturo hit a beautiful low shot into the green and the ball checked up about ten feet from the cup.

From forty yards Charlie hit a low pitch that carried above the hole and spun back close.

Clark handed him the putter. "Nice shot. You're gonna do all right. People been here years and still can't figure that out. They try to roll it up there but you won't believe how the ball acts on the Poa."

As he waited to putt, Charlie circled the green, getting his bearings straight. Where was the wind? Where was the ocean? And as they all headed to the second tee, he looked back over the first hole, then high above, to a patch of blue sky framed between the tallest pines.

After nine holes, Charlie lingered on the practice green while the others went into the shack for a snack and a soft drink. He putted ball after ball, never two in a row from the same place, and closely watched how each rolled. His brow furrowed and his mouth contorted, he nervously bit his lip as he tried to figure out the strange turf. Occasionally he felt the wind pick up, looked up at the trees and noted the time. He made some five-footers and two out of three fifteen-footers, nodding his head as he walked quickly up to pluck the balls from the holes. Finally he looked up to see William Moorer and Sam Deacon waiting by the green.

"How you doin', kid?" William asked.

"D-d'you cut your hair?" Sam asked.

"No," Charlie said, beaming at the two of them. His hair was tousled and his right cheek streaked with mud. His old blue sweater had holes along the neckline and hung loosely over his square shoulders. His shirt collar stuck out on one side, and his right pant leg was dirty where he wiped off the ball.

"Looks like you're havin' fun," William said. "Your caddy got a towel?"

"Yeah," Charlie said.

"You look like you could use it."

"Th-that's one of the things a c-c-caddy does," Sam said.

"We win," William said, "I'm a buy you a new sweater."

"This is one helluva golf course," Charlie told them.

Sitting by the bag rack, Jack held up a hand. Charlie acknowledged him with a nod.

"How was your trip?" William asked him.

"Good," Charlie said, then shuddered, his smile diminishing. "Buried my dad."

"You seem different," Sam said.

"Do I?" Charlie glanced over at the tenth tee, where his group waited for him, and suddenly refocused. "Let's go. We got one day to learn this course. Jack!" he barked. "Give Clark the new sticks. Just ride along and let me know what you think."

The three teed off. Arturo walked, so Jack jumped on the cart with Adrian; the boy smiling ear to ear to be in such company.

"You know smoking is bad for you, sir?"

"No it's not," Jack said. "That's bullshit."

Grady and Arturo played their game as Charlie and Jack discussed shots and strategy.

"What'd you shoot on the front?" Jack sounded quite comfortable, but he was still taking in the place that had once been home.

"I don't know," Charlie said.

"Greens in regulation?"

"Nine," Charlie said.

"Kicked away three putts," Clark said, "they were so close."

"What'd you hit into number five?"

"I can't remember."

Clark spoke as if reporting the traffic. "Seven-iron, Jack," he said.

"How ya doin'?"

"All right," Clark answered, then pointed at Charlie. "Played the whole nine with his irons. One eight-five he had left to a par five and he hit a seven-iron. I can't imagine how far he'd hit a new driver."

Around the back nine they went. Sam and William looked on as Charlie hit shot after straight shot, occasionally dropping a second ball if he sensed he'd missed something, the wind suddenly shifted or he wanted to land the ball on a different part of the green. "You could never work here," he told William. "They don't have a caddy master and the starter's a jerk."

"Sign of the times, kid," William said, still marveling at the comfort with which Charlie was playing.

On thirteen Adrian missed an approach shot and Charlie trotted over to him, whispered something, adjusted his hands on the club, then whispered again and pointed to Sam. Those that knew him couldn't believe their eyes. Charlie was so loose, seemingly devoid of a single thought except for the boy, until he stood over his own shot. Then, the same as always, his concentration locked down again.

"You played *Hogan*?" Adrian blurted, staring at the old caddy.

Sam nodded his head, then Adrian held up his club to show him his grip. "That's it!" Sam said. He pointed at Charlie. "Someday you'll b-beat the pants off him."

"I'm an old Olympic Club caddy," Grady said to William. "Made my way down here 'bout thirty years ago . . ." Various conversations continued in and around the shots. Histories were put together, where their paths had crossed, the cities traveled to and courses played, down to the specific shots and where and when they hit them.

Grady suddenly exclaimed, "What's the prettiest hole in the world?"

"Easy," William answered. "Seventeen at Lincoln."

"No shit!" Grady said. "And a fuckin' public course at that!" Take Pebble, take Cypress, take 'em all! Get up on seventeen at Lincoln Park and that Golden Gate's loomin' over your shoulder like God! Two thirty downhill and wind blowin' like a bitch. Like those Scottish motherfuckers say, 'Nae wind, nae golf!' " The two men laughed and leaned shoulder to shoulder like they'd known each other their entire lives.

Charlie stood over his ball, and Grady quieted. "This boy's a motherfucker," he whispered.

"I ain't never seen nothin' like it," William said.

Charlie struck his ball and sent it left-to-right, dead on the pin. He dropped another and hit it right-to-left, landing it a few steps from the first. Then he hit one straight as could be ten feet above the hole, and it spun back not a foot from the other two. Shot after shot, hole after hole, the foursome played. William and Sam looked on and Jack sat in the cart and smoked. At each green he'd get out and putt one or two balls, as if to refresh his memory.

Meanwhile, Charlie seemed to gain energy as he played, buckling down just before each shot, striking nearly every one perfectly and putting from all sides to see how the ball rolled. The play was slow but no one minded. The golf course was theirs.

"Hey," Grady said, waving William over, and Arturo handed him a plastic cup.

William took a sniff and knocked back the drink. "Whew," he said shaking his head. "Needed that."

As each hole went by they, both players and observers, became more enthralled with Charlie. Sam threw balls into traps, giving him impossible lies. Charlie flopped them onto the green as if he were tossing them out underhand. The bunkers were deliberately inconsistent and he noted which were soft and which had hardly any sand.

After Charlie birdied the par-three seventeenth, William said, "No way that pin's gonna be there tomorrow."

"You're right," Charlie said, pointing his putter where it had been the day before. "It'll be there."

"That'll bring that bunker into p-play," Sam said.

"Tough little three par, my friend," Arturo said. "It can ambush you. And eighteen? I see many come here even and finish two or three over."

At this, Charlie's mood suddenly darkened and he walked slowly from the group. Seconds later, with everyone else behind him on the eighteenth tee, he pulled his persimmon driver and ripped three tee shots down the middle, two landing in the neck of the fairway, the third one-hopping into the barranca.

"Two ninety," Clark whispered as Charlie walked slowly off the tee, submerged in his thoughts. By the time he approached his drives his face was set in a scowl.

"What's he thinkin'?" William asked Deacon. "He's got to lay up. Wind's comin' right across the water and that green looks like a fuckin' shot glass out there. Ain't nowhere to land the ball."

"Three hundred to clear the water," Clark said.

Charlie walked over to Arturo and laid his hand on his driver. "May I?" he asked.

"Of course."

Charlie pulled it out, a new, high-tech model with a black graphite shaft and a composite-steel head. It was light and evenly balanced. He and Arturo were about the same height, and the loft and shaft, Charlie thought, were perfect. He studied the two shots. The ball on his right was the longest, but he looked at it and turned away.

"S-s-sitting down a little," Sam said to Adrian. "Lie's t-t-too tight, need a little grass under it."

The boy nodded his head.

The second ball was sitting up, so Charlie lined up his shot.

"Yeah," William whispered.

"Lookin' a little right," Clark said. "That's good. A high hook and let it ride the crosswind."

"Uh-huh," William grunted.

"I don't know," Grady said.

Charlie stood easily, attentively looking at the trees, trying to feel just when the wind might pick up and come down on his right shoulder where he needed it to be. His wait was just seconds. They all felt the wind shift from the west and collectively came to attention. Charlie spread his feet a bit farther apart than usual and, balancing his weight between them, dug his right toe deeper into the ground and took one look at his target. The club came back a little slower than usual, then down quicker than ever.

With an unbelievable sound, the ball rocketed skyward and Charlie took a step after it, his right foot crossing over. He'd hit it just as hard as he could and soon the wind would catch it. Arturo jumped out of his cart and came alongside Grady as the ball rose higher and disappeared into a bank of gray cloud and all eyes quickly focused on the tiny green. A split second later the ball landed on the front edge of the green, took the slant of it and

began to roll back, bumping the edge of the fringe, and then trickled down into the still water.

Charlie fished out his ball and tossed it on the green.

"That's wh-why you practice," Sam said.

They sat down in the grass like at a picnic and watched Charlie
roll ball after ball, over every inch of the surface. Now and then a
group of caddies played through, and eventually Arturo, Adrian
and Grady said their good-byes.

Charlie plopped down next to them above the green.

"Kinda h-hot down here," Sam said. "Drink p-plenty of water."

"How you feelin', kid?" William asked.

"Ready," Charlie said. "It'll come down to this, right here, and
I can't leave it to his putter. He's too good. Christ, these greens are
tricky."

"The grass," Sam said.

"Jack knows 'em," William said. "He was lookin' around pretty
good. He's got a good feel and great eyes."

A popping sound came from behind them and they turned to
see Jack standing on the first tee chugging a beer. "Let's go," he
said. "I gotta go over the front nine."

30

GONE EXPLORING was scribbled on a pad next to the phone, so Charlie shed his shoes, pulled a club from his bag and headed for the beach in the bright, hazy afternoon. Bouncing a ball on the clubface like a circus juggler, he wandered down a short set of steps and onto the sand.

The wind was dying and the surf flat, so he walked along the edge refreshing his tired feet and examining the scorecard, again going over what club he'd hit off each tee and to where in the fairway, imagining the shape of each shot. He saw the first hole differently now, having spotted a weakness, but guarded this secret like a thief would a bag full of money. Determined not to follow his opponent's lead, or to wait for something to happen, he meant to take every advantage and play the course his own way.

One by one he tried to recall the shapes of the curious greens and the coarseness of the grass, to understand it and make it his own. The slopes were strange and almost imperceptible, something to sense rather than see.

"You can feel it with your feet," his father used to say. "If you feel like you're leaning when you're standing over a putt, you've got to factor that in."

"Play it, don't ignore it," Charlie whispered, finishing his father's credo.

"Where would water run?" his father asked him. "That's where your ball will go."

Today the grass was so coarse in the late afternoon that the ball had hissed when he putted uphill and he wondered if anyone else had heard it. The greens hadn't been cut since maybe two days ago, making those putts hard to judge. But tomorrow they'll be quiet and fast as lightning, Charlie thought. And that was okay. It wasn't the speed he was worried about.

He had Jack. It was strange that he'd never once seen him with a bag on his shoulder, and Jack hadn't set foot here in years, but none of that bothered Charlie. He himself remembered every slope, curve, break and mound of any course he'd ever played and he trusted that Jack did too. He was now trying to fix this newest one in his mind.

"Put it there," his father said, pointing at his temple. "That's where it has to be first. Shot by shot, move by move. Then play."

Charlie took hold of the club as his father's voice echoed in his head.

"Work. Work! There's no magic here! No tricks! Just work. God doesn't live on a golf course. You'll 'feel' after you've hit five hundred balls a day for five years. You'll know by elimination, after you've already made every mistake a thousand times. You'll *know* what to do. You'll have worked it out in your head and reasoned it out through your body until you can *only* hit that shot! The shot you need, when you need it!"

Charlie stepped back into the dry sand, took a slow, graceful swing, then imagined the ball sailing through the air.

"That's a very nice swing you have," he heard.

Charlie turned and immediately recognized the man who'd met with Siegal after his round. He could see himself reflected, in miniature, in the oversized sunglasses, and he sniffed the aroma of his cigar.

"My grandfather used to smoke cigars, Mr. Miller," Charlie

said, then breathed in deeply. "Every time I smell one, I think of him."

"A pleasant memory, I hope," Ben Miller said, clearly a man of the old order, a soldier from wars past who saw the modern world as more and more complicated and unnerving.

"Yes," Charlie said and smiled. "It is." He glanced at the two large men standing at the foot of the steps he'd descended.

"Don't worry about them." Miller shrugged. "These things are necessary. What did your grandfather do?"

"He was a coal miner, then a steelworker."

"And your father?"

"Same thing."

"Workers," Miller said.

"Yes."

"I heard you can hit it a mile. And that's how you became so strong—following in their footsteps?"

"I'm pretty strong for my size," Charlie said.

"Hard work will do that. Make you strong or break you."

"I always liked it."

Ben Miller shook his head slowly and smiled. "I never did," he admitted, then laughed. "But I always respected the men. Took care of them. Paid them well." He rolled the cigar in his fingers. "Your father? He passed away recently?"

Charlie looked at the two bodyguards, then back. "Listen, Mr. Miller, if you want to try to get inside my head, go ahead. But I can tell you it won't work. Not for tomorrow."

"No," Ben Miller said, holding up his hand. "No, son. I just wanted to offer my sympathies. I haven't a need to be vicious. I understand you've had a rough time, that's all."

"A bit," Charlie said. "It's better now, but I won't make the mistake of saying it wasn't hard."

Miller's words came slowly, apologetically. "There was a time when I would've used such information to my advantage, believe me. To hurt people, coerce them . . . even break them. Who knows what we're willing to forgo to get what we think we want? No one makes as much money as I have honestly. They took it from someone. They hurt people or hid behind their knowledge. They knew the laws better and maybe knew other people better than they know themselves. Sensed their weaknesses and exploited them, bent the rules until they forced someone to change the rules. They break the law only after they estimate how much they'll make after the indictments and the fuckin' lawyers' fees. But never mind."

"You've had a change of heart?"

"I have," he said. "It's too late. But I have."

"Why'd you come down here?" Charlie asked.

"I wanted to meet you. Ask you about things."

"Me? What could I tell you?"

"I think you may know things I don't, because you're maybe the best at what you do. I like to meet such people. Besides, it was a nice afternoon, so I took a walk. And here you are."

"Here I am," Charlie said, knowing this encounter was no coincidence. There was a familiar desperation in Ben Miller's eyes, and Charlie wondered if anyone else alive had ever seen it.

Ben Miller poised himself and then spoke. "I know about your loss. Your losses."

Charlie began to ask how but dismissed it as frivolous. They were all bound together, closely now, right through to the end.

Miller's forehead was furrowed in thought. "Would you change anything?"

"I was going to ask you the same thing," Charlie said.

"Please, after you." A delicate smile crossed his face.

"It seems silly to even think about it, but no," Charlie said. "Listen more, maybe, but if you can't hear, if you're not ready—"

"Not a thing?" he asked, and Charlie shook his head. Miller had another pull on his cigar. "Wouldn't say anything more to the people now gone?"

"I said what I could then," Charlie said, "but it's taken me a while to realize that. I've played it over and over in my head, a thousand different scenarios. But the only one that matters was the one that played out. I can't live the others, not now, not on this earth."

"None of the things that happened to you? None of your friends?"

Charlie blinked back tears but spoke clearly. "I wish I could have some things back, sure. But not at the cost of what I know now."

They began to walk down the shoreline and Charlie, stealing a glimpse behind the dark glasses, sensed that Ben Miller, for all his money and power, was scared. He pitied him and somehow knew that for himself, the worst was over. The panic he saw in Miller's eyes was no longer in his own.

"Did I see Sam Deacon today?" Miller asked.

"He was at the golf course, yes."

"Helluva player," Miller said. "Maybe the best. It was a good thing Larry caught him on the way down."

"And on the way out."

A smirk slowly spread across Miller's face. "Too bad he pulled that damn putt."

"William said he misread it, that the putt broke."

"Do you know the putt?" Miller asked.

"Stood over it today."

"And does it break?" the Czar asked.

"Easy putt," Charlie said. "I'd play it straight."

"And what does that tell you, young man?"

"That there are more important things," Charlie said. "That when it's time to go, it's best to move on."

"And you'll know that time?"

"I can only hope," Charlie said, then laughed and shook his head. "But it ain't tomorrow."

Miller laughed too, and together they turned and headed

back, side by side. "Now I think Larry is on his way down," Miller said.

"I saw him swing. He's a player."

"Yes, he is. But he may have had one hot dog too many. He's younger than you and could pass for your father. He thinks he can just turn it off and on. Golf isn't like that."

"Nothing is."

"But he's my friend," Miller said, "and he'll be taken care of— win or lose." He then looked over the top of his sunglasses, his deep brown eyes tired and red. "I'm glad to have met you, to see what you're like." He paused. "The people you work for, that you've become acquainted with, aren't such nice people. You should look out for yourself."

"I think I can do that by playing my best," Charlie said.

"All right, then." Miller dragged heavily on his cigar. "Do you think you're going to win tomorrow?"

"I'm going to play the course and see what happens."

"But do you see yourself beating Siegal?"

"If I play well," Charlie said.

"The course record is sixty-five. Larry set it years ago and he's done it six times since. He can play this course perfectly."

"I see it differently than he does."

"How?"

Charlie hesitated.

"What's the difference if you tell me?" Miller said. "It's golf. It's not like he can play defense. He can't counterpunch."

Charlie nodded. "I'm longer than he is, Mr. Miller." He turned to face the setting sun. "I'm longer than most with a one-iron. That's all I'll say."

Ben Miller laughed, and Charlie laughed with him. "Eighteen in two?" he said. "That hole plays over six hundred yards, without the wind."

"I almost got there today," Charlie said, and then gazed out over the ocean as Miller puffed lightly on his cigar, watching him. "There's a lot of oxygen in this air, isn't there, Mr. Miller?" he said. "I feel great."

"There's a good deal of money riding on you, son," Miller said.

Charlie braced himself. "So all those guys, Sam, William, they bet on me?"

Miller nodded his head, seeming surprised that Charlie could take this information in stride. "A good many members too. And some money from back East."

Charlie thought briefly of Stephen and his father, then shook his head. "And Jack?"

"Yes, he's in for a bundle. I don't need to tell you that at three-to-one they all could do pretty good."

"Good for them," Charlie said. "Bad for you."

"There's enough down on the other side, more than enough to cover my losses. I'll do fine. And frankly, I don't care." He smiled. "And it doesn't seem like you do either."

"I don't think about it," Charlie said, "and I won't."

"Then you're strong," Miller said. "Stronger even than you know. That comes with purpose."

"We'll see," Charlie said. "You'd like to see Lang lose."

"I think you know that."

"He doesn't like you either," he said.

Miller pointed at him. "Because of what I am," he said, and Charlie saw his demeanor shift from pliable and gentlemanly to vicious. Then he gathered himself, taking a moment before he spoke. "I'd like to live in a world where deeds determine treatment." He shook his head. "Not in my time. But that's all right. I've dealt with it all my life," he said, waving the thought away as if he were shooing flies from around his face. "He's a sad, empty man who can never have enough."

"He hasn't lost anything yet," Charlie said. "He wants to keep it all."

"Well, you can't," Miller said. "I've learned that not so long ago."

Sadness swept over Charlie and it felt strange that he and the Czar stood on the same ground. "Did you love her very much, Mr. Miller?"

"I know you've lost some things, young man."

"I lost everything," Charlie said. "But I found some others."

"You're young, you have time. I'm old and sick. My wife was the only thing I loved. She was true. She was good. I was lucky to know her."

"How long ago did she die?" Charlie asked.

"Not quite a year. You?"

"My wife?"

"Yes."

"Divorced." Charlie answered.

"Divorced? Ha! What a crazy fuckin' world. What are people looking for—perfection?"

"I still don't know."

"How long were you married?"

"Forever, since we were kids, it seems," Charlie said. "I don't know. I've had some thoughts."

"Some thoughts?"

"That's all."

"How do you stand it?"

"I don't know," Charlie answered. "How do you?"

"I can't. I feel smaller, thinner, every day, like the wind itself could carry me away. I imagine it's killing me."

Charlie thought of how quickly his father died after his mother. "So what do you want now, Mr. Miller?"

He didn't have to think. "I want to see a good match. I want to live one day longer than I'm supposed to, but I won't. No one can. It's cruel. My time is short, but I want to see you play the way they say you can. But most of all, I want someone to push Larry and

make him play like I know he can. That's what I want before I
leave this earth, before he loses me. I think it's important for him.
To be pushed. To be frightened into realizing that things do end."

"He doesn't know that?"

"Hasn't ever lost a thing," Miller said.

"That he cares about," Charlie added.

"That's the only time it counts."

The two of them walked along to the crash of the waves and
the cries of seagulls.

"How'd you know I was down here?" Charlie finally asked.

"I own the motel you're staying in and a few others along here.
I live right over there." He pointed to a little bungalow nestled
against the hillside and the dunes.

"This is a great place, Mr. Miller."

"Ben, please," he said. "What do you plan to do after the
match, Charlie?"

"I don't know," he answered.

"How much do you have down?"

"Not a dime," Charlie said.

Miller stopped in his tracks. "You're joking. Maybe I will win."

"I wouldn't bet on it," Charlie said.

Just then the sun dipped below the horizon, and they both
sensed their time together drawing to a close.

"We'll talk," Ben Miller said, extending his hand. "Good luck
to you, my friend. Tomorrow and in the days to come." Then he
turned to go.

"Do you play?" Charlie asked.

Miller turned back. "No, nothing that you'd recognize as golf."
He pointed his cane at Charlie. "But I've always enjoyed those who
could." He raised his voice to be heard above the wind and the
waves. "The players. I've seen them all, known them all. Hogan.
Snead. Deacon. Palmer. Player. The Mexican. A guy up North
name of Harvey—a tremendous player, but he drank too much.
These new guys, they knock it a mile but I wonder how they play

with their own money on the line. It's been wonderful and Larry's the best I've ever seen."

Charlie waved good-bye as Ben Miller walked and puffed his way down the beach, his bodyguards a short distance behind him. His white shirt flapped in the wind, his bare feet trudged deeply into the sand, and his cane was propped jauntily on his shoulder.

31

Sarah ordered in pizza and beer and they ate as Charlie cleaned his old clubs. With a tee he scraped any bits of dirt from each groove, then wet the grips with his towel and rubbed them dry until they were tacky. He swung each club to feel the weight of it in his hands. When he was done he laid them next to the new set, took a clean white towel and draped it over them like he was tucking in a baby.

"Which ones are you going to use?" she asked.

"The new ones are better," Charlie told her. "I'll ship these back home."

Sarah took a swig of beer to hide her smile. "So you have everything you need?"

"I'll buy a couple balls at the pro shop. The new ones go farther."

"Just like the commercials say," Sarah said.

"Right." Charlie laughed. "Just like they say." He sat down on the floor and unfolded his legs before him, stretched his back for a minute or so, then leaned on his hands, his mind in thoughtful awareness.

"You ready?" she asked.

Charlie nodded and winked at her confidently. "I met him on Sunday, the guy I'm playing. All he has is this game."

"And?"

"He's miserable. It's hard to watch."

"Why?"

"He's spoiled. Always got his way. He can see the shot, knows what to do and how, but it's not the same. He hesitates. If he gets in trouble, he plays it safe. As good as he is, I know he used to be better."

"Wouldn't you have been better too?"

Charlie shrugged. "I suppose," he said, the last years flashing before him. "I feel sorry for him."

"Can you afford that?"

"Pity?"

"Yes," Sarah said.

His face clouded. "No. There's no room for that." He nearly winced, and a bitter smile pressed on his lips. "God, I'm just like him."

"I see no hesitation in you, Charlie. Not now."

"No, and there won't be any. But we're in the same place, he and I."

"But you're going up, not down," Sarah said.

Charlie knelt in front of her. "Maybe."

"Don't worry. I said it for you."

"You'll be there?"

"Only if it will help."

"It would." Then he moved onto the bed beside her, and for a time, they lay still in each other's arms.

32

Charlie arrived an hour before the match, the gate opened and Jack stood waiting on the other side.

"Place is quiet," he said as they walked through the parking lot to the clubhouse.

"Like a Monday," Charlie answered.

Everyone had been given the day off and the shack was empty. But as they walked up the long path, a small group of people began rustling toward them and when they rounded the corner, between the first and tenth tee, men and women were chit-chatting like extras in a French Impressionist painting, dressed in bright tropical colors and sipping coffee and drinks from a mobile bar complete with a bright yellow umbrella shielding it from the sun. Jack immediately reached into his shirt pocket and threw a cigarette into his mouth.

"Nervous?" Charlie asked.

"You bet your ass, Pittsburgh," he said.

Turning to catch a glimpse of the challenger, each was uniformly surprised, and surely disappointed by his stature and raggedy appearance. Charlie had on his caddying clothes: a blank white polo shirt, khakis and an old blue sweater slung over his shoulder. He was unshaven and had yet to tie his brown, worn-out golf shoes.

But when he approached they parted as if for royalty. Jack

threw the bag onto the iron rack and began pulling out clubs, methodically cleaning each one again.

"Don't wear the grooves off," Charlie said, then stepped inside the pro shop.

Alone and unobserved, Jack felt his worry swell. The crowd didn't bother him. It was Charlie. He'd played well the day before, spectacularly, his practice and habits impeccable, workmanlike and exhaustive, as always. But he recalled his conversation with Spider. There was little trace of the ferocity that Charlie played with before. He was too calm, too light, like the weather here, sunny and mild, with a breezy air about him.

Fuckin' place makes me want to take a nap, Jack thought. But Charlie also seemed less fragile, safer. And that made Jack a little more comfortable, a bit surer that Charlie was ready. Too late now anyway, he concluded, and returned to his business.

The pro shop looked like an upscale Kmart. Sets of clubs lined the walls along with all the paraphernalia: hats and pants and shirts and sweaters, every new club and ball, fifty putters leaning in one spot, all the gimmicks that supposedly helped improve your game.

Through the clutter, he found what he needed: a sleeve of three balls. A wooden rack stood off to the side and on it the latest series of woods; three-woods, five-woods, seven-woods. In the corner, another rack was filled with drivers. As Charlie pulled one down—the same model as Arturo's—he felt someone walk up behind him.

"Good morning, Charlie," Ben Miller said, and he could sense Charlie's growing concentration, even calmer than the day before, consciously falling into a hypnotic state. Marvelous, Miller thought, truly marvelous.

An assistant walked up to them and nervously cleared his throat.

"I'll take this," Charlie said, "and this sleeve of balls."

"I'm sorry, sir, but this shop is for members only."

"Put it on my account," Miller told him.

Before Charlie could argue, the door opened and Daniel Lang walked in, followed by Grant Evans, Shaw, and Schmitty.

Miller followed Charlie's eyes. "If you lose, you pay. If you win, keep it. Deal?"

Charlie nodded his acceptance. "I guess I do have a bet."

"Daniel!" Miller called, as if greeting an old friend.

"Ben," Lang said, unable to hide his contempt.

"I was just talking to your boy here," Miller said.

Lang quickly acquiesced, stepped forward and shook Miller's hand.

"Boys," Miller said to Lang's companions. Each gave a dutiful wave in return, but they all, even the boisterous Dr. Smith, looked as though they'd rather have stayed outside. They'd never met Miller, only heard of him, but standing before him, they now found his presence intimidating, his clout that stretched far beyond finance and property, overwhelming.

"Charlie," Lang said. "Jack here?"

"Everybody's here."

Lang drew a deep breath, regripped a brown leather satchel and gazed at Charlie but could not read him.

Miller pulled a cigar from his shirt pocket. "This is going to be fun," he said.

"What's with all the people?" Lang said. "Is there a luncheon or something?"

"No luncheon, just the match. They all paid. You'll get a cut."

"There must be a hundred," Lang said, trying to sound calm. "Is that okay with you, Charlie?"

"It's fine," Charlie answered, then turned toward the door. "I think I like it. Just like high school."

After he left, Lang hissed, "This is bullshit."

"Everyone's fine with it, Danny. Your boy doesn't care. These

people, they want to see and they bet big money. They're enti-
tled to."

"Fine," Lang spat. "Let's do this."

The two of them stepped into a small room at the back of the
shop and shut the door behind them, then Daniel Lang laid down
more cash than he ever had in his life.

With his nine-iron Charlie began hitting small punch shots and
Jack kept thinking, Find that rhythm, babe. As his body warmed
up, his swing became longer and the force of the move more powerful. He turned the ball at will with each club—left to right, right
to left—as effortlessly as ever; sent low, driving three-irons into
the far fence; then fluttered high, drifting draws with the same
club. He was in such command that Jack, confounded by his
almost leisurely ease, began to relax. Charlie's concentration was
deep, the darkness that had seemed to threaten him replaced by a
quiet awareness that was expanding second by second, breath by
breath, as if each swing took him farther and farther from his
troubles. Occasionally there was the grimace of old, but it radiated
from sheer physical exertion, and then the calm returned like a
cool gust of wind through a hot summer's day. Charlie's lips moved
but his voice was inaudible, his conversation private, as in his mind
he was playing his way around the course right there on the practice tee.

"How are you, Jack?" he suddenly said, then hit another ball.

Jack dragged heavily on his cigarette. "I think I'm okay."

"Just point me in the right direction," Charlie said. "You read
'em, I'll knock 'em in."

"One shot at a time."

"Play the course."

"That's all you can do, Pittsburgh," Jack said, and cackled.

Charlie pulled the driver out of the bag.

"Big sonofabitch, ain't it?" Jack said. Much larger than anything else in the bag, it was grossly conspicuous and the bright red headcover resembled a flag at the head of a parade. "Ugly too," Jack said. "Now those old persimmon drivers, they were pretty. You could look at one of them all day."

Charlie rolled a ball onto the grass, made a clean strike and the composite metal gave a dull, lifeless thud and the ball soared easily over the far fence.

"You gonna use it?" Jack asked.

"Only if I have to," Charlie said. "I don't like it. I can't feel the ball off the face." He hit three more balls with the same result, then slipped the club back into the bag.

"Ready?"

"Ready," Charlie said.

When they turned to go, Larry Siegal was standing there behind them, waiting. "I'll be a sonofabitch," he said.

Charlie put out his hand. "It was unintentional. I just wanted to caddy, to see the place. I had no idea I'd draw you."

"How could you?" Siegal said, smirking. He extended his hand, and Charlie felt a cool clamminess that matched his sallow skin and watery eyes.

Siegal nodded to his old caddy. "Jack."

"Larry."

"Got a smoke?"

Jack tapped a cigarette out of his pack.

"How are things in San Francisco?" he asked as Jack offered him a light.

"A bit cool, but I like it. They let you smoke."

Siegal smiled. "Yeah, we got some little Nazis running things around here these days." He blew out a billowing cloud. "I hear you have yourself a player." He pulled a glove from his back pocket as he waited for an answer, but none came. "You want a little side bet?"

"I already made my bet," Jack answered.

"Mr. MacLeod?"

"Fives, three ways," Charlie said. "Pay on the eighteenth green."

"In front of all those people?" Siegal laughed loudly. "Oh, that'll hurt. That's good, that's very fuckin' good. I'll see you on eighteen."

"I'll see you on one," Charlie said.

As they walked away, Larry Siegal's smile dissipated, and he stared at his clubs as if he'd never played. Then he pulled a nine-iron and began his warm-up.

A player's game hangs on his nerves. Some go their whole lives and only their physical skills deteriorate, while others battle every day just to hold it together. Then, for an array of reasons or maybe just a single good one, the time comes when what once was simple becomes irrationally impossible, be it a drive anywhere in the fairway or a straight three-foot putt. And no matter how many tournaments you've won, or how great they say you are, you can't keep your hands from shaking as you step up to that little white ball.

These thoughts had never occurred to Larry Siegal. The other guy was always the one to crumble. Over the years he'd psyched out most of his opponents before they'd gotten to the first tee. His presence was spooky, even if his swing wasn't quite what it used to be. Gone was the command of just a year ago. No one really knew except him, but now there could be two.

He kept swinging, getting close, turning the ball left or right at will, knocking it down or hitting it a mile high, and he assured himself that he could still putt the lights out. He did have it in him, but maybe a bit too deeply under the booze, the bullshit, the drugs and the fat.

Sam Deacon was here and, like years ago, the giant of a man by his side. Still fresh in his memory was the look on William Moorer's face as he towered over his player, bluffing, hiding his look of utter shock. It was an easy putt and Deacon pulled it. And he'd taken it so well, simply offering his congratulations. Still fixed in his mind were the calm, serene eyes and the warm hand of Sam Deacon. This had never added up. Alone, doubt crept in.

What if Deacon had made it, what then? He'd always thought that by upsetting Sam all those years ago he had won Ben Miller's confidence. What if he'd been the one who had choked? Would Miller have been so generous then? And could all this admiration, money and fear he'd garnered be the result of a thrown match?

But he couldn't imagine Deacon being bought and could think of no other reason why anyone would willingly lose.

And what had he just seen? He doubted if he'd ever done with a ball what his opponent just had, so easily and with such authority. And even though there are a million ways to hit a golf ball, and just as many ways to win, he had to ask himself if he was ever that good.

He reached into his bag and took a snort of vodka. There was one thing he was sure of—it was too late to do anything about it. What he had left was all there was and he would have to go with it, regardless of how much he'd pissed away. He lit up a fresh smoke and rolled another ball into place, hitched up his pants and continued to fire away.

33

The Front Nine

The crowd was gathered around the first tee and scattered down the edges of the fairway. Larry Siegal strutted by like a king, bounced up the wooden steps to the first tee and handed his bag to a boy standing there waiting.

The head pro, a tall, rangy man, tanned and rough-looking, peered out over the gallery. "Ladies and gentlemen, this is match play between Mr. Siegal and Mr. MacLeod and I'll serve as marshal. Gentlemen, if you could come forward." Charlie stepped away from his bag and stood elbow-to-elbow with Siegal as the pro flipped a tee into the air. It came down and was pointing to Siegal. "Mr. Siegal, you have the tee," he said, and the match was on.

Everyone fell silent as Siegal flicked his cigarette aside and sent his tee shot flying down the left side of the fairway. The ball bounced and caught the slope as it had on Sunday, kicking forward and coming to rest some fifty yards short of the green.

"Chase that," Siegal whispered, just loud enough for those close by to hear, and a wave of suppressed laughter rippled through the crowd.

But when their collective eyes shifted to Charlie they found him gazing back at them. William Moorer loomed over everyone, with a serious, somber look on his face, and Sam Deacon, standing beside him and two heads shorter, winked. Charlie dropped a ball onto the ground and rapped the edge of an iron into the soft green earth, raising it. Puzzled by what he was doing, people craned their necks to get a better look. Charlie rolled the ball onto the mound, backed away, then set up well inside the trees on the left side of the fairway, a wall of pine and thick brush. Jack followed the line to the top of the trees and felt his heart come up in his throat. At the corner of the dogleg, two tall pines towered above the others and, at the very top, barely visible in the glaring morning sun, formed a V-shaped opening. Christ, he's gonna cut the leg off, Jack thought. So much for playin' the course.

Charlie hitched his pants, took one last look up and let go a smooth, graceful swing. The sound was terrific. Grass flew and the ball shot toward the trees. Abandoning the bag, Jack ran to the front of the tee box to keep it in sight and then, incredulous, turned to see Charlie, head cocked, listening rather than watching. A few mute seconds ticked by, a silence suddenly jolted by a single voice crying out from beyond the trees.

With a nod of satisfaction, Charlie flipped the club onto the bag and started walking as a spectator, still yelling, appeared at the corner of the fairway.

"What the hell's he carrying on about?" the pro snapped.

"Helluva shot," Jack whispered, and shouldered Charlie's bag.

Word traveled back up through the gallery and people peeled off, dropping all social pretenses as they scurried toward the green like they were running to a fire.

"It's on the green," someone called. "It almost went in!"

William Moorer and Sam Deacon strolled a few paces behind Charlie shaking their heads, while Danny Lang, Grant Evans and David Shaw stood motionless by the tee, trying to maintain their cool. But Doctor Alan "Schmitty" Smith ran up the fairway like a kid, cigar in one hand, Bloody Mary in the other. Ben Miller, driven along in a cart and sipping a drink, eyed Siegal walking toward his ball alone.

The crowd was buzzing and the pro shouted, "Quiet, please!"

Siegal, seeing Charlie's ball directly between him and the pin, was impressed but not unnerved, and he hit his approach shot to what appeared to be just outside of it. I make, he misses, he thought, we're all tied. But as he walked up to the green he fought to cover his creeping astonishment. Charlie's ball rested not two feet below the hole and his own ball some ten feet back. Never willing to be upstaged, he marked his ball and turned to the crowd.

"I'd love to give you that putt, as any gentleman would," he said, "but many of these people will tell you, I'm no gentleman at all. Besides, I just love to see eagle putts. So please, mark your ball."

Laughter rolled through the gallery as Charlie marked his ball and tossed it to Jack. He looked half asleep, almost bored, his silence unnerving.

Siegal's putt lipped out, and he mumbled a curse.

"That's good," Charlie said.

"And yours," he answered.

Charlie scooped up his mark and headed to number two, one up.

Both men parred the par-four second, but Siegal felt like he'd dodged a bullet. After he lagged his putt close and tapped in, Jack pointed to a spot on the green and from fifteen feet Charlie rolled the ball right over it, but it caught the right edge of the hole and spun out. Jack thought it was in, and so did Siegal.

"Too hard," Charlie muttered. "I thought it was uphill."

"I told you it was flat," Jack said.

Everyone had moved on, and they were alone on the green. Lang trudged up the right rough by himself, looking tired and nervous. Charlie considered how little he knew him and felt sadness threatening to take hold. Why did he and Siegal have to play under such circumstances—the threats, the lies, the money? Why couldn't they play alone, and in the end say who'd won? It was hard, this choosing sides and deciding who was to blame. His resolve returned when it dawned on him that everyone was. He putted again, and split the cup.

"It's flat," Charlie said, handing Jack his putter.

"Just like I said," his caddy told him.

Both players hit the fairway on number three, Siegal's driver just short of Charlie's one-iron.

Siegal struck his approach shot, and the crowd applauded lightly as the ball landed on the green.

Charlie pulled a club. "Have you seen any redheads in the crowd?"

"One right over there, kinda close," Jack said. "Sharp."

"Good." Charlie smiled. "Glad to see your head's in the game."

"Yours too," Jack said.

Charlie hit a low penetrating shot into the wind and started walking after it well before the ball dug into the green, hopped once, then sat down close. A few people applauded, but most stood by not quite believing what they were seeing. Undeterred, Siegal walked whistling to his ball, marked it and handed it to his caddy, then hit a putt from twenty feet, draining it. He was tromping off to the next tee even as Charlie's putt fell into the cup.

Charlie made his first error on the fourth hole, coming off his tee shot and blocking it right, into the rough. "He's human," Siegal announced, and laughter ran through the gallery again. Even though he was down, the crowd was his and now he had an opening. He snatched his driver from his bag and sent the ball down the center of the fairway.

Charlie was a hundred and seventy yards out, the early morning sun hadn't reached the thick, wet rough and a large pine tree blocked his line to the green. "Plain old grass," Jack said. "I think you can get to it."

Charlie took a seven-iron and looked up through the trees, then put it back. "Give me a four," he said, looking left of the tree.

"I like it," Jack said. "Slice the shit out of it."

It missed the tree by a foot, bent left-to-right, ballooned high in the air, carried the left greenside bunker, and settled softly on the green.

Forgetting who they were rooting for, the crowd roared.

"Came down like a butterfly with sore feet," William Moorer cried.

"Bent that ball f-forty, maybe f-fifty yards like it was nothing," Sam added.

Larry Siegal made his second birdie of the day but gained no ground. Charlie trusted Jack and played his downhill putt straight, and it rolled in the hole.

"Thought it might break right," Charlie said.

"God-damn slope holds it up," Jack told him.

Each birdied five, then parred six, seven, and eight and Charlie was still one up.

Number nine was a short par four whose narrow fairway tilted hard from right to left. The same water that fronted eighteen wrapped around the green, which sloped back to the water, with a large bunker framing the back of it. Both players drove it just into the left rough, Charlie's hitting the fairway but taking a hard bounce and coming to rest deep in the shade of an old pine tree.

"We should've played that a little more right," Jack said. "My fault."

But it was Siegal, just a foot in the rough and a clear shot to the green, who drew the worse lie, the ball barely visible in a deep thatch of kikuyu. He was away and didn't think twice about laying up, grunting as he hacked his ball out with a sand wedge.

All eyes went to Charlie. He had no club in his hand yet, his arms folded in front of him, his eyes closed. The ball was down, invisible, but he'd caught a break. The grass, though thick and long, was dry and lying toward the green.

He took a stance, then went through the motions of a full swing. "What's the yardage to the front, Jack?" he said. He studied the lie again and walked back out into the sunlight to see the pin, calculating as he went what holes were left to gain or to lose. Jack leaned the bag.

"Today," Siegal whispered just loud enough for Jack to hear him.

"When he's ready," Jack shot back. "You got one fifty-five to the front edge."

"The wind's against me?" Charlie asked.

"Everything's against you," Jack said. "We're up. Make him come and get us."

"Oh, he will," Charlie said. "And I don't want to be there when he does."

"That's exactly what he wants you to do," Jack said. "Think. Play the course, like you're always sayin'. Play the course, beat the man. Ain't that what your old man taught you?"

"Yeah, that's what he'd do." Charlie pulled a club. "But I ain't him."

When he realized Charlie was going for the green, Siegal turned to hide his delight.

But there are times in any competition when the players know the odds and what should follow. It's not unlike poker. The games go along hand by hand or stroke by stroke, and players can be lulled into that rhythm. But an extraordinary player recognizes when it's time to move out, to break from the book and go with what your gut tells you. This moment comes at different times, and no one knows what causes it; the stars might fall into alignment, or an opportunity is glimpsed, or an instinct recognized. The player breaking out knows it first. A second later his opponent realizes what's happening, but it's too late. The bet's down, the play's being made. Helpless, he can only watch as the cards are turned over or the shot is made.

Siegal found himself the spectator. Hopes raised just a second ago now sank as the ball came out low and hot, cleared the pine by inches and rocketed toward the green.

"Get down!" Jack yelled, and the ball seemed to obey. The wind caught the ball and pushed it higher into the sky, where it arced left to right, hung a bit, fluttered and then plummeted, hitting the green and rolling within a few paces of the pin.

Lang, Shaw, Evans and Schmitty were shocked. Sam Deacon would freely admit that he'd never even dreamed of such a shot, since he'd never possessed the strength to hit it.

"Shot!" someone yelled, and astonishment ran through the crowd like a train, grown men holding their heads in disbelief, their mouths wide open.

Ben Miller thought it was the greatest shot he'd ever seen. The lie seemed impossible and there were so many hazards, yet Charlie had stiffed it. What balls this boy has, he thought, and took his drink to cover a smile.

When the buzz settled, Siegal hit a short wedge to the middle of the green that checked up and then spun back, five feet from the hole. After all the shots he'd seen Charlie hit—the tee shot on one, the radar-like approach on three, the cut on four—just seconds ago he'd believed he would make it through the front nine even. He felt deceived, like the gods were playing with him and there wasn't a thing he could do about it. About to go two down, he began to panic even as he smiled and lit another cigarette. Then he missed his putt.

"That's good," Siegal said as he swiped his ball off the green.

Charlie picked up his mark with his left hand and hurried away toward the caddy shack, his right hand buried deep in his pocket.

34

The crowd moved to the tenth tee, many on their cell phones and they weren't talking business. By the time the players reached the tee there would be fifty more spectators; midway through the back nine, a hundred.

Ben Miller caught Siegal as he walked off the ninth green and pulled him aside, laying his hand gently on his shoulder. "What are you thinking?" he said. "Who the hell do you think you're playing?"

Siegal was in a fog. "He's tough," he said. "That last shot. The tee shot on one. Christ."

"You're out of your game, my friend. Play your game. Play it out. There's no lay-ups, for Christ's sake. This guy doesn't have a lay-up in him. He's going to go every time. How many holes does it take for you to understand that?"

He hadn't raised his voice in years and didn't know why he had to now. But Siegal looked terrible, slouched over, sweating profusely, his shirt hanging over his pants and his hand shaking as he took another drag from his cigarette.

Miller took a towel from his cart and handed it to him. "Wipe your face," he said, wondering if he really knew his man at all. He quickly decided that he did. He looked up to make sure the crowd had passed. "Take a drink, Larry."

"What do you mean?" Siegal said.

Over all the years, Ben Miller had placated Siegal's every desire, had stood by and winked at his habits as a young man's right. But Larry was no longer young. So should he lay on the whip or just let him go? If pressed, he might break under the pressure, and he needed his cockiness in order to have any chance of winning. It saddened Miller to know, even though he felt a paternal affection for him, that their relationship was as irrevocably determined as the rising and the setting of the sun, the path altering from time to time but the destination always the same. When Larry Siegal finally lost, be it this day or the next, their friendship would be gone too. So Miller decided to use his power to delay that from happening.

"Don't fuck with me, Larry," he snapped. "Take a drink. You can't play if your hands are shaking." He unzipped the golf bag's side pocket. "Go ahead." Then he stood guard, as he so often had, as Siegal took a good, long chug of vodka. "You and me. All we have left is this game," Miller said, "and we're on the back nine. Make it your best nine. That's all I'm asking. Right here. Right now."

The old Larry suddenly emerged, strange and cold. He angrily pulled his glove on. "Sure," he said. "I got nine more."

"That's my boy," the Czar said.

35

When Charlie didn't appear on the tenth tee, Jack went looking for him, walking quickly through the caddy shack. Charlie was in the bathroom bent over in pain, with Sam and William on either side of him.

"What's wrong?" Jack said, but he already knew. Gone was the serene state of mind. Charlie was in a panic.

"I can't feel anything," he said, "from my elbow to my hand. It's all numb."

"He's done," William said.

"Let me see," Jack said, and gently took hold of Charlie's arm. "Maybe it's just the crazy bone. It'll go away."

Charlie felt a warm rush and a sharp pain on the inside of his elbow, growing.

"It's swelling," Jack said. "I'll get some ice."

"He's done," William said again.

"Fuck that!" Jack snapped, just as the bathroom door flew open and Lang, Evans, Schmitty and Shaw stormed in.

"What the hell's going on?" Lang asked.

"It's his arm," Jack said.

"Everybody out of my god-damn way," Schmitty barked. He took Charlie's arm in his hands, pressed a spot just inside the elbow, and Charlie grimaced. "That's a fuckin' mess, son," he hissed between his teeth, then began massaging Charlie's arm from his elbow up to the armpit.

"Medial collateral, some bicep maybe," he concluded. "The more you play, the more shock you put on it, the worse it'll get. You could tear it completely. Happened on that last shot."

"Yeah," Charlie said. "I felt like I was going to throw up."

"Unbelievable shot," Schmitty said absently.

"Will it hold up?" Lang asked.

With expert hands Schmitty continued massaging the arm as he spoke. "Medical opinion? Out of the question. If the tendon detaches, I'm guessing he already has a lot of scar tissue. I can put it together, but play again? I don't know."

"I don't care," Charlie said.

William Moorer stepped forward. "I do," he said. "This is the boy's life." He pointed at Charlie. "Don't you do it. It ain't worth it. Fuck the money! You can play anywhere!"

"Stay out of it, Moorer," Lang said.

"And fuck you too!" William shouted, leaning toward him like a giant bear. But Sam stepped between them and Moorer stopped.

"You're out!" Lang yelled.

"I don't give a fuck!" William spat back. "You might be able to screw us caddies over, but you ain't gonna hold this boy up! Fuck you!" Everyone began pushing and shouting.

"I'm playing," Charlie said, but only Deacon and Schmitty heard him.

"Don't step onto the grounds! You or him!" Lang pointed at Sam. "I'll have both your asses thrown in jail!"

"I'm playing!" Charlie yelled, and the small room suddenly went quiet. He straightened up and, for the moment, by sheer will, dismissed the pain. "I'll do whatever it takes to win. And I'll be a sonofabitch, but I don't care if I ever play again." He heaved in a breath and blew it out. "Dr. Smith," he said, "will you try to fix my arm? When this is all over? I don't have a dime but I can work it off."

"Charlie, I can't promise—"

"But you'll try?"

"Yes, God damn it, of course I will."

"Thanks," Charlie said.

Schmitty resumed massaging the arm. "Best fuckin' shot I've ever seen. Give my left nut to hit a shot like that. Fuck, I'd give both." He turned to Lang. "If he can stand the shock, the pain, he'll finish. It's gonna hurt like hell, but he's strong."

Lang was silent, but the consequences were obvious to everyone.

"Do what you want, kid," William said. "You been doin' everybody else's biddin' for a long time. Gettin' out of the way, buryin' people, sayin' good-bye when you didn't want to. So now just do whatever the fuck you want."

"It's only m-money," Sam said. "We can c-c-cover you."

Charlie weakened and suddenly he looked like a little boy. "You know, all I have riding on this is a five-dollar Nassau. What do you say, Jack?"

Jack glanced at Lang. "I can't tell you that, Charlie." They all waited for his answer. But they didn't have to wait long.

36

The Back Nine

Larry Siegal was on the tenth tee, swaggering and smoking, and when Charlie finally arrived he immediately sensed that something was wrong. And once Charlie bent and straightened his arm, he knew he was hurt. To what degree he wasn't sure, but it boosted his confidence. "Take a nap?" he asked.

But Charlie was distant, invulnerable to his sarcasm. He quickly came to address, digging his feet into the grass as words and images from the past rolled over him. He summoned them, gathered strength from them, let them roam freely once more inside his head and consume him. His face turned small and mean, and he let go a ferocious swing as the crowd hooted and cheered. No one present had seen a ball hit so far, so straight; it was as if a machine had launched it down the fairway. Charlie grimaced, then quickly tucked his hand into his pocket.

Siegal collected himself and hit a big drive, then the two players walked separately down the fairway. The gallery grew steadily. Golf carts lined the hole, parked in clusters, and people scrambled for position.

Sarah walked along the fringes of the crowd. On the front nine Charlie seemed loose and open, his abilities transcending her lack of knowledge of the game, his talent potent and irresistible even to the novice. But now she snuck closer to him and saw the change. Startled, she wondered what had happened and was concerned not only for him but also for herself. Was this how he had to play in order to win? Or was this what he was like and always would be? Most important, did it matter, as Charlie said just a day ago, that he needed and loved her? Or did he love winning at any cost? The differences in him were unsettling: as tender as could be at one moment and then, in the blink of an eye, and to her knowledge with no provocation, he could switch it off and shut everyone out. And now he was tight, aloof, his eyes cast down, his stature shrinking, a sea of people sweeping him away. Her trust began to waver.

When Siegal's approach shot hit the green and jumped close to the pin, her heart sank. She turned to find Charlie, hoping she would catch a glimpse of the man she knew and believed in. But he was gone, changed, a dark stranger, forty yards down the fairway but miles away, staring at the pin, his hand grazing over his clubs as he made a decision, even as she was, about what to do next.

Sarah made up her mind first: she would go see other places and people, as she'd planned. Having lost him to a game, she cursed the day he first set foot on a golf course. Just one more shot and she'd be gone.

It was straight and true and rolled inside of Siegal's. Sarah held her place as the buzzing crowd sifted by her. But then Jack walked back to replace the divot, and unexpectedly he and Sarah were alone, yards apart but eye-to-eye. Maybe it was her body language, or his timely skepticism, but he seemed to read her mind. He knew. A trite, cruel smile sprung to his face and she felt as if a dark, heavy cloud had just passed over her. How fitting, she thought, then sensed someone behind her. Alarmed, she turned to see a gigantic black man, looking stern and sad, standing there, offering his hand. "Hi, we're friends of Charlie's," he said and nodded to an older white man standing next to him.

Smiling through her anguish, she said, "You must be William." She turned to Deacon. "And you *must* be Sam."

"Th-that boy n-needs you," Sam said gently, as if she was the only one who didn't know.

"He damn sure do," William choked.

"He's hurt."

Sarah spun around to find Charlie approaching the green slowly, his right hand frozen in his pocket, and at that moment, she thought her heart would break.

Sam held out his hand. "Come on."

Sarah let him take her elbow and the three of them hurried to the tenth green. She looked at Sam but was speaking to William. "They're two of a kind," she whispered.

"Lucky for us, darlin'," William said. "Lucky for us."

After two birdies Charlie stayed two up. They matched pars on eleven. Twelve was a short par five and guarded by trees and sand on both sides, its narrow fairway winding left to right and then down a hill. Charlie's drive carried all the trouble and left only a mid-iron to the green, and Siegal hit one deep down the left side of the fairway. As they walked off the tee, it was apparent to Miller and Lang, as well as Sam and William and Jack, who now held the upper hand. Each shot seemed to take everything Charlie had. He walked alone, sadness set on his face, as Siegal strolled easily to his ball, talking to the crowd and enjoying himself. Occasionally he'd zip open his bag and take a snort of vodka to the gallery's delight. They all knew of his antics, but this was the first time they'd witnessed them. He was bigger than life. He could tell Charlie was hurt, that his swing wasn't what it was, and with his confidence rising he tagged a five-wood to within twenty feet of the pin. The crowd whooped it up as he flipped the club to his caddy, tucked the putter under his arm and strutted down the fairway.

When Charlie reached his ball he pulled an iron without asking Jack a thing, took one look at the pin, and quickly hit a shot that settled just outside Siegal's ball, and they both two-putted for birdies.

The lead was finally cut on thirteen, a short par four that doglegged right. A miscalculation on Charlie's part, he hit his one-iron off the tee, and even though he cut it, it was too much club and the ball shot through the fairway. Siegal then took his driver and cut the corner, giving him a hundred yards to the green with a straight shot to a back left pin.

Charlie stood just inside the tree line, his ball buried in deep rough. The sun had turned hot and he seemed to want to stay right where he was, in the shade of a tall eucalyptus. Jack waited until Charlie took another look at the green and made his decision, chipping out into the fairway with a pitching wedge.

"That's all right, kid," Jack said. "Make him play a good shot."

As Siegal's ball soared toward the pin his caddy pulled out his putter, but Siegal didn't even look at him. The ball hit once, bounced past the pin and spun back down a short incline, slowed and took a small break in the green, the crowd roaring as it fell into the cup for eagle two. Siegal never broke stride or acknowledged the applause, but then suddenly stopped and pointed to Charlie's ball. "Oh!" he called. "That's good."

Charlie was one up with five to play.

Having honor for the first time since the opening hole, Siegal drove down the middle of a long par four. Charlie opened his left foot at address, swung easily and sent the ball down the left side, turning it lazily back toward the middle of the fairway; it hit and rolled just past Siegal's ball. After Siegal hit the green, Charlie took more club than he needed and again swung easily, the ball starting even farther left but finishing just inside Siegal's ball. When Jack pulled out the putter, he said, "You hold it. Please. I can't think. I don't have to beat him from here, just tie. I'll just stay inside of him."

Jack shook his head in amazement. "You can do that?" When Charlie nodded, he said, "Good. That'll drive him fuckin' nuts."

The strategy seemed to work. Marking his ball, Siegal realized that his putt would show Charlie the line, and that players of his caliber seldom missed once they see the line. If he didn't make his own putt, he'd be two down with only three to go and Charlie could dog it all the way to the clubhouse. Having no choice, he lined up his putt and from fifteen feet drilled it into the hole.

Charlie stepped forward to place his ball, and as he removed his marker, Jack drew close. "He had a lot of pace on that ball. It breaks a little right-to-left."

Charlie stroked the putt up the hill, where it lost its speed and drifted left into the cup. When the crowd cheered, he acknowledged them for the first time with a gentle wave of his hand.

Fifteen and then sixteen, the gallery roared and moaned with each shot. Few had picked up on Charlie's tactics, since to nearly everyone his swing hadn't perceptibly changed. The sound at impact had lessened but was still odder than anything they'd ever heard and if the flight of the ball was different, his command was still present. For every ball Siegal hit, he'd follow with a big left-to-right shot that allowed his arm to move freely.

"It's an in-in-tentional slice," Deacon said.

"Motherfuckers spend their whole life tryin' to get rid of it," William said, and the two of them laughed like kids stealing Bazooka from a candy shop.

Whatever patience Siegal had gained began to wear away. He felt he was being robbed, cheated, and no matter how well he played he wouldn't be able to make up the ground, even if eighteen holes can seem like an eternity.

Seventeen, however, didn't play into Charlie's hand. The par-three pin was, as he predicted, tucked in the front left behind a deep bunker, leaving him little room to bring the ball into the small, heavily undulating green.

Siegal's spirits lifted when he realized Charlie couldn't hit the draw it required. He took a little extra time, then started his shot at the middle of the green and turned it back toward the flag, staring it down as it hit then backed to within two few feet.

"Follow that," he whispered under the gallery's roar, then wearily dropped the club into his bag. He too was exhausted—but not by the match or the discipline he'd thrown away over the years, not even by the money. Only one thought weighed on him: what would he do if he was no longer the best? For the first time he was playing with desperation, and for his life.

The inside of Charlie's arm was now completely swollen, and to hit the draw would surely damage it further.

"Take what you can get," Jack said. "You got one fifty-five to the front edge. Take one more club and give yourself a putt."

"I've got to get it close."

"Don't do it," Jack said. "We're up one. Hit a fade to the middle and give yourself a putt."

"I have to birdie, Jack," Charlie said. "He's not gonna miss that."

"So we get him on eighteen," Jack said.

"With what? Three to the green and another putt?"

"Then we'll go extra," Jack said, trying to relax him.

Charlie took a breath, attempting to gather himself. "I don't have it," he said and pulled a club.

His shot started twenty yards left of the green, and the crowd moaned; it climbed above the trees while all eyes struggled to keep track of it, turning right and fighting the wind.

"Get up!" Jack yelled, but it landed in the front bunker.

Suddenly energized, Siegal hustled off the tee and Charlie followed him down the short hill.

Buried under the lip of the trap, Charlie reached down and plucked his ball out of the sand just as Siegal marked, and the whole crowd gasped. "That's good," he called to Siegal.

"It's the smart play," Sam said. "Smart. He can't hit that shot, not with his arm."

Everyone headed to eighteen, the match all square.

. . .

Larry Siegal grunted and his tee shot landed in the middle of the fairway and stopped short of the barranca.

Now a good caddy can club any player after a well-struck iron and with a single stroke of the putter he can tell if he'll need to spend his day coaxing him as he would some two-year-old. But until now Jack hadn't been sure—not because he lacked skill, but because his player was so extraordinary—just what Charlie's next move might be. A good caddy, though he wouldn't necessarily do it, could pull the club and hold it out even before his player has stepped off the yardage, just by instinct; the numbers, yardage and odds might vary, but it's clear this is the play. So when Charlie reached for the new driver he found it exposed, the silver metal cold and shining, the gaudy red headcover already in his caddy's hand.

"Rip it," Jack said.

The late morning wind had shifted, now stirring out of the northwest, and Charlie felt it on his right shoulder. Lining up toward the giant mounds on the right side of the fairway, he grimaced when he pulled his right elbow tight to his side, then backed off the shot, shook his arm and re-addressed the ball.

On his downswing, the stiff graphite shaft bowed under the stress as Charlie threw the full weight of his body down into the ball and hot, electric pain jolted through him as he struggled mightily to keep his elbow tight to his side. The clubhead snapped forward at impact, and he cried out when he felt something give, but by then the ball was soaring toward the pines, surrendered to the wind, the fates and God himself.

"Where the fuck is it?" Jack muttered.

"It's over," Charlie whispered, dropping the club to the ground.

Jack winced. "Don't say that, kid."

A tremor ran through the gallery as a few of them raced forward in their carts like the cavalry, heading toward the mounds to look for the ball. At the barranca they jumped out, hit the ground running, and began a frantic search while others broke from the pack, bumping and pushing one another across the narrow, rail-less bridge, their eyes scanning the muddy, rocky ditch below for that little white ball.

"There it is!" a woman cried, pointing and running while holding her skirt in place, as if she'd discovered a long-lost treasure.

Indeed, the ball had cleared the ravine, caught the slope of the mounds, and shot down and across the far side of the fairway.

Charlie had reduced the impossibly long par five into a reachable par four.

But the shock in his arm had traveled from his elbow right up to his neck. His temple throbbed and he felt numb from his hand to his ear. He no longer could hide it and cradled his right arm in his left even as it swelled from the inside out. "We still got work to do," he said.

Jack sighed heavily. "Yep."

Shuddering in pain, Charlie wriggled his hand in hopes of regaining the feeling as yet another hot rush of blood started swelling his arm, stiffening it. Again he felt something pop and he didn't dare move it for fear he might cry out. The wind helped dry the sweat now pouring over him, but in an instant he became faint. Jack came up and pulled Charlie against him. "I'll hold you up, kid," he said.

Larry Siegal stood at his ball coolly, smoking and taking in the chaos around him, absorbing it as he had his whole life, digesting it until finally he felt quite comfortable with it. He knew the ball had cleared the ditch the moment Charlie hit it. On the first tee he'd spotted the new club in Charlie's bag and began wondering when he might use it; he had hoped it wouldn't come down to this, but when it did, he was ready, having come to expect such things from this newest opponent. He quickly ruled out going for the green. That's exactly what he wants me to do, he thought. Make a dumb play and put it in the water. That's what the tee shot was for. No, he wouldn't take any risks. He'd just wait and see if Charlie had another shot in him. He hit a crisp iron to the one-hundred-twenty-five-yard marker, then took his pitching wedge and walked behind Charlie and Jack as they approached their ball. When he finally saw Charlie's face, he felt something most unusual: open respect and admiration.

Sam Deacon couldn't have beaten Charlie on his best day. The pros that had come by and lost, the occasional outstanding young amateur, they all ran like a parade through Siegal's head. None of them, he thought, could touch this guy. His best days are gone, and he never even got to play. He'll be forgotten, a myth no one will believe. Of all the players he'd faced, none even remotely compared. If Charlie was healthy, he could never beat him and would've been closed out on this match holes ago. Then he returned to a frame of mind that would see him through, win or lose. There was territory to protect and a kingdom to defend. He looked to Charlie once more and hardened his heart. "Tough shit," he mumbled.

As it was on Sunday, the hole was cut just five paces onto the green, dangling just above the water's edge.

Charlie pulled his one-iron from his bag, then put it back. "What do I have?" he asked Jack.

"Two twenty to the front, wind still right-to-left, from this side of the fairway, maybe a little against you."

Charlie took back the one-iron.

"That's a lot of club," Jack said.

Charlie managed a smile. "Not the route I'm goin'." He began his pre-shot routine.

"Left-to-right?" Jack asked. "Hang it out over the water?"

"I can't hit it any other way," Charlie said.

"Ain't there nothin' I can say to stop you?"

Charlie took a practice swing. "Time's runnin' out, Jack," he said. "I gotta go."

He set the club down, lining his feet and body well left, and took a gentle practice swing. Another shot of pain rushed through his arm. He tried again, letting his arm hang as loose as he could, but the pain was still there and expanding by the minute.

So Charlie took a little extra time pulling back the club, like he was swinging at a slow-pitch softball. He cocked his wrists, his elbow flew out away from his body; he did everything wrong except strike the ball, sending it flying out over the water. Halfway there it began bending right into the opposing wind.

Good, Charlie thought. Blow hard now.

Jack screamed, "Go, you motherfucker!"

"*Get up!*" Daniel Lang yelled with genuine enthusiasm.

It was close. The ball hit the wall of wind and fell to the green, bounced once and began a feeble roll toward the water, then stopped no more than a step from the pin.

Never had Larry Siegal seen anyone get to this green in two. He'd made eagle here, but from the fairway and never with this pin. Now he had to hole out from a hundred and twenty-five yards and he gave it his best, he fired at the pin, but when it hit, a few feet past the hole, it spun back too far, took the slope and tumbled into the pond.

The match was over, the course as quiet as a graveyard. The gallery stood motionless as the players walked up to the green. Siegal stopped short at the edge of the pond, and in just a foot of water he could see his ball, the logo clearly legible. Charlie took out his coin and leaned over to mark his ball. "I think that's good," Larry Siegal told him.

Epilogue

I n a room reserved for card-playing, the doors were shut and the Czar handed Daniel Lang two brown leather gym bags.

"Is that everything?" he asked.

"I think so," Lang replied.

"Your boy's a helluva player. Good luck."

"Thanks," Lang said. "See you around."

Ben Miller shut the door, and that was the last time the two men ever saw each other.

Lang came through the gate with Evans, Shaw and Schmitty, walking four abreast as they did each Friday, Saturday and Sunday.

William Moorer, Sam Deacon and Jack were waiting in the parking lot with Charlie and Sarah, Charlie squeezing a bag of ice between his body and his aching arm.

"I'll see you in my office tomorrow, first thing," Schmitty said, handing him a plastic bottle and his card. "Take these."

Lang tossed one of the satchels on the hood of Jack's car. "There you go," he said. "I guess we won't be seeing you guys for a while."

"Not me," William said. "I'm goin' home to Mississippi."

"Me neither," Jack said, reaching for the bag. From inside

Jack's car a strange man, with bulging, muscular arms, came bouncing out of the back seat. Lightning-quick, he snatched the bag from Jack, and everyone, even William, took a step back.

"I'll take that motherfucker," he spat, and Jack didn't move to stop him. Then, with equal quickness and agility, the man ducked down behind Jack's car. Charlie and Sarah expected someone, maybe Lang, to do something, but they all just stood there as if they were waiting for a bus. Lang nonchalantly cast his eyes down like he was about to pick up a penny. Shaw and Schmitty had turned their backs, and Jack lit a cigarette while William and Sam leaned against their own car. So Charlie and Sarah waited too.

"Here!" The leather bag flew up over the car, and Jack caught it. A moment later the man rose. "Thanks," he said, slinging a green backpack over his shoulder. "I took a little extra for my pains. I've had a lot of 'em."

"That's cool, Randall," Jack said.

"Randall?" Charlie blurted. His hair was short, neat and clean, the mass of tangles cut out. His face was worn and handsome. Dark, round sunglasses covered the wrinkles that surrounded his eyes, and he was clean-shaven.

Randall stepped close to Charlie and studied his face. "Who the fuck are you?"

"That's him," Jack said, "Charlie."

"That right?"

"I met you a while ago," Charlie said.

Randall removed his sunglasses, and his blue eyes twinkled. "Where?"

"At the club," Charlie said.

"What club? Just kiddin'. No," Randall said, and a great emptiness threatened to swallow him. "I don't remember." He leaned and whispered. "The last weeks have been kind of a dream."

Charlie nodded. "I understand."

Randall thought of something, then shook his head, said,

"Fuck it." He held up the backpack, and its contents raised his spirits. "You must be a helluva player to beat that boy 'cause he's a motherfucker. Good luck with all that shit. Bye." He stepped away, then quickly turned back to offer his hand to Lang. "Thanks. I'll be seein' ya, I think."

With each step he gained speed, gathering momentum as he approached the front gate. When it failed to open promptly he threw his bag over and then, like a great ape, grabbed the top of the fence with both hands, vaulted over and was gone.

"I guess we won't see him for a while either," Charlie said.

"Nope," Jack said.

"N-no," Sam said, "n-not till he r-runs out of money."

"How long will that take?" Schmitty asked.

"Not long," Charlie said. "Jack?" he said, pointing to his clubs. "Could you?"

"I got it," Sarah said, and Jack hoisted the clubs onto her shoulder. She felt the weight of them and smiled. "Light," she said.

"They're not all like that one, darlin'," Jack said.

The two of them headed to Charlie's car. He opened the trunk and began to change his shoes.

"Wouldn't they let you do that inside?" Grant Evans said.

"This is fine." He winced as he pulled off his shoes and tossed them into the trunk.

Someone yelled, and Larry Siegal came walking out of the gate and stopped in front of them. "Well, isn't this an unusual gathering. Slummin' it, Sam?"

"Just t-t-today," Sam said.

"I owe you five bucks," he said to Charlie. "You got me two ways, front and eighteen. I got you on the back." He held out a twenty. "You got change?"

"Yeah," Charlie said, reaching into his pocket. "There you go."

"Good-bye," Siegal said, and turned to go.

"We should play sometime," Charlie said.

"You'd have to give me one a side," Siegal answered, still walking, "and I ain't quite ready for that."

"I understand," Charlie said.

"I don't get out much anyway," Siegal said.

Storms pummeled Northern California that winter and Charlie's arm was in a cast the whole time. When the rain stopped, he went back to work, carrying a single bag over his left shoulder, comfortably inside the etiquette and rhythm of the game, speaking only when spoken to.

The cast came off in the spring. His arm again was shriveled, atrophied beyond recognition. Schmitty handed him a tennis ball.

"Squeeze that till it hurts, then ice it and take two aspirin. Do it every day and we'll see you in rehab."

In May, Schmitty gave Charlie the go-ahead and he began to practice, lightly at first, then every day. In the middle of that summer he lingered one Monday between the first and tenth tees, but everyone had a game and Charlie, again, was unbeatable. Billy and Figgs passed him by.

So he played alone. William Moorer had indeed gone home to Mississippi and seemed to have taken a little piece of Sam Deacon with him. He rarely came by. "J-just like a caddy to up and leave," he told Charlie one day.

Charlie and Sarah took a place near the beach. He bought a bicycle and pedaled to work. He practiced till near sunset every day, and his game began to return, day by day, swing by swing.

In the cool evening he put on a sweater, crossed the great Pacific Coast Highway and walked to the edge of the water. White-capped waves rolled toward the Golden Gate Bridge and giant tankers glided west across the open water, in minutes merely specks on the vast horizon. A seagull circled in the patchy fog, calling out for its mate.

Sarah was walking the beach and heard an unnatural sound carom off the rocks down the shoreline, the echo reverberating through her and out over the water. She spotted Charlie standing tall, his shoulders turned and his hands clasped together high above his head, the metal shaft shimmering in the light of the falling sun.